THE PENNY DROPS

By

Catherine Sedgwick

First published in 2022 by Amazon

Copyright Catherine b. Sedgwick 2022

All Rights Reserved

Nanna,
With all good wishes,
Catherine

Front cover from original watercolour by

C.B. Sedgwick.

This book is dedicated, once again, to my ever patient and caring husband, son, parents and family.
I will forever be the tortoise.

THE PENNY DROPS.

Chapter 1

I took a deep breath and sighed loudly…....here we go again. Susie teetered over to the table on five-inch heels. Her eyes narrowed she leaned forward, almost spilling out of the tight, sheer number she had painted on earlier.

"I've got this one Penny, hook, line and sinker. He's a real prize salmon. He's giving me a lift home….....and I may invite him in for a coffee." It was inevitable, every time we came out pubbing or clubbing. She couldn't help herself, or them.

"You don't mind making your own way home? You'll be okay, won't you?"

"Never mind me Suse what do you know about this bloke?" I craned my neck trying to weigh him up as quickly as I could. She caught me with that look, her green contact lenses catching the light, like some beguiling, feline, she purred.

"I've seen his gold card, I've checked his pockets and fingers, for drugs and wedding rings, he's given me his mobile number, his home number and the registration of his Mercedes soft top, he's luscious, loaded and layable, stop worrying chicken."

(Chicken was her pet-name for me when she knew I was doing the mother hen bit!)

I sighed raising my eyebrows. "Well, just you remember, make sure you ring me when you get home." She laughed.

"Yes, Mum" I tutted, which just made me sound even more like her mother.

Susie was walking away giggling and about to join her, 'man of the moment' She said something and he turned and looked over, I shot him the 'evil eye'. I squinted at him, narrowing my eyes, trying to focus without my specs, it was more, angry mole, but he wasn't to know. It was a warning glare. 'Mess with my friend and you'll have me to deal with pal!' He caught my look, smiled and mouthed across something like, 'don't worry, she'll be safe with me'.

I watched Suse gaze up at him, the classic eyelash flutter, the sugar pink pout, his arm sliding round her waist as they disappeared into the crowd and I wondered if Crippen, had uttered those very same words, "Don't worry she'll be safe with me."

Snap out of it. She's an adult, entitled to some fun, to do what she wants. She's had her fair share of hurt and experiences that make her need this sort of attention...... No, let's be totally honest, she just loves this sort of attention!

I got up quickly as I saw a crowd of girls heading towards the door, there were always a few going in my direction, on their way out, so I'd walk closer, mingle, pretending I was in their group. Some girls were so squiffy, I was part of their group! "Hiya! Thought you couldn't come tonight, what's yer name again?" I'd smile, "Just got out of work, so a bit late!" And off they'd stagger as I rushed off in the opposite direction to my car.

I had to get home to await Susie's call. We always rang to check each other were home, it was a friendship made with love, care, concern and of course, on my part, ……..just a little bit of envy! I wanted to make sure that at least one of us was having some fun tonight. A sort of sex life by proxy!

Knowing Suse, I will have re-lived all the intimate details by lunchtime tomorrow. There are only so many descriptions of men's underwear I can cope with. I'm more the… judge a man by his clean shoes and whether he bothered to pull a comb through his hair, but with Suse it's a man's underwear that, maketh the man.

Calvin Klein or Dolce & Gabbana boxers – he is well fit, likes quality and style, but has a bit of mystery about him.

Briefs - (as long as not in loud colours, or patterns,) he knows what he's got and what he wants, he's confident and switched on.

Posing pouch, or thong …… (I'm usually wincing at this point.) You know exactly what I've got and there is no point hiding this much of a good thing. (Yuk!)

Y-fronts - still lets mum do his shopping, or….is old enough to be her father. (Which in Susie's book means, they have to be loaded and will need a shopping trip to menswear, if they want to see her again.)

The phone rang just as I put the hall light on. "Everything okay Suse?" I asked anxiously.

"Late start tomorrow, I'll catch you for coffee sweetie" she says breathlessly.

"Okay Susie, if you can't be good be careful and if you can't be careful be very…very good?" I whisper, trying to be saucy, anything but prudish. She giggles, then to my embarrassment, but not hers, I heard the rich Mercedes voice asking if she wants milk and sugar in her coffee. I suddenly feel *very* intrusive.

"Oh! Night Suse. Speak to you tomorrow, take care".

As I lay in bed, my cat Ferdy one side, a couple of magazines on the other, I imagined what it must be like to have a night like Susie's.

Not that I am some thirty-seven-year-old, virginal, saddo you understand. No....no! I have even had the odd spontaneous, one-night stand of passion, (odd being the operative word!).

I'd been 'whisked' off my feet, after a couple of Martinis, by an assistant chef, Charlie, (truly embarrassed to admit I didn't get his surname.) Tall, blonde, with twinkling eyes and a gorgeous smile. It was at a hotel we stayed at, down in York.

A wild hen night! Not mine I hasten to add. If I'd had the chance to get as far as the alter there is no way I'd have my head turned by the promise of a lifelong supply of prawn vol-u-vents, or brandy snaps. (Chocolate Eclairs and I might have wavered!)

It was late evening and he'd just finished in the kitchens and had come into the bar for a quick drink and I squiffily complimented him on *his* chocolate eclairs and it was lust at first sight, we had a truly memorable night.

Later, as he went to leave my hotel room, he'd said, he wasn't really someone who made a habit of one-night stands and he really liked me and felt that he'd blown it and maybe we could start again with dinner sometime? I was taken aback and a bit embarrassed, as he wrote down his phone number, kissed my forehead gently and pressed the piece of paper into my hand, saying, he *really* hoped I would ring. Yes! He had......*actually* ......fancied me!

It took me over six weeks of Suse badgering me and for me to pluck up the courage to ring the hotel kitchen. I was convinced it would be a fake number and feel disappointed and humiliated.

But the hotel kitchen said he'd left just over a week previously, got a better job and prospects, they couldn't remember the name of the place, Hay Wain, Wheat Barn, something like that. Typical! Not to be, the one that got away and I really did regret not calling sooner.

That was nearly three years ago and no more one-night stands. (Nothing would match that one!)

I then found myself in a ten-month steady and surprise engagement, to Warren. That is until he changed jobs and found the office, 'floosy' more to his liking. A blessing in disguise Suse had said. That is certainly not how it felt at the time.

The next was a five month, 'un-steady', to Carl. Who was incredibly insecure, immature and possessive. In fact, to be honest, a touch scary! For several weeks after I had finally decided to finish the relationship, he would just keep appearing, outside work, pubs and clubs, hovering in the background till he got the opportunity to talk.

He would be friendly at first, then he'd start asking questions, trying to find out if I was seeing anyone, then he'd get pushy. It was annoying and unnerving in equal measure. Why couldn't I give him another chance? I didn't know the real him. I think I knew more than enough thanks!

Put me off dating for quite some time I can tell you. But the girls rallied round and saw him off and we were all back out there having fun and loving the single life.

But watching Suse have such fun with her blokes, I was really starting to miss some male company and of course, I wasn't getting any younger, time wasn't on my side, body clock ticking etc.... as my mum kindly pointed out at very regular intervals every time I visited her and dad.

Susan, Susie, or Suse as she liked to be called, had been my best friend for years. We were sort of thrown together at school, two odd fourteen-year-olds that got picked on. Susie was given a hard time, for……just being a beautiful person really. There were jealous girls who just couldn't stand the competition.

One bitch of a girl had grabbed Susie by the hair, dragged her into the empty cloakroom, pulled out scissors and cut out a chunk of her gorgeous long hair, warning her off a lad she fancied, threatening her with worse if she told anyone. (We were children of the seventies, we put up and shut up sadly.) Not sure why the bully thought that would get her the lad she was after. As if any decent lad would have looked twice at that charmless, bint of a bully. Susie could knock spots off that lot, even with a now, very dodgy mullet!

Back then of course she wasn't the full-on temptress she is today. She was quite shy, lacking in confidence. She just didn't see what others saw. That's where I came in, short, dumpy, picked on for the blatantly obvious really!

'Oi! Fatty fish-face, what you looking at?'

I desperately wanted to cleverly retort, "Not sure I'll just consult my, 'Peat-bog Creatures' handbook" but if they took a chunk out of my less than lustrous locks, I'd have looked like I'd tried a Rod Stewart cut with blunt scissors, so it wasn't worth the risk. We were talking serious seventies rag-cuts back then.

Susie was standing in the girl's toilets trying to assess the damage to her golden mane, when I shuffled in.

"Can you see at the back how much has gone? Mum and dad will kill me." She said, her eyes watering.

"It's not too bad, it's only about four inches up, a decent hairdresser could grade it with layers"
I said knowledgeably, thinking back to that issue of 'Jackie' and the latest haircut section.

She sighed heavily, leaning on the basin, "I just don't know what to do to make those girls like me. I just can't seem to make friends here."

She'd moved up from the Midlands, to the beautiful, but strangely 'competitive', City of Durham, she'd only been here a term.

"Don't worry, they'll soon get bored. You're the new girl, they're just letting you know they were here first, they're a bit sad really" I had tried to sound grown up and dismissive, but I knew exactly how she felt.

"Ignore them, I do. Either that, or get the tallest, handsomest lad in the school as a friend and protector. Tom, in 5A, the one with all the muscles, the sporty one, that'll get rid of 'em!"

She giggled then, "That's great advice, you should be an agony aunt in 'Jackie'."

"You read 'Jackie' too! It's the best, isn't it?" I grinned.

She linked my arm and we wandered off down the corridor towards the classrooms comparing notes on our fave popstars, fave colours, fave fashions. As we parted to go to different classes, she asked if I'd come round her house Tuesday for tea, listen to records and have a gossip. Would I?!...
Try and stop me, my new friend was the nicest in the school.

It was the start of a very special friendship. Especially, two months after we met when she proudly introduced me to Tom. Definitely the tallest, handsomest, sportiest, lad in the school.

Just the way they looked at each other, they were all, well……
'Puppy-Loved' up.

"I took your advice Pen, what do you think?" I was no judge but he was, in the words of T. Rex, a real………'Teenage Dream'.

We had some great times growing up together. Those awkward teenage years were so much easier when you had someone going through the same to whinge with. Oh, and did we whinge! About everything! Parents……lads……spots……fashion and of course, both being fat and gross. Suse was a petite size eight, I was only a curvy size twelve, but I seemed small and round next to her, which probably started her confidence soaring and mine waning. But our friendship, never waned.

Dating in our late teens, was predictable. The classic scenario, every time we went out, the good-looking lad would make a beeline for Suse and behind him he'd have………
'his friend'.

Often the slightly greasy haired, spotty sort, who was either very brainy, but conversational skills nil and the sense of humour of a gnat. Or, a……… 'Mr Funny'?!

You know the sort, thinks that prodding his finger into your clavicle, sniggering, 'What's that' and as you look down, he brings his finger up to flick your nose, is hilarious?!

After the tenth time in one evening the forced grin turned to clenched teeth and I turned to Suse. "Make up your mind about the bloke you're with, otherwise the clown gets it okay! He's driving me round the bend!"

Of course, it got more difficult as the relationships became more serious, more intimate. Suse would be all, 'gooey eyed' with some real hunk, they would snatch the odd kiss between us all chatting over a basket-meal. I swore to Suse this was my last date with, 'Mr Funny'. Cornered at one point, he tried to put his arm round me. With his clumsy attempt he elbowed me, in what little I had at the time for breasts.

He childishly sniggered and said loudly, "Oops sorry, did I shift yer hankies." Shocked and affronted, as a girl would be, that he had implied I had stuffed something down my top to resemble a bosom, I glared at him and blushing pink had said, "No, but if we're talking about tits will you stop behaving like one!"

I know it wasn't ladylike, but if it shut him up, it was worth it. It put paid to a relationship with Mr Funny, but of course it also put off the hunk Suse was with. He felt awkward seeing her, when his poor sad clown of a mate had no one. She told me this, two days after the 'tits' incident, sobbing into her tea.

"Oh, come on Suse, what sort of bloke is he, if he gets persuaded by 'Mr Funny the clown' to give *you* up?" I put my arm round her and whispered. "Honestly Suse, not much of a loss, is there really?"

She pulled out a couple of tissues, wiped her eyes, smiled and said.......

"Nah! They were both a...... *pair* of tits really, weren't they?" We fell about laughing. Then of course we'd start making arrangements for our next girly night out. Best way to get over one bloke.........go out and find another!

In Susies case, another and another, she ploughed on through 'hunk-dom' with enthusiasm and gusto. I on the other hand appeared to have ploughed through cakes with the same game spirit!

"Penny, Pen! Hi honey, sorry I'm late. My boss didn't really want me to take a lunchbreak as I got in work late this morning.

I said I had to nip out to get……. 'women's things' for the monthlies, poor bloke, went the shade of my hall carpet!"

Susie had that way of throwing things back at people, she made *them* feel guilty, for her faults, it was a gift, an absolute gift.

"Well?" I said pushing her lukewarm, black coffee towards her, while I poured a second cuppa from the chubby, floral teapot of Parker's Café.

She took a sip, a broad smile lit up her face as she leaned back and sighed.

"Oh Pen! He is just so gorgeous, so sexy, so much fun, I could really get so used to this man being around!"

"Oh! Come on Suse, you met him last night, you slept with him, after knowing him barely five hours, do you really think you should be planning the wedding list already, you know what you're like……and what they're like!"

I bit my lip as soon as I said it, I felt so critical, bursting her bubble, before she'd even got her balloon half inflated.

"Yes…thank you, walking oracle of wisdom. For your information, I did *not* sleep with him…….and he's picking me up Friday night and taking me out for dinner……at that flashy restaurant, 'The Straw House'."

Her smile widened, she looked me straight in the eye, raised her eyebrows, as if to say, go on then, try and put the dampers on that, chicken.

"Wow Susie! That is so exclusive, how did he manage to get a table there? Sorry, I jumped to conclusions. You know I hate seeing you get hurt."

I was genuinely excited for her and really hoped this wasn't another dork, full of false promises. She leaned forward, as if imparting a huge secret.

"His brother is high up there, he rang him last night, managed to wangle a little corner table for two." I looked at her glowing face, was this finally a bit of real romance, I hoped so, she so deserved it.

I dawdled back to the office, enjoying some late November sunshine, as usual trying not to look towards the shops. I caught sight of myself in that damn mirrored window of, 'Pinks Boutique'. They have obviously put it there on purpose.

No doubt as the tall and willowy, beauties of this parish pass they will admire their reflections. Then look at the same shaped mannequins in the window, draped in dark blue velvet nipped waist jackets, barely there silk and chiffon dresses and think, 'yes, I must go in, that outfit would look wonderful on me.' Instead, the real world and me, dart past thinking, 'yikes, it is me! It really is time to get my roots done and that is one hell of a price to pay to look like an ornamental kite.'

Back at my desk I gaze at the clock, willing the pointers to go faster, not that I was rushing home to anything, just bored being here. Harkass, Jenkins & Preece Chartered Accountants. Not exactly life in the fast lane. Susie worked at, 'Farriers'…. Durham's top travel agent. When she got a bonus, it was either a weekend at a health spa, or an all-expenses paid week away to do a holiday resort review.

We on the other hand were either showered with an extra twenty quid, or had Mr Jenkins creeping up behind us with a bottle of cheap Asti and the offer of staying behind to help him finish the bottle. (Poor June still hasn't recovered from him showing her his trick with the cork, at last years office Christmas party!) I never wanted to be stuck in an office nine to five. (Well, eight till four actually, flexi-time.) My mind starts to wander. I had always hoped to do something a little less routine. I wanted to work with animals, do something more hands on and helpful to the environment. It wasn't the classic Beauty Queen speech. But what if…….my mind drifted as I gazed through the office window.

What if………. Beauty Queen Pageant 1997, stage right. Creepy, presenter approaching.

"Penelope Wiseman, ladies and gentlemen, isn't she stunning in her crocheted one piece, aqua-marine, swimsuit. Well, my darling and what would you like to do in the future Penelope?" (Seedy wink and a leary look in his gimlet eye).

"Well Garth, (voice going up two octaves and acquiring a cute lisp) I'd weally like to work wiv fluffy animals, help all the poor people in the world and twavel." …Reality check!

"No, *actually*, I'd like to work very little and get paid an extortionate amount, have a gorgeous man whisk me to the country and do absolutely nothing Garth, or should that be, 'arth'? Oh, me and my lisp……and just so you know Garthy baby, my face is not six inches above my waist, you over coiffured, perv!"

Hands now covering my crocheted daisies, I saunter off, stage left.

"Aha, er, Penny Wiseman ladies and gentlemen, isn't she just, er too……..honest?"

As I smile to myself, my fingers clicking away on the computer keys on autopilot, my daydreams are sharply interrupted by my second-best buddy, trolling into the office.

Maurice, (or 'Maureece' as he would say, we're talking Bucket and Bouquet here!) He is the office Prince, he would say Queen, every girls bestest friend. He is an absolute love, knows everything about, fashion, style, health, beauty, men, but more importantly, all the office gossip before it's hit rumour!

"Hellooo, sweetie! Sorry I didn't get down to you this morning, but Mr Preece insisted the weekly figures were on his desk by noon, me fingers are worn to the bone and me wrists… no, not me wrists, they're always this limp!" He let out a loud, hyena laugh and everyone began to giggle.

He made all the classic camp quips, loved wickedly joking and teasing everyone he could. Underneath 'the fluff and drama' there was a genuine, intelligent, caring and trusted friend.

He just loved all the attention and happy, smiling faces. Some days he was my one saving grace, in this boring building, he was the brightest and gayest, in the very truest sense.

"How's our Susie baby?" He asked, eyes wide in anticipation of her latest man marathon and weekend fun. Of course, I told him everything.

"Oooo! He sounds a bit spesh doesn't he? I'd be purring too with that hunk whispering sweet nothings in my ear, the lucky minx. Not that I'd ever swap my Rojere. (Roger to you and me.) He may not be the hunkiest thing walking this planet, but oh heavens, he's a boon in the kitchen and bedroom!"

"Ewww! Too much information Morry," I said quickly, about to wince.

"Oh girl! Mind like a whore's handbag. I meant he can get to grips with those darn duvet covers. Last time I wrestled with one of those, lost me balance, Roj found me fifteen minutes later sprawled on the floor in a muted blue Jasper Conran, prostrate like a discarded teabag! *Never* again!" He sat down sharply, wafting his hand across his forehead.

"Anyway lady, how's your lack of love life, enticed anyone into your web of mystery yet?" He says, moving closer for possible gossip.

"Oh, ha ha, Mr Sarkypants, there were a couple of possibles the other night, but you know me, I hate to rush things, I'm just *not* the pushy type."

He propels himself backwards, on the castored chair, then begins pulling himself along past my desk making locomotive movements and chugging sounds.

"Woo, woo! Rush things! If your train gets any slower lady, there'll be no one left at the station and the tunnels will be all bricked up!"

I purse my lips in mock disapproval. "Yes, thank you for your Freudian observations, but this well-built express, likes to get to her final destination without picking up one-stop time wasters on the way." I say wryly.

"Well, you're hardly the Virgin Intercity are you love, any slower on those tracks and they'll be shunting you into a siding with all the other old boilers getting short on steam."

"You cheeky sod!" I say, throwing a pencil like a dart at his chest, he feigns reeling pain, says he's mortally wounded. Tells me to run and get Dave Hardy from the second floor to give him mouth to mouth. He then drags me off to the drinks machine saying, I've upset his blood sugars, he needs a large Cappuccino with three Demeraras and I'm paying.

"Look, I've told you before, I know a few gorge guys. I could set you up with a couple of blind dates, get you back on the market, what do you reckon babe?"

"Thanks a million Morry" I say, sounding insulted, "I've gone from being an old boiler of a steam train, to a rather past her sell by date, Jersey heifer, you do know how to boost a girls ego. How would you like it if I referred to you as a, tarnished old hook!" He looked puzzled. "A what?"

"Rusty, ageing and bent?" I say matching his hands on hip stance. "Oh! I refute that, I just had honeycomb highlights put in at 'Boden & Sangs' last Wednesday, Brett says I don't look a day over twenty-seven!"

We both fell about giggling, but then pulled ourselves together quickly like two guilty school children, as Mr. Harkass passed brusquely, muttering something about, overpaid deskies.

"Go on. Think about it babe." Morry whispers, as he starts back up the stairs to accounts. "What have you got to lose?"

"My dignity, my street cred?" I said with raised eyebrows.

"I rest my case!" His hyena laugh still audible, as I sat back at my desk, fingers back in position, typing up yet more boring files and letters. Lucky Suse had travel brochures to look through day after day, I had the joy of accountant's letters.

Ten minutes later, when June and Anna were out of the office, I made a grab for the phone and rang Morry. "OK. I'll do it!" I said in a low whisper.

"Pen, I'm only setting up a blind date love, I'm not sending you off to spy for England." Morry says loudly.

"Shhh, I don't want everyone to know, I feel a right saddo! Oh, God Morry, these two blind dates of yours they are straight aren't they, I couldn't cope with any of those undecideds, bi-sexual, or on the cusp conversions?"

He sniggers, "Oh, come on lady, I'm hardly going to send you on a romantic date with someone who's going to try your lipstick, gaze at your shoes, count the sequins on your halter-neck, then ask if you fancy a duet of, 'I'll Survive' on the Karaoke. Do you really think I'd waste him on you!"

"Who are these blokes then?" I ask, feeling slightly relieved, (but strangely, quite liked the sound of that evening.)

"Philleep, (Phillip) he's my cousin and Rafe, (I know, I know, Rolf!) is Rojere's older brother, okay?"

"How old is older?" I ask concerned. Morry paused to think.

"I think Roj said around thirty-nine. Is that within your age range of suitable males?" He says cheekily.

"I am a young thirty-seven," I state defensively. "Don't you dare say anything about old boilers again, just sort something out and let me know, I'll have to go Morry, the girls are back."

"Okey, dokey love, I'll let you know as soon as, bye!"

As I drove home that evening, I did feel quite excited, at the prospect of a couple of blind dates. If nothing else it would be a change of scenery. Get in a bit of, woman to man conversational practice.

And......I wasn't really lying to Morry when I'd said, there had been a couple of 'possibles' the other night.

The first encounter was a bloke that had wedged himself up against me at the bar, his beery breath wafting over me, as he charmingly said. "I'm supposed to say to you, do you come 'ere often, then you are supposed to say, if you get any closer, I may already have! Eh! Do you get it, uh, do you get it?"

He sniggered triumphantly. "Yes, I *do* get it actually, from someone considerably more subtle than you, fortunately."

I retorted, glowing in my cutting put down. But he looked so deflated I nearly apologised………but I didn't.

What was wrong with me, Suse would have added, 'the look' turned on her designer heels and done that slow walk she does, just to let him know how much of a fool he really is and just what he has lost with his tasteless crudity.

The other bloke had tried several attempts at conversation, but he had a dose of laryngitis. The music was so loud, he was straining to speak clearly. He began some sort of dodgy sign language. Then began scribbling on bits of paper from his pockets with one of those tiny pens you get from Argos, or bookmakers, (so I'm told). It kept running out and he was getting more and more frustrated, in the end I got up saying, I must go as my friend was leaving. He passed me a bit of paper which said something like, *'ou nave ov ly big cycs I ow bo t datc'*. Suse reckoned, when I showed her the bit of paper later, he'd had trouble with his, 'e's! I think, she was being very kind!

I rang Suse later that night to tell her about what Morry had said at work, about setting me up with a couple of blind dates.

"Oh yes, definitely Pen, go for it." She said enthusiastically.

"Would you go on a blind date Suse, honestly?" I asked needing her reassurance.

"Oh hell, yes Pen, if I was you. Sorry, that sounded awful, as if you're desperate."

I sighed. "I know what you mean. You don't have to blind date, you've got men queuing up to take you out. Tell me truthfully Suse, do you think I am being desperate?"

There was a silence. Then Suse says gently.

"All I know is very few men in my queue are there because of my brains, or possible wifely, motherly qualities. But I do know……. that any man that is lucky enough to start your queue, will be there for the right reasons." She then went quiet.

I swallowed hard. I could feel my eyes watering. Suse, for all her full-on personality and figure wasn't really any different to me deep down. Underneath, we just wanted exactly the same from a relationship.

We both loved and enjoyed our lives, but still hung on to the hope that there was that Knight in shining armour. (Or in my case, Jason Durr in his 1960's 'Heartbeat' police uniform and those black leather motorcycle boots. Each to his own I say, white chargers and shiny armour do it for some, black leather and vintage motorcycles do it for me.) Now smiling, I change the subject.

"Right Suse, how about we going shopping on Saturday? It's been at least three weeks and I think my bank balance has just about recovered from the last time we hit the high street!"

"Yes! Absolutely Pen, you'll have to get yourself something new anyway, for all these blind dates you'll be going on!" She says excitedly.

"What do you mean, *all* these blind dates? I thought I was meeting the man of my dreams on the *first* blind date, first in the queue you said?"

"Er, sorry Pen, but unless yer fave man, Jason Durr is going undercover as Rolf, Rafe, Ralf, whatever, I think you're out of luck." She laughs.

"Right, that's it Suse, I must stop sharing bottles of wine with you. I don't think I've got a single fantasy left that you haven't weaselled out of me when I've had one too many sweet whites!"

Chapter 2

Friday 11.45am. Only another fifteen minutes till I can escape for lunch.

There's a flash of dark blue velvet, passing the office partitions. God, I hope it's not that Tiffany Mills, she'll have been to 'Pinks'. She will have bought that, gorgeous jacket, in a tiny size eight. Then she'll saunter past collecting files, not a hair out of place, like a 'wig on a stick.' Meow! I can't help it! She just brings out the worst in me. Some people are just obscenely perfect.

She always hovers, just long enough to give me that pitying look, then moves towards June and Anna, to tell them loudly, about her gorgeous fiancé and how, '*thee* wedding preps' are going, the house in the country, the designer gown, the gold leaf table settings, the honeymoon in St. Lucia.

She stands around 5ft 10inches, her court shoes always in ballet third position. (If like me, you were a sugar plum hippo ballet first grader, when young, you'll know this one. Right foot heel to the middle of the left foot.) She always has her left hand up in front of her, ostensibly holding a file, but she is actually showing you that the greatest ever 22carat African diamond is amazingly, on her third finger left hand!

No! I'm mistaken, it's not Tiffany. The flash of blue velvet is actually Morry, in the mens version of, 'Pinks Boutique's, nipped waist jacket. Then again, I notice which side the buttons are on.

"Morry! You haven't taken the jacket off that poor mannequin's back?"

He twirls quickly. "You've got to admit it looks better on me, than on that stiff in the window. Mens clothes are *so* conservative, I don't know a Burtons, or a Next that can give a man a nicely cut bit of velvet." I crease with laughter.

"You said that with a straight face Morry, how do you do it?" He looks sideways.

"There is *nothing* straight about me girl, not even my humour, thank Gucci!"

He pulls a chair up and squeezes in next to me, then says, rounding the words slowly, in a half whisper, as if I'm hard of hearing.

"Do...you...want...me...to...tell...you....about...the...first... blind...date...or..... shall...I...write...it...down?"

"Morry, if you think that will keep it secret, you're much mistaken, *all* women can lip read, it's inbred!"

"Oh, sorry sweets, I'll just tell you then. Monday night 7pm, meet Philleep, outside the Odeon, so it'll be safe for you, there'll be loads of people around, you'll see a film, so not too taxing on the conversation, that okey for you babe?"

I look worried. "What's wrong with him, why should there be loads of people, why can't he hold a long conversation?"

Morry looks skywards. "Safe for you, you muppet! In case you're not keen, you can grab a taxi, make a bee-line for your car. You won't have given too much away if you're watching a film, so there's nothing lost, is there? Heavens above Pen, he's me cousin, not Fred West!"

"Oh sorry, just me, I'll be fine. I'm actually quite looking forward to it all. What type of girls does your Phil, sorry Philleep normally go for? Have you told him anything about me?"

"Of course I have. He's looking forward to meeting you. He likes, from what I can gather, what you'd call 'girly' girls? Frilly, feminine, genteel. I think you'll appeal somewhere in there." He says, looking me up and down with amusement.

"Thanks a bunch, a compliment I presume?"

Morry leans in again. "Anyway, if our Philleep doesn't do it for you and Mondays a damp squib, I've got you Rafe fixed up for Wednesday!"

"Two dates in a week?" I look shocked.

"Excuse me lady, you're hardly awash with a tidal wave of dates now are you, it's hardly what you'd call a relay, get a grip girl!" I start to panic.

"Yes, but two different men, so close together!"

Morry looks as if he's about to snigger.

"It's not an orgy for God's sake! Hell's teeth girl, you'd think I'd fixed you up for a threesome!" He can't help laughing now as he carries on. "You'd think you'd spent the last two years in a convent, they're men, not bloody aliens!"

"I know, I know, Morry, it'll all come back to me, I'll get the hang of it again, don't worry."

His laugh got louder as he squealed. "You shouldn't be hanging from anything at your age girl, not on a first date!" I could see the girls prick up their ears.

"Shhhh, Morry!" He quickly caught sight of the interested faces and adds.

"No, it's those parallel bars lovey, you stick to the running machine first time, get those thighs toned, the sauna's open till *seven*, okey dokey? Good luck."

He over winked and rushed off, climbing the stairs two at a time. I wasn't sure, whether I'd rather the girls thought I was going on a blind date, or that my flabby thighs needed toning up! Both pretty mortifying, in their own way.

I got home late, tired and stressed after sitting in endless traffic, I really should have walked. These were moments when I longed for that rich man and a retreat in the country.

I tried to stay with those thoughts, as I steered a hungry Ferdy with tin and spoon towards his bowl and away from trying to remove the contents of my sandwich with his claws. Silly me, nearly put myself first there, won't do that again in a hurry.

The doorbell rang, I nearly jumped out of my skin, it was nearly twenty to seven. I chucked several magazines under the settee, along with the current, soppy novel I was engrossed in, (I know, romance by proxy too?)

Why was I panicking, Jason Durr wasn't passing through Durham was he? Royalty wasn't in the area? Family are all well, I'd only spoke to mum on Wednesday.

I just didn't get callers, unannounced at this time of night. For goodness sake! I suddenly realised that I was panicking... because the *doorbell* had rung. As it rang again, I rushed towards the door thinking......I really should get out more.

"Penny! Why did you take so long to answer, have you tidied your hair? Who did you think it was going to be?" Suse grinned, then wiggled in.

"Oh my God, Suse! You look stunning! That dress is just beautiful, so...... sophisticated."

She did a slinky catwalk stroll across the room then turned slowly. "And you think I can't do sophisticated?" She held eye contact.

"You can do *anything* Suse, especially sophisticated, but that dress, it must have cost a fortune." The said creation was, emerald green, the colour contrasting with her pale gold, auburn highlights, but matching her contact lenses exactly, she looked like a movie star about to go to a premier. Long, with corset bodice and fish-tail, showing off her fantastic figure. Her hair tumbled over her left shoulder the right side held up by a green jewelled clip, matching earrings and necklace. Her five-inch heels in cream silk with diamante ankle straps, just made her look …. perfect.

"Simon…Mr Mercedes, remember? He is taking me to 'The Straw House' tonight. I just wanted to look right for him…… I *really* do like him Pen." She, confident, beautiful Susie, was actually bothered what a man thought of her. She genuinely looked worried that he might not be impressed with what he saw.

"I've made such an effort Pen, the dress was from, 'Mimi Cherelles' it cost me just over three hundred. I got Paul, you know, who has the jewellery business, to loan me the gems, the shoes I already had, fortunately, from Ginny Lane's wedding. Do you remember?"

Do I remember? My mind drifted back three years to that hotel in York and Charlie. Suse noticed my eyes glazing over and the Stan Laurel smile appearing.

"Pen, concentrate! He'll be here at seven. I told him I had to borrow something from you, so to come and pick me up here. I want to know if you think I look the part, going to such a flashy place."

I felt really flattered that she thought my opinion counted in the fashion department. If I had been standing there in the very same outfit, she knows and I know, I'd look like a very shabby drag act.

"I don't know how you do it Suse, honestly, any man that saw you tonight, in that outfit and didn't think he was the luckiest man alive wants certifying, or at the very least, a trip to the opticians."

"Ah, thanks Pen, that's so calmed my nerves, you haven't got a small sweet white to calm them even more?" I thought quickly. "You don't have to drink to 'enhance' your personality Suse. Truthfully……. I think you should believe that Simon wants to get to know the *real* Susan Parks. Just be yourself, you'll be fine."

Now that was what I was good at, the boosting of others confidence, the emotional support and not the fashion advice.

The doorbell went again, "Never! It's like Piccadilly Circus in here, who will that be?" Suse looked amused. "You don't get a lot of door-chime action here, do you?" We giggled as we went towards the door together.

"Door-chime action!" I said through giggles. "If that's the same as, chandelier action, no I don't seem to be getting what's rightfully mine."

As I opened the door Suse quickly composed herself, she stood there calmly with a Mona Lisa smile, looking every inch a lady.

I on the other hand, nearly buckled at the knees, at just being part of the moment. I felt like some, tweeny, I should be curtsying and tugging my forelock, announcing the arrival of…'Sir Simon Mercedes and his white charger, Duke SF44.'

Close up, inches away, he looked and smelt so.... so.......utterly and totally, gorgeous!

I hadn't really got a proper look at the club the other night, I was being too vain to wear me specs, (kept them in the glove compartment of the car. I could risk ignoring people I knew, but not running them over.) I found contact lenses difficult, so I'd squinted best I could. As far as I could see, he just looked tidy, tall and dark. Susie's usual.

But standing in front of us was this, *very* tall, broad-shouldered male, in a dark suit and tie, cream shirt, showing off his healthy tanned skin to perfection. His eyes twinkled, the small laughter lines creasing as he smiled and what a smile, (where *do* people get teeth like that?)

He began to speak, I was transfixed, Susie nudged me quickly. Oh God, was I dribbling, had I got that nervous tick in my left eye again.

Then he spoke. "Susie's told me so much about this best friend of hers, I've been so looking forward to meeting you Penny....*and* you found your glasses?"

I quickly pulled them off, clutching them tightly.

"Ugh! Er, wwwhat" I stammered, trying to avert my stare.

"Susie said you'd lost your glasses at the club the other night. When I'd tried to speak to you over the room, I'd told her, I thought you looked in pain." (That was my best angry mole impression!) Then I laughed. No! Actually...Snorted!...Pig-like!

I was a drivelling wreck, but he just didn't seem to notice. If he did, he was being politeness personified......a total gentleman. His chocolate brown voice continued, as he took in the vision that was Suse.

"Susie, you look absolutely incredible, I am so proud to be taking you to dinner tonight, you look truly…. perfect."

That was it. That was the word, he'd done it. Suse was just glowing as she turned and hugged me goodbye and gave me a wink. I wanted to speak, to say something, but it just wouldn't come. I stood there, waving, with an inane grin on my face, like some small, demented child saying goodbye to emigrating relatives.

I slumped down on the sofa with sheer relief. I found myself saying out loud, as if making a wish. "I don't ever, *ever*, want to date a Mr Mercedes." (Let's be honest it would only last the one date anyway, because I'd have stuttered through it, goo-goo-eyed, like some bereft, love-sick, teenager). I would be too worried every time some woman looked in his direction, or man for that matter. Morry couldn't convince me that he wouldn't try a line, if he thought there was the tiniest chance of him being able to walk into, 'Hepburn's' bar with that specimen of man on his arm!

I just didn't want a man who turned everyone's heads. I just wanted a man that turned mine. When I thought back over the years, I had never gone, looks-wise, for the classic chiselled jaw, the 'Toblerone' physique, (large shoulders, small waist, kind of triangular.) It was always, the eyes, the smile, nice hands. I liked a man that made me laugh, that had character. Granted a couple of them had too much character, in fact so much so, that it made them positively weird!

It's not that I didn't…. or couldn't get the 'classic' man. That time when Suse was stuck with, Mr Rockstar for months on end. Well, she didn't see it as being stuck, she thought it was, 'glamorous and exciting.'

Mr Rockstar was the typical, 'Legend in his own lunchtime'. 'Yeah, it's all sex, drugs and rock 'n' roll man.'

He saw himself as a cross between Mick Jagger and Kurt Cobain. Personally, I thought he was more a cross between Iggy Pop and that dodgy pub singer we saw in Skeggy one year. He was always very……..'deep man.'

I ended up having to sit Suse down and tell her he was pushing dope and ecstasy after 'gigs', even to youngsters, I'd seen him. But she wouldn't believe me at first, so I told her which of the guitar cases he kept it in.

I told her he wasn't to be trusted. He could even be dangerous for her. She was risking becoming an accessory, if he was caught. Or worse, he could get her onto the stuff. She swore to me that she'd never smoked anything, or taken any tablets, ever. Well, not intentionally anyway.

She said he'd told her, he would never do drugs, as his 'cosmic level was on a much higher plane…..man'. His music was his drug and that took him to where he wanted to be…… man. Yeah right! As far as I could see, that 'man' was right up his own …….porthole!

Anyway, until I'd finally persuaded Suse that, 'Rockstars moll' wouldn't always be that glamorous. That, he would either pick himself another younger groupie at one of his, 'many gigs', on his next, 'nation-wide tour.' (Which consisted of two shows in Spalding, one turn after the drag act in Doncaster and a small village folk festival in Penzance, (bet that frightened the Pixies!)

Or worse, he would become famous and deluded, get all creative, religious, then paranoid and she'd end up holed up with him in a barn conversion, doing a Lennon & Yoko bed-fest in Kent!

He had even tried to make out they were married once and that Suse was his, 'Parallel Soul'? (The only, 'soul' he was to Susie was prefixed with…arrrr!)

They had had some spaced out, hippy, summer solstice ceremony at Stonehenge. Suse had shown me the photos. She was wearing, what appeared to be a sheet, a chain-belt and wilted poppies round her head. The person marrying them was apparently, a self-ordained Hell's Angel from Goole.

The guests consisted of the group's drummer, bass guitarist and three back packers who were just passing through and thought it was druids summoning up the gods and ridding evil spirits. Well, that can't have worked, or Mr Rockstar would have been carried off by, a three toed, winged beast, what a shame. Where were the Druids when you needed them?

Susie so wanted to be married, it took her a long time to accept that it was null and void in the eyes of the law and anyone vaguely normal!

But while the, 'romance' was, 'banging man' (Mr Rockstar's term for anything good.) I had to find others to, 'hang with…. man.' Well, it was all very amusing and infectious at the time.

So, I found refuge and much fun with other buddies, including my past college friends.
Bina. Full name, Ribena Khan. Mother white, Dad Indian. So named because, the story goes……..

They'd been so busy with the family business, mum just popped Bina out at home with the midwife in attendance, she'd shouted through, as Mr Khan was leaving for a three-day sales conference,

'What do you want to call your baby girl'? The midwife had hurriedly written it down.

Mum had rushed to the town hall two days later, Mr Khan still away, she handed the bit of paper over to the registrar, as she didn't want to get the spelling wrong. Then got home, got busy with the other children, new baby, house, business. Wasn't till dad came back, looked at the certificate, stunned he said, 'Ribena? Is this the English translation of Bina?'

Of course, she went through it at, infants school, not because anyone teased her, but because she used to go around snatching purple cartons and bottles from other children, she thought had taken her belongings, well, it was *her* name on the front!

Bina, was feisty, loud and very opinionated. She even made her dad promise, when she was 16yrs old, that he would never give her away in an arranged marriage to some old letch, or some young, but ugly leftover, just because they had money.

Her father had laughed and told her, there was no way he could inflict anyone he knew with such a loud, bossy, far too talented for her own good, female. He also told her, as far as he was concerned the luckless sap that crossed her path in romance, deserved every manipulative moment. But had added, 'That He better take care of you and love you, as much as I do, or he'll have me to answer to. No, sorry, *you* to answer to!'

She did meet her match, a partnership made in heaven, but that was not before gaining a degree in law and becoming a barrister.

Paula, on the other hand was very much single, said she'd tried men once and didn't like them. Couldn't quite see the point of having a man around when she was perfectly capable of wiring her own plugs. We didn't dare ask!

One evening when we were having a girly night in, too much Pinot Grigio had flowed and we hinted to Paula, in our inebriated state of logic, that maybe she was of …you know…… the other persuasion?

"Oh God no, I've never been into c__ts!" She said her nose wrinkling. Bina slid off the settee in shock.

Paula had said the 'c' word! I was stunned.

We never said the 'c' word! (Ever since I'd read spirit medium, Doris Stokes books and thought my gran and grandad may be watching over me from the other side, it took me all my time to say, damn and blast…at very worst, bugger!)

"Paula?!" I said in disbelief, thinking it just had to be the wine talking.

"No really Pen, once you say yes to them, next thing you know you'll end up naked and disappearing down a black hole, never to be seen again." She visibly shuddered and grimaced.

Bina and I were looking at each other, then at Paula. Does she know something we don't, has she been reading some, dodgy, imported, sex book?

"Paula" I ask tentatively. "Who told you ..…that you'd disappear, never to be seen again, etc?"

"Well, I had this friend at college who was approached by one." Bina and I leaned closer, totally intrigued by what was coming next.

"*She* said…… that they gave her a leaflet and told her that if she came to the prefab behind Tarran House at seven-thirty, she would be the chosen one."

Bina and I sat in stunned silence, then, as it all registered, we chorused.

"Oh God! Paula, you said, Cults!"

It took another minute for Paula to register, what we were referring to and what we thought *she'd* said……

"Oh no! You didn't think I said"……

We were prostrate with laughter, then Paula thought she was going to wet herself, which made us laugh even more, as she couldn't get up off the settee, then I realised, it was *my* settee! As I tried to move forward to help her up, Bina had the same idea, we then clashed heads and all just fell back in absolute hysterics…….

I really, really do hope grandma and grandad *weren't* watching!

Back to my 'classic man' encounter. Bina had got invites to an exclusive gallery opening. She said she'd only take me and Paula if we didn't show her up with our lack of artistic knowledge. *This* was coming from someone who thought, Leonardo De Vinci starred in 'Titanic.' "De Caprio" I said to her, trying to get through. "Don't they make those ornamental flower things?" She said seriously. "You're pulling my leg! That is, Capodimonte and if you say, isn't he the fruity fella that says, 'yes', I'll swing for you!" Her excuse was she only appreciated modern art, (that will be why she has a Picasso print, upside-down in her utility room loo then? I haven't the heart to tell her.)

Bina had said we had to dress, 'boho chic'? She said, think art student, child with a dressing up box, with a little charity shop mix n'match. I wasn't going to have a problem, that appeared to be my whole wardrobe.

Paula didn't get it quite right, looking more, boho Margaret Rutherford in 'Blithe Spirit' mode, eccentric…… but just a little bit scary too! I think it was the roses in her cleavage and the dying dahlia above her left ear that did it. She said she wanted everyone to know she was a florist, her bohemian side, being at one with nature.

I whispered to her, that was all very well, but some people might be a little put off by the greenfly in her hair and the small slug crawling over her right breast.

Paula missed the cheese nibbles, she emerged from the ladies twenty minutes later with her hair brushed to within an inch of its life, with so much static she looked like, the *actual*, Blithe Spirit, about to do a haunting! Her chest was red raw, as if she'd been trapped on a sun-bed for ten hours. Poor Paula, I had to accost the wine waiter to bring her another drink, for medicinal purposes only.

It was while I was on my way back from accosting the wine waiter that I saw, 'classic man.' The chiselled profile gazing up at a rather wishy-washy, grungy piece of, I beg to differ, 'artwork'? I took my position, standing at the next piece of work, putting on my, 'I'm just drinking it all in,' expression. He took a quick sideways glance, I let out a little sigh, and gazed on, as if lost in the artist's work. He caught my eye and smiled as he moved closer to look at the piece in front of me.

"Do you like their work?" I quickly looked at the card fastened beside the painting, which had the artists name on.

"Yes, I'm a real fan of Paul Saunders, I love the way he uses his depth of colours, the light and shade changing the mood, I can see what he's trying to convey."

"Really." He muses, obviously impressed by my artistic bent. Or so I thought.

After a little more artistic banter, he asked if I'd like to go out to dinner, 'Maison Rouge' perhaps? Would I! (It was more sophisticated than the usual chat up line, I'll meet you in the Snail & Lettuce, I'll be with me mates, you bring some of yours!)

Four days later, dinner was a stark white, minimalist, Bistro, bit trendy, but everyone took a second look when we walked in. I know it was at me, as much as him because he said I looked...... 'lovely' (not perfect, but 'lovely', of course from 'classic man' I think that's got to be pretty good.)

He does all the ordering, the wine and food, all in French, with a very confident manner. I gaze at him, rather pathetically, in awe. He tells me all about himself. In fact, he doesn't ask me any questions at all till we're halfway through what appears to be an overpriced stalk of dill with an inch square fish garnish.

He leans forward, with what I see as a slight smirk on his face and asks if I normally wear glasses. I look at him with slight suspicion, strange question. I've not left a couple of pairs on my head a la Professor Brainstorm, have I? I'd heard about these confident, good-looking guys, control all and everything in their working day, but like the dominatrix type of woman in the bedroom. I had visions of him moving on from glasses, to, do I own a pin-striped suit and a large wooden ruler! I leaned back, unsure how to answer.

Before I could answer, he started laughing. "I'm sorry, it's just last week, at the gallery, you were admiring the work by.......Paul Saunders? Paul Saunders was actually...... the owner of the piece, it was on loan to the gallery, so you were waxing lyrical...... about the owner...... *Not* the artist."

He continued to laugh finding it all so, *very, very,* amusing!

My admiration for 'classic man' suddenly disappeared.

"Yes, alright, alright, I think you've made your point, so I'm not an arty know all. Well, whoever painted it, hardly matters really, it was dreadful. Ed the chimp could have produced something more pleasing to the eye with crayons and a pile of horse plop!"

An immature response I know, but I was angry and it just gushed out, (bit like the horse plop!).

He stood up, obviously about to leave. I stayed put.

"You may like to know, that load of, 'horse plop' was done by a very talented artist and ex-girlfriend of mine……Fennella Black."

Determined to get the last word and to feel slightly less humiliated than I already did, as I watched him huffily turn to go, I called after him. "She obviously got her inspiration from the break-up………It was an interesting use of brown!"

Let's face it. If he'd been anything near a gentleman, he wouldn't have mentioned my faux pas. (See, I can do French too, when it's needed.) He brought it up just to put me down and flaunt his superiority.

That is not a plus in my book.

Needless to say, we didn't stay in touch and I still don't like modern art!

You can give me a………'Laughing Cavalier' any day!

Chapter 3

As Monday evening approached all too quickly, I drove home trying to work through my wardrobe. 'Philleep' it seems he likes, feminine and girly?

When I'd spoken to Suse on Saturday, while we were out shopping. Her advice was to go for... subtle but sexy?' I was stumped.

It was alright for her she could look sexy in a bin-bag and wellies. She'd bought two tops and a pair of gorgeous black, suede boots. She persuaded me to try a pair on, I swore under my breath unable to get the zip more than two thirds up my calf. What is wrong with designers, why do they assume anyone above a size 10 doesn't deserve to be fashionable.

It wasn't a good start to a day clothes shopping. The thought of standing there in my, 'adequate pants', holding my stomach in, wishing I'd shaved my legs and worn a matching bra.

Communal changing rooms………why?! What possible reason can there be for putting us, 'body unfortunates' in with those slim, lithe, forms, with hip bones like machetes and stomachs you could bounce watermelons off. Talking of melons! Not everyone is wearing a pull 'em up, push 'em out Wonderbra, so why do they all look as if they've modelled for Gossard, all up and out there? (Mine are more down and been there!)

Worse still, when there is a girl who stands in all her confident, swishy-haired, super slim glory and you see her strut out to do a twirl for her hubby and…… five children! If she can look like that after five, I'll be going into hiding if I'm lucky enough to have one. Without my, 'adequate pants', on a bad day, you'd be forgiven for thinking I was three months gone. At least pregnancy would give me the excuse to look like a Weebel. (Bit of a drastic solution for too many eclairs though I feel.)

I ended up, as usual, buying a lipstick, a caraway bar and two health and beauty magazines, promising myself, *this* time I'll get it right.

Susie had had a fantastic evening with Simon, who was now Mr Forbes, and not, Mr Mercedes, I knew it was moving on as he's now lost his nickname. He was driving her to, 'the country', next weekend. The wilds of Cumbria. She told me she'd rooted out her Barber jacket, white shirt, riding boots and soft, cream stretch jodhpurs, in case they had horses nearby.

She'd bought this apparel six years ago when she was seeing a horse trainer, Miles. It ran its course, (pardon the pun) when she got fed up never actually managing to mount a horse because Miles kept side-lining her into the stables to do a bit of mounting of his own. She said he was too highly sexed. I told her she should have put him out to stud.

I asked her whether she hadn't thought that perhaps the sight of her in jodhpurs, so tight over her curves, that VPL was an impossibility, a white shirt open to her ample cleavage, that maybe Miles found her just too irresistible and couldn't help himself? She said it was the, 'helping himself' she got tired of. She liked to flirt, tease and take her time, he was just *too* easy! (Heaven forbid, an easy bloke, not in my lifetime anyway.)

What if that outfit did the same to Simon, I asked her. She said that she was hoping the look would have the desired effect, as he was very cool and controlled, but in a nice way. She wanted to just ruffle his feathers a bit, (and his perfectly styled hair possibly?) I could only imagine that Simon was going to have no choice but to return from the country well and truly, 'ruffled'!

Suse would also be meeting his sister and parents (she'd already met his brother, briefly, working at the Straw House.) She said she was so nervous, but really happy, as she rarely got introduced to………'the relatives' and his brother had been lovely, so she had high hopes for the rest of his family.

She said she finally felt normal, she then laughed and said maybe it was time to swap wardrobes. She should have all my cover up, ladylike clothes and I could have her, 'pulling clothes.' It conjured up some hilarious visions, more mine than hers.
If I squeezed myself into some of her lycra, or leather numbers I think I'd be in danger of being harpooned, or gently covered in damp blankets by Greenpeace and hauled across the nearest beach!

I pushed Ferdy gently sideways, as he pummelled the mound of clothes I'd pulled from the wardrobe and drawers. "You're not helping my decision you hairy, fur-ball", then again it narrows down the choice if I can't wear the items covered in cat hair. Maybe Phil's an animal lover and that will appeal to him or, maybe he's allergic to fur, that wouldn't be a good start, leaving him red-eyed and sneezing.

The final decision was made, by the clock hands, ticking by quickly. Also, by my aching arms after twelve changes of clothes, six changes of shoes, four changes of hairstyle, a change of handbag, three lost earrings and a clogged-up mascara brush!

The final outfit being, sensible straight, mid-length brown skirt, with a burnt sienna blouse, my concession to sexy being, two buttons undone instead of one!

I remembered, 'girly' and had put on matching necklace and earrings of tiny yellow, glass roses. I was quite pleased with the result. Ferdy purred in agreement, as I scattered a couple of crunchy treats in his bowl and headed for the door.

Ten to seven, I walked towards the cinema. Oh my God, there were so many people about.
All there to witness my meeting of a, complete stranger! Could they tell I was a 'Blind Dater'? I felt, as I climbed the steps that I had a large arrow above my head pointing down and a neon sign stating, 'This woman is on a blind date, how sad and desperate is she?'

Morry had said… 'Philleep' would be carrying his paper and briefcase, as he was coming straight from work, he was in insurance, was that a good sign?

As the fourth male passed carrying a briefcase, I started to feel quite nauseous. I had so many butterflies, I just longed for a man with a large net and jam-jar.

Then, a rather red-faced male, with a windswept shock of white-blonde hair, appeared juggling newspaper and briefcase, he offered a hand. As he grasped my fingers and shook them firmly, he looked me straight in the eyes and like a rather amusing cross between Leslie Philips and Joey from Friends.

"Well, well and how *do you do?*"

"I'm very well thank you", I say with a nervous smile.

"You must be Philleep, er, Philip?" He leans in, his breath smelling of a rather recent gargle, or squirt of strong, minty breath freshener.

"Well, Henny Penny, you may be in trouble if I'm not!"
I looked worried. He laughed, a *very* loud laugh. "Yes, I am Philip and I believe we've got a film to see, any preference?"

Before I could say I'd seen Titanic, but quite liked the sound of 'Wings of a Dove' with Helena Bonham-Carter, he was ushering me towards the ticket office, talking as if addressing the whole lobby.

"Can't bear that Bonham-Carter creature, but there's a fine filly and a good bit of action in….. 'L.A. Confidential', are you game?" Game for what? I wasn't sure. Game for proving I wasn't jealous that he had a thing for Kim Basinger? (Who hasn't after 'Nine and Half Weeks.') Game for running up cinema stairs, as if your life depended on it? Game for talking like you're a 1944 fighter pilot, who's been left with, 'gunners' ear'? Who knows.

He managed to disturb several people while they tried to watch the film, with his loud comments.

"This is real edge of the seat stuff isn't it, eh? Grab yourself another mitt full of popcorn, you look like a girl who's got a sweet tooth."

But it was the Biggles guffaws in between, that got everyone's backs up. He seemed oblivious the film wasn't a comedy.
I shrank down into my seat feeling, oh so grateful we hadn't gone to see….. 'Good Will Hunting'.

Out of the cinema, I was all for taking Morrys advice and making a dash for it, but he insisted we were having such a good time we couldn't part without having a 'chin wag' and a coffee, or maybe something stronger?'

I then sensibly explained that I was driving and didn't trust my reactions with even the smallest amount of alcohol in my system. He looked slightly disappointed, but still insisted, "Coffee for two it is then!" He took my arm and propelled me into the nearby wine bar, 'Violas'. The waiter took us to a small corner table for two...... Oh lordy, *surely* he didn't think we were a couple?

Philip ordered coffee and a selection of biscuits, very loudly and with added hand gesticulation that looked as if he was semaphoring his fellow pilots into land! The poor waiter, who granted had a strong Italian accent, spoke perfect English and was certainly not deaf.

Philip was, to be honest and not always intentionally, quite amusing! He had a story to tell on every subject and when I finally got a word in, he did, actually listen.

"So, office life getting you down a bit then Penelope? Insurance is a bit like that for the ladies, stuck on the end of a telephone. Whereas us blokes are lucky, we get out on the road, the hard sell, don't you know."

I felt the world should be grateful they had his voice bellowing at them from across a table, or through a car window, rather than down a phone, will have saved many a ruptured eardrum, I'm sure.

We parted company around 10.30pm. He wasn't pushy in the slightest, but then hey I was no Kim Basinger! He shook my hand again, very firmly, pulling me towards him at the same time, I thought for one awful moment he was going to do the 'lunge and kiss' move, but no.

He said, (in what was for him a real effort at a whisper,) as the pain in my right ear subsided. "Morris has got my number Penelope. If you are short of a chaperone again, I'm more than happy for you to tag my name onto your list."

I wasn't quite sure what he meant but assumed it could only be gentlemanly coming from him.

"Oh, thank you very much. I've had a super evening." (I said, '*super*', I was turning into Gloria Swanson, I'd be saying...... 'gosh and golly' next. Why was it I always seemed to morph into female versions of the male I was with?)

As he turned to leave, his mop of hair falling forward again, his broad grin spreading across his glowing face, his long coat catching the wind, he raised his arm, waved his paper and called out for the population of the town to hear.

"Yes, it has been super. Got to dash, got an old dog at home needs feeding."

I didn't ask! I suppressed my giggles till I reached my car, as several people had gazed in stunned silence as that sentence echoed loudly in the night air.

Not the best start to my dating diary, but not the worst, thankfully. He was a man's man, in a man's world, who probably wanted a 'little woman' in his life to save him taking his laundry to Mother, or the local service wash.

He wasn't intentionally chauvinistic, just old fashioned. I liked old fashioned, but I also liked fun, parties and dancing. I think the nearest I'd get to that with Philip is a family and friends 'bun-fight'. Things on sticks, buns, Black Forest gateaux, Mr. Disco, consisting of the, Okey Cokey, Simon Says and the Dambusters theme tune. Followed at the end of the evening by Engelbert Humperdinck singing the 'Last Waltz' and of course,

'Please Release Me'. Sorry Philip, nothing personal, but you are just not my type, nor me his to be fair.

As I climbed into bed, my ears still ringing, like I'd had a five-hour stint in 'Ollies' nightclub, I stroked Ferdy as he stretched out, giving me that, 'oh you're back' look, through half closed eyes.

Anyway, presuming Philip's, 'old dog' he was going home to feed was canine, that made him a possible non-cat person?

I really had to have a… cat person. I drifted off to sleep picturing Jason Durr dressed head to toe in black fur, draped across my bed, purring. At least if I died in my sleep tonight, I'd have a *very,* very, big smile on my face!

Chapter 4

"*Well?*" Asked Morry, who'd come rushing to the top of the stairs Tuesday morning, after seeing me stroll into the building.

"What did you think of our Philleep, isn't he just an old fart before his time?" I hadn't wanted to tell Morry exactly what I thought, with Phillip being a relative, but he said it first.

"You knew he was like that, what made you think he was my type?" He gave me that look, checked the offices were empty then said loudly.

"How the hell should I know 'what is your type'! You've had the best part of twenty years dating men and you still haven't found a Mr Right yet. Not even a Mr Maybe, or a Mr What-the-Heck. You're thirty-seven years old, who are you waiting for? Cos' I'm sorry lady, you've missed the boat if you're still waiting for David Essex, Lewis Collins, Hugh Grant, Robbie Williams and all the other fantasy men you've swooned after over the years. You live in cloud cuckoo land lovey! You're going to end up a lonely and bitter old bag, with only a house full of cats for company!"

As he turned to continue his, 'tongue in cheek' banter, he looked shocked and guilty. I stood there, tears rolling down my face. They say truth hurts and the pain was all too visible, as the words sank in. He wrapped his arms round me quickly and steered me towards the file store where it was quiet.

"Oh Pen, I am so sorry, lovey, didn't realise it mattered so much." He said, hugging me tightly.

"I thought you and Suse loved being single, giving all these eligible men the run around. Christ, thirty-seven, you've got years yet, babe! Women reach their prime at thirty-five so you're well in it girl! We'll find you a fella, not a problem, someone really spesh. Hey! We get on, what the heck I'll marry you, if you're in a rush! You know, for babies, body clock ticking and all that?"

He hugged me closer. I couldn't help but smile as a rather bizarre picture of the wedding passed through my mind, me in the morning suit, Morry in a white taffeta meringue number and Roger as a bridesmaid!

He passed me a hanky, as I looked up at him through my, mascara-streaked eyes, not a good way to start the day.

"Much as I appreciate your kind proposal Morry and the sentiment behind it, I have to say no, for the fact that I'd have to fight you for the bridal gown. I really didn't mean to get so upset. It's just sometimes I feel life's passing me by. I love my life, my home and my friends, but I'd also love a man in my life and the possibility of a family before all me bits dry up."

Morry's nose wrinkles. "Oooo er! Things are more serious than I thought, I'm visualising old prunes and pot-pourri here, let's change the subject."

"I have got a suggestion though, if you fancy a quickie"
I stare at Morry in disbelief.

"God, not me you fool, I'm a no, no, before ten-thirty! No, I was thinking if you rush down to London Zoo, there's a large, male Panda that would go the distance after one look at you and those eyes!" He turns me towards the mirror in the corner. I gasp.

"I'll get my own back, just you wait." We both start laughing as he helps me wipe the smudged black rings from around my eyes.

"Right, Dolly Daydream, are you going to get into the real world with the rest of us and stop waiting for Mr Perfect 'cos he just doesn't exist."

I pretend to think hard, then say, "Can I just keep Jason D? For night-time dreaming only, pleeease?" He looks skywards. "Oh, I forgot about him, go on then for night-time use only remember?" (Oh God, Jason Durr for night-time use only……. yes please.) Morry makes sure that I am, 'looking gooood' before he allows me back to my desk, brings me a strong tea, one sugar, says it's to calm me down after my emotional outburst! (He obviously hasn't seen me in true emotional outburst mode, weeping into the chocolate biscuits, 'Hazard of Hearts' on the video, nothing fits me and I'm all alone in the world. Happens about four times a year and it's not pretty!)

"So, Philleeps not a goer then?" He asks with a sideways glance. I smile sweetly.

"No, not in any sense of the word I'm afraid, but there is Rolf, sorry Rafe to look forward to…… isn't there?"

Morry grins. "Oh, yes, now, he's very different from our Philleep." (Not a bad thing, too many Philips and we'd all end up in tweed suits, being very sensible and very loud! All frightfully nice, but maybe not much fun.)

"What's Rolf into then? Likes, dislikes? Do you and Roger see him much?" Morry looks coy.

"We don't visit often. He's very fit, Rojere gets jealous, if he catches me staring at him more than I should."

"You ogle your boyfriend's brother?! I know the sort of blokes that catch your eye, so he must be a bit of a hunk." I say excitedly.

"My Rojere's the only one for me, but you know, sometimes my imagination wanders." I laugh keeping eye contact.

"He's your Jason Durr isn't he, you little tinker?"

He raises his eyebrows trying to keep a straight face.

"Well, put it this way, I think there's more chance of him being your Jason than my George Michael, he certainly isn't fighting *his* way out of any closet!"

Tuesday lunchtime I finally got to talk to Suse again, we shared a pot of tea in Parkers and caught up with the gossip. I told her about Philip, she said all the right things, I knew she would.

"Not meant to be babe. You want your ears nibbled, not shouted in at twenty decibels! My dad always says, everyone has to kiss a few toads, (or frogs even?) before they find their Prince. I've had a few reptiles in my time Pen, I can tell you!"

"Honestly Suse, I'm fine about it. I've decided I'm going to treat this blind date thing as just a bit of fun, nothing more. Something to get me out of the house now and then. There's not much chance I'll meet my soulmate on a blind date is there? That only happens in books and movies."

Wednesday came and went at work. Morry had taken the day off to take his mum and dad to the hospital. He said he'd be dropping dad in Urinary and mum in Dermatological and flitting between the two all day, with a flask of tea and bags of Barley sugars and liquorice twists. (I didn't ask for any medical details, I'd have been there all day, he's like an old woman where, 'bits' are concerned!)

I was just locking my desk drawers when Anna came over, closely followed by June. Anna smiling, but looking slightly embarrassed. "Look I know it's maybe not my place to say anything but...." Anna was a lot younger than me, in her twenties. Big and bouncy was how she described herself! She was deliriously happy, with husband Mark, who worshipped the ground she walked on and their two little girls, Verity and Emma, (proof in many photos, lined across her desk!)

..."We couldn't help hearing that you've been on a...a blind date?"

I began to feel a little bit awkward. I don't suppose either of them would stoop to this level of desperation. They would prefer to stay single and proud!

"Yes, well, just the one, it was just a bit of fun really."

June looked a little shocked at the prospect of going out with a man, 'just for fun'! June had definitely not married Barry for fun. She had married for, mutual respect, for an intellectual equal, to share common interests of 17th century architecture, folk music, animal rights and beekeeping. Also, for the large house, gardens and seven beehives. No children, (they could not bring themselves to produce another life, forcing it into such a dreadful, decadent world.) But they did have five chickens and a one-winged turkey called Christmas! (Named in irony...... certainly not fun!?)

June stepped forward. "What Anna was trying to say is, if you would like to continue with the blind date concept, we both have male persons you could meet?"

"Oh, errr, well, I'm not sure, to be honest, I've actually got another date tonight."

Anna continued unabated, "In for a penny, in for a pound then, I've got hubby's friend, Angus, divorced, two sons, but coping, what do you think, a week Friday? Oh, do say yes, he'd be thrilled!"

The thought of someone thrilled at the possibility of a date with me was a definite plus, also I quite liked the thought of a ready-made family. (Whoops! Nothing too serious, no hints of desperation here.)

June hovered desperate to speak. "I have what I consider a step-brother, Ben. He's coming down for a break, end of next week, for a fortnight. He works for his dad's organic fruit and vegetable business. It will all be his soon, as his dad wants to retire, I can make arrangements for a week next Tuesday, that okay?"

This was getting better, own business, a possible big place out in the countryside.........Woah! But nothing too serious of course, just remember that.

"This is really nice of you both to go to so much trouble. Yes, I'd really like to accept both your offers of men and dates, count me in. I'll look forward to it."

June gave Anna a sideways glance, "I'm sure Ben is the kind of companion you're looking for." Anna bustled passed her giggling. "Oh, I think Angus is a much better prospect for stability, contentment and some *fun*!"

That word again, June tutted, as she gathered her duffel coat and crocheted satchel bag. Anna then grabbed her pashmina, couple of M & S carriers and rushed after her, making friendly enquiries about her bees and chickens, June softened, their voices drifting off as they descended the stairs.

Chapter 5

I was meeting Rolf outside 'Teddy's Bar' at eight. Morry said it was a bit of a poseurs paradise, but Rolf knew the place well and it was central too. I took my car again. It just gave me that extra avenue if I wanted to cut and run. I just didn't like getting into those awkward situations with some men and taxis.

If you take a taxi, they always seem to go to your home first, then you get the 'puppy dog' eyes and the line......'Any chance of a coffee, I'd love to chat more?'

I hate that situation, particularly if you like them, it really puts you on the spot, kind of emotional blackmail, nothing worse. If you say no, you feel distrusting, a suspicious prude, but if you say yes, you can almost hear his loins cheering. 'Wahay! We're on a promise here lads!'

I was almost on the *verge* of saying yes once, until I found myself almost on the *verge* of the pavement, as the man I was with lunged out of the taxi in his over triumphant eagerness!

I very quickly changed my mind, thinking on my trampled feet, I made the excuse that I'd forgotten my brother was using the settee for a couple of nights, in town for an interview. I didn't know who I then felt sorrier for, the spurned date, with his deflated ego and let down loins, or the poor taxi driver who would have to console him all the way back home!

As I turned the corner to 'Teddy's Bar' I saw the 'Adonis' that was Rolf. Approximately six foot three, with shoulders like bull bars. Morry wasn't wrong, a wonderful specimen of toned man. He was positively glowing with testosterone and vitality.

Thick, wavy, dark hair, very tanned. A sunbed job, but who could blame him, gilding the lily perhaps, but what the heck!

Wishing I'd made an effort with the contact lenses I squinted to make out, crisp pale blue cap sleeve shirt, hugging his biceps, open at the neck and classy black trousers covering his long, long legs. He looked more in his twenties, than thirties and I suddenly felt quite jaded.

As I slowly walked towards him, I could see it wasn't my eyesight playing tricks on me, he really was incredibly handsome and very fit. My mind was racing. Oh God, there is no way he is going to want to be seen with such an unhealthy lump of ….. womanhood, surely. I felt as if I'd just been awarded, 'frump of the year' and he'd been sent to make me realise what I could get if I made an effort.

I *had* made a real effort though, with my outfit anyway. After listening carefully to Susie's advice, she'd told me this time to try……demure, but flirty. I'd looked at again her in total blankness.

She patiently advised me to pick something stylish, but accessorise with something quirky, ultra-feminine, that would make me stand out from other girls. I had asked if a chignon of panty-liners would do for, 'ultra-feminine and quirky?' She suggested that perhaps I'd not just be standing out, but be standing out on my own, if I decided on that look.

I finally took her seriously and after rooting through numerous bags, hair decorations, boxes of costume jewellery, racks of belts and even my collection of hats. I came up with fairly demure, slightly flirty and a little quirky!

I'd gone for a coffee coloured 50's style, full skirted dress, with layered under nets, a soft, fluffy cream, bolero cardi with pink rose buttons. I put my hair up with two gold, rose pins.
I found my mid brown suede ankle strap shoes matched perfectly. Pulling together with my vintage cream bag, covered in hand-beaded pink roses.

Anyway, it was too late to hide, Rolf caught sight of me.
I suddenly felt like Doris Day at a fifties convention, or Sandy in Grease. When she suddenly realises that perhaps the man before her is more a tight lycra trouser man, instead of wanting to spend the evening with something that looks as if it should be covering a toilet roll in grans outside loo!

He suddenly grins, raises his eyebrows, (in utter disbelief no doubt?)

"*Wow*! Hello Gorgeous!" He says grabbing my hand, not to shake, but to twirl me quickly, making my skirt come alive, so that I look like some ludicrous ballroom dancer, being whisked off for a foxtrot, or quick step. (Penny Wiseman, senior admin clerk by day, partnered by Rafe, a mechanic,
(I later find out) and yes, she does sew on all her own sequins!)

"A great look. You into the fifties then, are you? Wow! Are you totally authentic then......?"

He says his eyebrows raised, grinning from ear to ear.
A look of possible testosterone overload about to surface.
I suddenly click that his mind is obviously a vision of twirling skirts and the sight of stocking tops and dependable white suspenders!

"Hey cheeky, you don't even know if I'm your blind date yet, never mind questioning a lady on her under-garments." I try to say humorously, without appearing too prudish.

"Oh! No, sorry, no really...... I didn't, actually mean the underwear! I meant do you listen and dance to all that fifties rock n' roll music?"

We both blushed, (a sight to see a towering, body builder going as pink as my beaded roses!). Fortunately, we both saw the funny side and were still laughing as we entered Teddy's Bar, just for.........'a quick jar' he insisted.

Four 'jars' later, he was more than a little inebriated, he's not normally a big drinker he tells me. Then enthusiastically tells me all about his fitness regime. His strict high protein diet, (steak and egg whites, yummy! Bet chocolate éclairs aren't on his list?) his weight training and of course, his muscle definition.

Possibly, if I'd had the same amount to drink as him, I'd have been sitting agog at his absolute determination, time and effort in his quest to hone the perfect body.

He suddenly started clicking his fingers and bobbing a little, which was a disconcerting sight with his large frame on a metal bar stool. He looked rather like one of those springy toys that you lick and stick down then wait for it to suddenly free itself, launching itself skywards! There would certainly be a lot of injuries if he did the same!

"Which one would you be then, which one are you most like?" I look puzzled.

"Sorry, which what.......which.... what?"

"Spice Girls, spice girl, which one would you be?"

He says pointing his finger towards the ceiling as I realise,

'Who Do You Think You Are' is coming out over the speakers. How old is he? Morry had said late thirties, same as me. It's the sort of question I'd have asked my 8year old niece. She'd have squealed with delight and shouted, 'Baby Spice, no Posh, no all of them!'

"Well, which one?" He's now bobbing even more enthusiastically to the song, mouthing the words.

Now then, he obviously has a favourite, so I've got to be careful which one I pick, (I can't quite believe I'm giving precious thought to this decision!) If I say, Baby he'll think I'm trying to recapture my youth, if I say Posh he'll think I want to be skinny with delusions to grandeur.

Scary Spice?...... no he'd just think I was ....scary.

Ginger possibly? No, I'd had my experience of short skirts and platform boots when I was fourteen, they didn't do me any favours then! Trying to impress a boy in my new, red leather platform boots, slid on some ice, the younger boys had so nicely polished earlier, went flying, ending up showing him two sets of red cheeks, instead of one! I felt scarred for life!) No, no, you couldn't call me Ginger! So, it had to be Sporty! Never in a million years could I be classed as, 'sporty' but *he* wasn't to know. I'd often *thought* about taking up jogging, rushing out for an hour round the park before work. I thankfully managed to persuade myself that it was not only unsociable to Ferdy to remove his quality time of, owner and cat bonding, but also that it was very unsafe, all sorts of strange unknown people out at that time in the morning, (paper boys........ milkmen, you know the sort.)

Rolf was still oblivious to me thinking carefully about the question, he was now doing what could only be described as a sort of manic hand jive!

"I think I'd have to be Sporty Spice, she's very fit, healthy, doesn't cover her face in thick make-up, always bouncy and natural." He smiled sympathetically, obviously realising I was quite deluded.

"I actually like Baby spice." (God! Really......... why were men so predictable?)

"Oh, of course and I know why," I said trying my best not to be *too* catty.

"You like all that long, girly blonde hair, those big blue eyes, that innocent pout, high heels, those pretty little girly dresses."......He looks a little put out.

"No, actually, I really like her singing voice. I think she's the best singer, if they ever split, she'd do really well solo! But if we're talking looks...... that Ginger babe would get me going anytime...... now *she is hot*!"

Damn, I'd got it wrong again! The platforms and short skirts do it every time, (well they might if you could stand up in them...... but then probably flat on your back with your legs in the air is a man's preference, would he even notice the boots?) Rolf's hand jive had now moved to his feet, he's now off the bar stool and doing little shuffly, clicky steps in his shiny black loafers, he's looking like Lionel Blair warming up for a tap dance marathon.

"Look" he says doing a little sideways slide towards me.

"I just love dancing, you don't fancy an hour or two at 'Ollies' club, go on, say yes, it'll be great!" He looked so excited. I think he was holding his breath waiting for me to answer.

"Yes, great, why not! I love a good dance too! I may look

like a fifties throwback but I do like most of the current chart stuff as well." I couldn't be certain, but I'm sure he did a little skip hop out of the door, his long legs striding out and up the street then breaking into a strange leggy trot!

"Are you alright in those shoes, it's not far." He called back slightly concerned. Surely my shoes would give me a good enough excuse for not having to run like an over excited teenager trying to get a Spice Girls autograph! Anyway, these were shoes……. not platform boots, I was in control.

It was quite obvious that he wasn't in control. Hopefully it was just the lager, heightening his senses, as I watched him almost leaping like a startled Gazelle.

"Come on gorgeous, can't wait to get you on that dance floor!" He grabbed my hand, I caught my breath as he propelled me up two flights of stairs. I hoped to God he was only planning to dance on the dance floor! He quickly ploughed his way through the crowd at the bar and came back with two mineral waters.

"Don't want anything to ruin my concentration." What on earth was he planning on doing out there? Before I could worry, the pounding beat of ..Gina G and 'I Belong To You' fills the air, people are up and throwing caution to the wind, within minutes we're doing the same. Last time I ran that fast onto a dance floor they were playing Wham, 'Wake Me Up Before You Go-Go' in the mid-eighties, with all the girls and too many martinis!

Rolf had already got into……'shaking his funky groove thang,' I was still warming up with something that looked alarmingly like a Nolan Sister's routine!

"Come on sweet thing, let yourself go!" I'm sorry but from where I was standing, if letting myself go was gyrating my groin towards my partner, grabbing my crotch at regular intervals, a la' Jackson, you could count me out! I *was* enjoying the music and loosening up a bit and couldn't help noticing all the girls flashing just a little hint of 'green eyed monster' in my direction. They couldn't help looking at Rolf's amazing physique, muscles rippling as he moved around me keeping perfect time with the beat. There was no denying, he was a sight to behold and he certainly liked to make a girl feel special.

Suddenly he lunged towards me, then turned me round, pulling me close he began to gyrate behind me, his big strong arms in a lock around my excuse for a waist. He was totally uninhibited and the sentence, 'can't wait to get you on the dance floor,' appeared to be taking on another meaning!

I hadn't danced like this for years, the most memorable being the in-house disco at the hotel in York. Charlie and I only had eyes for each other, (granted I was probably as uninhibited as Rolf back then. Three Martinis and I'm a dancing fool!)

It had been more than that though, Charlie's touch was electric, we had definite chemistry, we were oblivious to others in the room, we just had so much fun. We'd laughed so much, dancing to, 'Dizzy' by Vic Reeves and the Wonder Stuff, then it got all sensual and touchy feely with 'I Wanna Sex You Up' and 'The Right Thing' by Simply Red. By the time we were locked together for 'If You Ever' by Gabrielle and East 17, we had planned our escape, mmmm....magical memories!

I suddenly realised as I'd got carried away with my thoughts, Rolf had turned me round, my head buried in his chest and his gyrating lower half just getting a little too intimate for a first date. I was sure I could feel the banana, (he said he kept in his pocket as a high carb snack when his energy flagged) move!

Then undeterred, I felt his hands move to my, fortunately well-covered, bottom!

Just as I realised, I may have to do my best Joyce Grenfell impression...... 'Excuse me, would you mind removing your hands from my posterior, thanks awfully.' The music changed. He lifted me so far into the air I nearly had vertigo.

"It's our song baby, listen!" He then proceeded to sing to me, loudly, the few words he knew of Babybirds, 'Your Gorgeous'! Had I been anything other than an exhausted heap I'd have been very flattered, that only three hours into our first date, we had an 'our song' and more importantly, he thought I was, 'gorgeous'?! We danced and danced there was no tiring the man! He'd grab my hand as a gap came.

"Yeah! Hurry up! Get a quick drink before the next one. Yeh! Come on, quick! It's Robert Miles, 'One to One', I love this one!" with that I'd be whisked back into the throng!

Even when I went out for a, 'we're not even going to look at men' dance-fest with Bina and Paula, we didn't stay on the dance floor this long!

I was beginning to feel, very slightly unattractive, sweat is not an appealing attribute. I could feel it trickling everywhere. ... I must look dreadful. I had to get to the ladies, just for five minutes. As the next record faded, I told him I was just nipping to the...and pointed in the general direction. He patted my bottom playfully and shouted as the next record started up.

"Don't keep me, or this dance floor waiting too long gorgeous!"

I staggered into a toilet cubicle. It was so small that when I sat down my skirt and nets stayed up the wall. I didn't even have to hold them up! Which was just as well because I felt incapable of movement, I hadn't even got the strength to pee.

Oh! God and my poor feet! They felt as if they'd swollen two sizes, (now I'd never be able to fit me glass slipper!) I shouldn't have sat down. It was then so much worse when I did finally try to stand. I could hear Morry's voice ringing in my ears saying, 'for Heaven's sake girl, you're thirty-seven not eighty-seven! Me mother is seventy-six and she can stay on that ballroom floor for six hours and she's got bunions and incontinence!' (To be honest I think I had the makings of both, with swollen feet and soaked nether regions……but hoped to God it was just sweat!)

As I emerged from the cubicle looking like, Bette Davis from, 'Who Killed Baby Jane', the room went quiet, just the odd snigger. I straightened myself up reaching the mirror, casually taking a lipstick from my bag.

Several young girls jostled in and began giggling, I heard one girl say. "Woah! She's gonna need more than lipstick to fix that, hope she's got cement in that bag o' hers."

It was like going back to the school cloakroom, skinny girls, all dressed inappropriately, jeering and laughing, usually at mine, or Susies expense.

Well sod 'em, I'd had enough. I didn't like it then and I didn't like it now.

I kept focused as best I could, on the mirror, my hair had frizzed, like it does when I get caught in the rain. I took a deep breath, patted my face dry with a tissue, applied just a little touch of powder, Bette Davis is not a look I wanted to nurture!

I carefully unclipped my hair, brushed the frizz back into a high 50's ponytail. Reapplied my lippy, ran my wrists under the cold tap, cooling me down.

There I was, fresh faced, lips red, hair neat, my skirts swishing I went towards the door, but not before turning to the half-dressed ensemble and saying.

"Maybe if you worked up a sweat on the dance floor instead of posing at the bar and hanging around in toilets, you'd get the chance to re-apply your make-up. You never know, you might get it right second time around!"

With that I rushed out to disappear in the crowd, I wasn't taking any chances, one girl had so many tattoos and sinewy muscle, she looked as if she could have challenged Rolf to an arm wrestle.

Anyway, where was he, the big, dance obsessed hunk, seconds out round two! I got to the edge of the dance floor to find, that apparently the 'flirty dirty girls' had got there first!

The girls who had been eyeing him up earlier, like wolves to the prey, had waited for the lioness to leave, then seen their chance, he was, from what I could make out, being ravished alive!?

One girl in a tiny skirt, or was it a big belt, hard to tell, was shaking her booty in fine Kylie styly, so close to Rolf it looked as if he was getting a car wash! She was quickly, swishing and flicking round him. Rolf was in his element. His long legs were slightly apart, gyrating those hips, his muscular arms above his head, eyes closed, enjoying every minute.

The other girl in white shiny, satin hot pants and a very, low top, nipples like chapel hat pegs, had both hands over his left bicep, hanging on in there, she was astride his thigh sliding up and down. He was the human pole in her lap dancing routine! She pushed her huge, (I'll bet silicone, meow!) breasts into his side and her right hand grabbed his left buttock!

All this on the dance floor! The phrase, 'get a room,' had never seemed more appropriate. As I turned to walk away, his eyes flickered open he looked from one nubile girl to the other, oblivious to me standing there.

As I left 'Ollies' following a group of swaying girls, the cold night air hit me. I shivered and cursed my old aching feet as I tried to struggle up the street to my car. I caught sight of myself in that damn shop window again and sadly conceded that perhaps a Darby & Joan afternoon tea dance should be my next port of call socially. I stumbled in my heels doing Dick Emery proud.

I clicked the heating on for an hour and of course the kettle, as soon as a got in. It all seemed like another world. My little sanctuary. My peaceful haven. Comforting and familiar. I eased my beautiful shoes from my not so beautiful feet.

It was after 11pm and I had work tomorrow, but I ran a bath, a shower would not do, I needed to escape and relax and wallow in the bubbles. As I lay in the deep foam, the heat of the water going through to my cold, numb bones, my tea next to me, fluffy towels waiting, I closed my eyes.

Rolf had certainly been an interesting and different date than I was used to. I wondered what he would have done if I had gone back to him on the dance floor. Would he have peeled the girls from his manly torso and come back to dancing with me? It didn't seem likely and to be honest and I hadn't wanted to take that risk.

Until that moment it had been fun, tiring, but fun. I couldn't complain that I didn't get to dance! Normally, it was a quite a feat itself trying to get a man onto a dance floor. Usually only when they are too drunk to care, then you wish you hadn't bothered because you end up partnered with something that moves like a lobotomised gorilla, or launches into the running man, for every record!!

Let's face it, if I'm being totally realistic about Rolf, we'd probably have only made good friends at most anyway.

I couldn't, no *wouldn't,* compete with fit, feisty young girls, with bodies like gymnasts. The thought of getting to the, removal of clothing part of the relationship made me shudder. (Well actually the thought of Rolf naked made me smile, wonder where he keeps his high carb snack then?)

Then the thought of Rolf seeing me, makes me feel quite nauseous. His tanned, muscle bound, finely tuned body, next to mine that resembles a large lump of bread dough, the contrast was quiet disheartening, but it wasn't going to happen, so I wasn't going to be hitting the sun bed, or toning tables at the faint possibility it might!

Suse and I always agreed on the fact that Mother Nature gave you what you have and it is this that your soul mate will love about you, when he finally appears. There was sometimes that tiny niggling doubt, when I was feeling down, or feeling a little inadequate next to Suse. Did Mother Nature have an off day with me? On good days, I thanked her for my big brown eyes, my slim ankles, my kind heart and forgiving nature, (which I was obviously using on *her* in these moments) and of course my sense of humour.

I would be happy to find a man with similar attributes. Of course, I won't turn him down if he hasn't got slim ankles, hopefully he's not going to be wearing heels much, (or at all really!)

It was after midnight when I switched off the light, a warm, curled in a ball Ferdy positioned himself on the bed next to my feet. Exhausted, I drifted off and I saw myself back on the dance floor, looking like a brunette Kylie. I was in a swishy, little skirt with huge, red platform boots again, but I could move in them this time and boy could I move! I shimmied and wiggled. I was in my element and I had two devoted, well-toned male dancers running their hands up and down my body, my eyes were closed in sheer ecstasy. Jason and Robbie! (I must remember not to listen to the radio before nodding off!) They were oiled up and ready for anything hopefully! Well, it is *my* dream!

I really must get in touch with a dream analyst, why is it I appear to have more of a life when I'm asleep than when I'm awake?

Chapter 6

"Oh Sweetie! You look well knackered! Been burning that candle at both ends? Come on give girl, I want all the goss!" Morry was in fine form and far too bouncy for his own good!

"What can I say Morry, the man wore me out, banging away for two hours non-stop, a very sexy man." He was stunned. Pushing me into the corner of the office so no one else could hear. "You little minx, you got my hunky fantasy Rafe into a compromising position?" He looks all excited at the possibility of some very hot gossip. I take my time answering, giving him a sideways glance.

"No, he's quite capable of getting *himself* into compromising positions! We were on the dance floor! No sexual olympics. He'd have been good with anything to do with poles though!" Morry looks puzzled. "What have the Polish community got to do with it?"

I then retell every detail of the evening, Morry listens, eyes wide. Oo-ing, ah-ing and tutting at appropriate moments. He also tries unsuccessfully to hide a snigger when I get to the part where I'm in the ladies.

"God I'd have killed to see that girl!" He says, keeping his hand over his mouth.

"Which, me looking like Bette Davis, or walking out looking like Sandy after assertive therapy?"

"Oh! I can't believe that Rafe……… the old tart!" Morry says.

"Well, not so old actually."

"What!" I look at Morry over my glasses, with narrowed eyes.

"I should have rung you yesterday I know, but I didn't want to put you off. It's just that Rojere said I'd got Rafe mixed up with his older brother Ray." He gabbles on, oblivious to my panicky expression. "Well…… he's got six brothers, they live all over, I forget which is which. There's Rojere, Rafe, Ray, Ronny, Ramon, Robin and……"

"Never mind the family tree run down Morry, how old is Rolf, Rafe, he, him?"

"Well, you said you enjoyed yourself, it was just a bit of fun…."

"Morry if you don't tell me his age, I'm going upstairs to your desk and I'm going to rip the heads off your gonk collection!"

"You leave my gonks out of it….he's twenty-two." He takes a couple of steps back at seeing my expression.

"Twenty-Two!….*Twenty- Two*!" I shout in disbelief, grateful that Anna and June are not in the office yet. "I spent two hours, closely gyrating my body, entwined with a man, nay boy, (well it might as well have been a thirteen-year-old schoolboy for the guilt I felt!) fifteen years younger than me?"

"Look where's the problem, six foot three, handsome, he looked the part. You didn't do anything that's an arrestable offence. Anyway, he is over the age of consent for God's sake, if you had got that lucky!" I ignore that last part as I'm too stunned to care.

"No wonder all those young girls were ready to pounce, they probably know him, probably thought I was his Great Aunt or something. I'm mortified!"

Morry looks towards the heavens and tuts loudly, pursing his lips. "Now you're just being silly. There isn't a straight guy I know that would get down and dirty on the dance floor with his Great Aunt.....well maybe Tina Turner's great nephew, but he's an exception!"

"No, you're right Morry, I did have a great time, for late thirties he'd have looked fantastic, but at twenty-two. If he carries on with that sun-bed malarky he's going to have skin like a horse's arse by the time he's, twenty-six! He did make me feel good though, but even if he'd been the same age...no ...no. Complete opposites, too exhausting to even contemplate."

"Oh God, Morry, last night, while I was in the bath, I tried to picture him naked!" I could feel the shame wash over me......

"Well, if it'll make you feel any better you can pop in and see my priest for a confessional but bagsy listening at the door while you describe that one! It'll be six Hail Marys and a promise you come back every Thursday to confess the rest of your wicked fantasies! Let's face it babe, we all fantasise about people we know naked!"

"Tiffany Mills?" I asked with a smile. "Oooh! Only if you've got an insect fetish!" He retorts with a wicked look in his eyes.

I then told Morry I had two more blind dates on my list, courtesy of Anna and June, so I was trying to stay positive in the light of my disasters so far. He went on to tell me that they weren't disasters, just experiences. That everyone had different qualities and I just had to keep dating different men to find the one with more pluses than minuses!

Of course, he was right again. I'd changed so much over the years, what was important to me ten years ago, (could he dance, have a firm bum, was he on the property ladder and know the difference between, Ben Sherman, D & G and Topshop for Men!) Now I couldn't have cared if he was a surfer Joe, a builder Bob or a banker Bill! As long as he was good to me, had respect, humour and affection, (a firm bum as well would be an added bonus!). Not too much to ask, is it? *Is it?*

I'd left a message on Susie's mobile, hoping she'd come into Parker's at lunchtime. I'd only just sat down, pouring a much-needed cup of strong tea, when in she came. She was fresh and glowing with the cold autumn breeze, she removed her soft camel coat, smoothing down her windswept hair, she sat down beaming.

"Don't want to put the dampers on your news, but can I tell you mine first?" She said excitedly.

"Must you," I said teasing, "I can feel a male underwear moment coming on!" She giggled like a lovestruck teenager, she'd obviously managed some serious, 'ruffling' in Cumbria!

"Pen, I don't know where to start." She said in mock coyness.

"I'm presuming that wasn't a line Simon used this weekend?" She giggled again.

"He was…so wonderful, gentle, romantic. It was just a perfect weekend. We even managed to get some riding in."

"Yes, I think you mentioned that! Oh sorry, you mean horses?"

"Don't Pen you'll make me blush!" She looks genuinely embarrassed.

"He must be really special you've gone all coy and ladylike? I bet you won't even tell me, if he's a boxers or briefs kind of guy?" I raise my eyebrows waiting, as she slowly pours her tea with a very satisfied smile appearing on her face.

"My …… *boyfriend's* underwear is not open to discussion, but I can tell you that he, his under garments and his outer garments are making me, very, very happy!"

I continue to make her happy, by allowing her to laugh out loud as I tell her of my recent novel date with a young Spice Girl's fan!

"Oh, God Pen, didn't you feel as if you were on a, 'Grab a Granny' night?" She says through tears of laughter. "Thankfully, I was blissfully unaware of my, 'embarrassing mother at the school disco' status until the following day!" I said trying not to feel too insulted that Suse had used the word, 'Granny' in her description!

She senses my hurt look and says excitedly. "Look I'll tell you what, we'll have to have a girl's night out before this blind date thing puts you off men for life. Who and when is the next on your list?" I rummage in my handbag, pulling out a small rose covered diary.

"It's Angus, Anna's hubby's friend, divorced, two sons, next Friday." Feeling suddenly daunted by the prospect of being with someone who's been there, done that and got the 'Divorced and Still Standing' T-shirt, I sigh loudly.

"What am I doing Suse, I must be mad, sad, or desperate….. I'm sure people will think I'm all three!" Suse looked at me, raising her eyebrows, but said nothing.

"What happened Suse? I was never a go-getter, never a career comes first girl. All I ever wanted was to be swept into the arms of Mr. Right, to be married by twenty-four, at least two babies by the time I was thirty, pottering at home, gardening, cooking and collecting antiques!" I continued pouring out my maudlin thoughts.

"Now look at me. I am the antique! A forgotten relic, left on the shelf, gathering dust with no one to admire me, cherish me and let me take pride of place in their life. Just left with a few passers-by, man handling me from time to time, assuming I'm just some worthless piece of junk ready for the skip." I could feel the tears welling in my eyes, I bit my lip, I was just having a bad day and instead of feeling twenty-five inside and ignoring the outside, I suddenly felt every day of my thirty-seven years.

Susie was never trite, or jokey at these moments. Even she felt them from time to time, her thirty-seven years had been much more glamorous and well-travelled than mine. But she'd said that recently she'd had an awful moment. In the middle of a loud, wild party, she had felt so totally and utterly alone and so very out of place, it had really frightened her.

"Right then!" Suse said loudly to break my thoughts.

"So, we've got nearly a week of girly pursuits, let's show the world, but more importantly Durham City what we're *really* made of!" She leaned forward with that knowing look.

"Firstly, I shall make us an appointment with Boden & Sangs for Saturday morning, I'll have a word with Aubrey, he'll fit us in. He's a dear and knows I can keep him in gossip for a month." She said, keeping eye contact, hoping she was working her magic and not her ticket. I tried a smile. Hair salons were not really a favourite place of mine.

"Yes, I suppose that would be a start, what else have you got up your sleeve for a 'get us up and out there' week?" Knowing this was her forte.

"Ooh, I know! "I'll...check...."

I quickly put a hand up to stop her. "Not that, 'Well Women Clinic' thing again, all those tests and checks to make sure all our bits are healthy, functioning and raring to go! It's okay for you, that nurse never gives you the look of sympathy! Not on my list of, 'exciting things to do'. Not going, no way."

Suse suppresses a snigger. "I was actually going to say, I'll check if, 'The Full Monty' is still on at the cinema Monday night. Very similar to a, 'Well Women Check', watching that film will certainly let a girl know her bits are 'functioning and raring to go!" I wrinkle my nose laughing at her analogy.

Suse, undeterred continues. "Before that though Saturday night, we'll get our glad rags on, paint the town… red! Will *you* ring the girls?" She asks trying to shake me out of my thoughts of Saturday morning, I hate hairdressers, not them as people, having my hair done! Suse knows it's something that stresses me. I mentally slap myself for being such a miserable sod, how can the world know what I've got to offer if I don't get it out there and serve it up on a silver platter!

"Which girls…… Morry and Roger?" I say, now grinning.

Suse giggles. "Well, I was thinking more Bina and Paula, but the more the merrier, we haven't had the whole gang out in yonks!" She smiles with relief at me poking my head out of my self-pitying wallow hole and now she's on a roll.

"Right then! Monday night cinema, Tuesday we'll have tea here, after work. Large pot of Yorkshire, plate of cream cakes, not forgetting your fave eclairs! Wednesday we'll visit family, get spoilt rotten by mums for two hours, they'll tell us how proud they are of us, boost the ego, always a plus on a bad week!"

"Then on Thursday I'll come round to yours around seven with a bottle of sweet white and we'll sort your outfit out for Friday and have a giggle at the same time."

The giggle would probably be at me trying on twenty outfits while becoming merrier and merrier! Last time we did it we ended up in hysterics, as I stood there in striped over the knee socks, sequinned strapless top for a skirt and two small floral hats over each boob!

I think it was the tangerine feather boa and Paula's red clogs that really made the outfit zing. Having said that we decided, had I been on a Jean Paul Gaultier catwalk, I would have been his muse, his inspiration and well ahead of my time!

"Hang on, hang on, I've just thought where does your amazing new 'boyfriend' Simon fit into all this female fun and frivolity?" I ask puzzled and a little worried.

Suse looked down at the table, running her beautifully manicured finger round the rim of her cup. "Well…..to be honest, this next week is as much for my benefit as yours. Simon has been called away by work……..for *two whole weeks*! I can't bare the thought of not seeing him for so long, I need my mind occupied." She gazed down into her cup.

"I told you Simon is in the wine trade, supplies The Straw House, Fennymans, all the top establishments. Well, they've got a new line coming out from France, I even got him cheap flights!" With all these new feelings she was obviously finding this relationship was very different for her.

I leant forward and did the eye contact thing myself and smiled. "With the way he is with you I can't imagine him not ringing daily and missing you like crazy, don't worry, we'll make the time fly."

She smiled back, looking relieved. "Well, he did say if it hadn't been such short notice, I could have gone with him, he wouldn't have said that if he didn't think something of me, would he?"

I raised my eyebrows. "I can't believe it, Miss Confident, questioning what a man thinks. It may be a revelation to you, but there is absolutely no doubt he thinks the world of you and you're obviously very special to him."

Suse stood up to go, buttoning her coat, gently smoothing the fabric, a little twinkle in her eye. "I think I might just let him know, that the best thing about being apart is looking forward to catching up on *everything* you've missed!"

Confidence restored, for both of us, we hugged and went our separate ways.

Back at work I had tons to type up and file. Which for once was a blessing. I just busied myself, avoiding socialising with the girls. I just wasn't in the mood for blind date talk, or competitive descriptions of the men on offer. Or worse, Tiffany's perfect find in her fiancé, Jasper Quinn and her magical quest to be Mrs Quinn, not today thank you!

Even Morry was conspicuous by his absence, he'd rushed past, blown me a kiss saying he couldn't stop as Mr Harkess was on his back about a file deadline. Then grimaced as he realised what he'd said, sniggering, 'he should be so lucky' under his breath! I didn't even have time to ask him about Saturday.

I'd tell him tomorrow and he'll have a go at me for not giving him enough notice to get his highlights blitzed and to prime Roger. I'll probably ring him tonight, I thought, smiling.

Home at last. I felt drained. I was in the bath by six and into me, 'baggies and sloppy joe by seven-thirty. Both Ferdy and I were fed, watered, warm, content and well relaxed by eight.

Ferdy had washed and preened while I was in the bath, paws up and over his face and ears time after time, eyes half closed, it was finally all too exhausting for him, he yawned. Wobbling slightly as he surveyed his numerous comfy spots, slowly making his way to the small fleece cat cushion by the radiator, he circles slowly several times, lowering himself while pummelling the cloth lovingly. Then curling himself into that beautiful feline ball, he nods off, every now and then one eye opening, just in case, heaven forbid, I head towards the kitchen without him.

I try my best to curl, feline like, into the chair by the phone and ring my list of prospective Saturday night revellers. Just an hour later and I'm feeling so much better.

Morry says he's definitely up for it, he'll just bribe Rojere with a new silk shirt and a big box of Thornton's continental and they'll both be raring to go by eight. He then says if he manages to get that large bread maker Rojere has had his eye on. (No, not that young hunk in, 'Bessie's Bakery') But the expensive machine in, 'Hopkins Homemakers' he thinks they may be able to stay out after midnight!

We then have a giggle about the prospect of Roger turning into a pumpkin and him not having the feet for a glass slipper. Before he puts the phone down, he says we both have to come into work tomorrow wearing something tasteless and it can't be me on his arm because that would be cheating. Thanks Morry, you're a true friend! The one who gets more of a reaction gets bought our competition cocktail, a .... Titchmarsh-Donkey, (vodka, whisky and Peach Schnapps......tastes like weed-killer but kicks you into the back of next week!!) by the loser, only Morry could come up with that!

I then ring Bina, who is more than happy to spend an evening not thinking of court rooms, liability cases, smelly nappies and Denzel's plans for a two-storey extension in between running his own Property Development company and building a large herb garden around the back patio. She secretly loves it all really.

At work she is Bina Khan, (kept her maiden name as she built up her revered reputation before she married Denzel), she is competent and hard working. She's also ambitious with an amazing strength of character. But at home, Bina Donovan is a patient and loving wife to Denzel and doting mother to her two children, Cosima, now a bright six-year-old and Alfie nearly ten months.

Her family were thrilled with Denzel, who although her dad pointed out was a strange choice of colouring, (they do say opposites attract.) Denzel having a thick thatch of red, (nay 'ginger') hair. Which Bina confided, turned her on so much, she was grateful he felt the same way and proposed so quickly, as she said there was a serious chance of her forgetting all her beliefs and not being as virginal as she'd hoped on her wedding day!

They were made for each other, both working hard to produce a comfortable life to bring their much hoped for babies into. The age gap between the babes being well planned to accommodate Denzel's business expansion, Bina's studies, exams, etc and allowing her to have time off with her children. She was only part-time at present, loving the time with Alfie, crawling about playing trains, chewing toys, using Mr. Pointy finger to get attention. She did say she must try to limit these habits to home, or her reputation may take a tumble! (In Lego, or wooden blocks I'd asked!)

Anyway, it was a yes from Bina. Denzel was more than happy for a recuperative Saturday night, (Bina's full on 'Frisky Night' he called it!). She would tease him saying it was the only night she had time to do it all! Her special 'hot, hot' curry, low lights, soft music, glass of wine or two and into her sexy outfit! No, not the old black lace stockings and suspender job that is the male standard. Denzel's turn on, was her traditional sari! He loved all that beautiful fabric around her body, unwinding her, he said it was like unwrapping his favourite sweet, very, very slowly.

Each to his own, if you're the sort that can make a chocolate caramel sensual, you go for it. Knowing my luck my mind would never get past a Werther's original or an Old English Humbug!

I made a quick cuppa before ringing Paula, knowing she'd never be a straightforward, 'yes,'
and I wasn't disappointed! Paula sighed, she ummed and ah-ed. I told her it was just a night out with the gang, I wasn't asking her to do the floral arrangements for St. Pauls!

She asked if Susie was still with the new fella, or whether she was on the prowl again, she couldn't cope with all that eyelash fluttering and cleavage?

I always sensed there was a little jealousy on Paula's part, she wasn't the sort you could imagine losing her inhibitions and Suse could be a little wild at times!

The nearest she'd got to wearing a short skirt was when she got her tie-dye floaty number caught in a lift! Bina and I so horrified she'd disappear up four floors as a pancake, pulled at her and the skirt so hard it ripped, leaving her in approximately twelve inches of ragged cloth. She was horrified. We told her not to worry she had great legs, just a shame she'd decided to wear her Snoopy knee socks and purple docker boots! It wasn't a look she was comfortable with, so Bina had lent her a long rain mac. (Now Susie......she would have just pulled those socks up and walked on out!)

It was difficult, Paula was just a little old fashioned. Suse would tease her a little, asking if she wanted to borrow one of her dresses. (They would look pretty bad on me but poor Paula, you can't wear tight red leather with a curly perm and pop socks!) I think secretly she did want to go some way to being sexy and alluring, but she just didn't know how to pull it off. Not that I'm an expert but I don't think Laura Ashley have added back-less, halter-neck cat-suits to their floral Periwinkle range just yet, but when they do, I'm sure Paula will be putting down her deposit!

Paula was good for the conscience though, she watched out for us, slightly motherly, firm but caring and amazingly for her lack of need of a good man in her life, she could weigh up the male of the species, very astutely.

She finally agreed to come a long, if we promised not to try and fob her off with some boring fart in a cardi just because she said she liked her men, just a tad more conservative than our choices!

I promised as long as she wouldn't comment on Susie's outfit and......not talk to Roger about dried flower arranging. Morry was sick of him going on about oasis, Physalis Franchetti, (Chinese lanterns to us layman!) and ornamental teasels!

Chapter 7

Friday consisted of everyone having that excitable, 'the weekends nearly here' feeling. Started by Morry winning hands down on the, 'tasteless accessory' challenge he'd set me up on last night!

He walked into the office wearing what looked like, his grandfather's fishing hat complete with, 'Bead-eyed Buggers' and 'Dibblers Nymphs'? (Which he tried to convince us were names of fishing flies!) Anna let out a shriek when she looked down to see his purple woollen leg warmers and Marc Bolan, girly red tap shoes.

"Morry! Tell me you didn't walk all the way to work like that?" I said trying to sound shocked and stifling my giggles.

"You know me if I've got a look to test, I like to get public opinion. I got four speechless gawps, two wolf whistles and a, 'what you wearin' you big woofter!' Can't say fairer than that......maybe the hat was overdoing it?" He says twirling like an over excited Anthea Redfern.

"You got a better reaction than me Morry, I'd have given anything for two wolf whistles. Having said that I was a complete coward and came in the car!"

"You call those tasteless accessories?" He laughs pointing at my orange tank top, my brother's cub scout snake belt and large plastic Christmas cracker earrings.

"I wore that very look in Hepburn's bar last May and everyone was wearing the same by mid-June, it's positively chic!" He says, doing a catwalk strut past my desk.

"Oh! So, I'm more, last season than tasteless, okay then, you win, suppose I owe you a Titchmarsh?" I say giggling as June eyes us sideways looking puzzled.

"It's a cocktail June, in case you were wondering."

"I think you'll find it's a gardener Penelope." She says gliding towards her desk, having corrected our obvious ignorance. Morry and I turned away trying to suppress our laughter.

After that frivolous start, although we managed to get our work done, there was constant light banter, double entendre from Morry and general silliness around the whole office. Which Morry prayed was catching because the second floor were in dire need of some belly laughs, unless you counted Mr Jenkins, 'corridor dancing' with Dot the cleaner.

"Is it another wet one this morning Mrs Trattles?" He asked before his brogues begun to slide out of control on the newly washed floor. Not wishing him to end up headfirst in her bucket she'd swung the mop up to stop his fall, both doing a sort of Celtic reel. They'd danced and circled each other till poor Mr. Jenkins had come to an abrupt stop with a large wet mop-head in his nether regions and at least six members of staff witnessing the sight!

Fortunately, Mr. Jenkins was the one out of our three directors that had a sense of humour and pulling himself up had chuckled loudly, as poor Dot thought she'd committed a sackable offence.

"Not to worry Mrs Trattles, no bones broken, though it's a good job you hadn't been using that large electric polisher, or I mightn't have lived to tell the tale, eh, what!"

Morry and I spent the rest of the afternoon ringing each other, between files, to discuss outfits and possible pub and club itineraries for tomorrow night............. Well, what else are Fridays for?

Saturday morning arrived all too soon, a morning that could make or break my mood for the day, with the unpredictable hairdressers awaiting our presence.

Was it really worth the almost certain humiliation against the very slim chance of..........

'Yes, it's great, I really like what you've done', I asked myself as Susie enthusiastically dragged me towards the salon doors.

I watched Aubrey deftly trimming Susie's prize mane of hair. I looked back to the mirror in front of me. Surely, I had more hair than this? Washed and combed, I sat waiting patiently hoping someone would hurry up and remove my frightening resemblance to Max Wall, (if that's before your time, think of a Chuckle brother in a straight black wig!)

"Warra you wantin' done then? Yuv boooooked in for a trim, but yer could do wa' a total re-style?" I stare in disbelief at a gum chewing teenager, brandishing a comb and scissors.

"Er, this isn't my normal hair-style." I say stupidly.

"I just wanted a trim and a bit more body in it, just a bit fuller?" Instantly feeling intimidated as she lifts up a lock and looks at it and drops it from her fingers as if I'm totally deluded.

"Yer, 'airs reeeelly fine, I'll just bung a bit o' layering in.... t' giyit a birra welly?" I was by this time having visions of the old dodgy Rod Stewart mullet of my past coming back to haunt me. Layers...... layering.....didn't that mean rag-cuts? What worked for the Bay City Rollers in 1974 was not going to travel well to a thirtysomething in 1997! Then in fear and possible shock, I could hear myself timidly saying.......

"You're the expert, you just do what you think is best, what will suit me."

Dear God, I was leaving the poor straggled excuse I had left for hair to someone wearing psychedelic plastic trousers with twenty zips, ripped vest and a hairstyle that looked like a chainsaw had been through it!

I took a deep breath as she started cutting, pinning, combing, her unusual tattoos reflected in the mirror as her arms moved quickly. I caught sight of the words, 'A Cut Above' with a pair of scissors cutting through the stem of a rose on her right upper arm and, 'Only the Good Dye Young' complete with bleeding red heart with purple and green drips, on her left forearm! *Very* 'Stylist'.

As I gripped the arms of the chair, biting my lip to stop the tears, thinking I'd have been more relaxed at the dentists, I suddenly hear Susie's voice above the noise of the dryers.

"Chantelle is Aubrey's protégé Pen, don't look so worried!" She smiled encouragingly.

Aubrey then adds, "You know what they say about stylists, you should always go to the one with the worst haircut, because then you know there is a very good chance, *they* will have cut all the others stylists' hair."

As his hand gesticulated to Chantelle's less than perfect head of straw then out towards his other staff who all looked incredibly normal, thankfully, (well as near normal as you can get for budding stylists! Had they never heard of mousy brown, minimalist highlights and fringes that came somewhere near to your eyebrows?)

I couldn't quite believe it when she'd finished, it was nothing like Rod Stewart, not even a touch Suzi Quatro. It was amazingly more a little Kate Bush, a little Belinda Carlisle, possibly even a little Gloria Estevan, full, wavy and bouncy……..I was stunned……...but delighted.

Visits to salons usually left me rushing from the premises distraught. Think back to the 'Purdy' cut! For heaven's sake, what possesses stylists to think, mmmm yes, if Joanna Lumley can wear it so can the rest of the population! We all ended up looking like our mothers had got the pudding basin out after an episode of the Avengers and two sherries!

I'd rather have a tooth pulled than end up wearing a woolly hat, for a fortnight, dodging questions about head-lice or bad home hair dyes!

But this was so different and such a blessed relief. "It's great, I really like what you've done." I say still in shock.

"Thanks very much, I'll remember your name for my next appointment….. Chantelle." I say politely, as if I could ever forget that name, or hair.

"No point, ave bin 'ed unted by that posh slon in Edinbru, waris it Aubra, 'Crispy Feathers', or summat?" Aubrey winces, then looks genuinely hurt.

"It's 'Crispin & Quills' girl! They took her from right under my nose, last month, at the Hair Awards. But what can you do, they've made her a better offer than I can, I'm small fry here. I'll miss her, the skinny little back-alley urchin!" He says with affection.

"Yeh! I'll miss yer too, yer fat, baldy old Queen!" (At least she'd had enough education to choose the word Queen?)

We left them with their arms around each other in mutual admiration, thanking us for our custom.

Our smiles were quickly wiped from our faces as a huge gust of early winter wind blew our newly styled hair up and around until we both had something that resembled a mound of candyfloss on our heads!

"Bloody weather," Suse says, pulling out a soft, stretchy hat.

"The 'Beehive' is a style I've never been able to get away with!" We both laugh.

"We've got hours to re-style it before we go out." I say flippantly with my newly found curly mane and confidence.

Only seven hours later. Well, my hair is almost as good, as I try and hold a small mirror up to see the back. A couple of last tweaks then it's sprayed to within an inch of its life. If I have to wear it as a helmet to keep it looking great, so be it! I'm so much more relaxed this evening, I'm not out to try and impress anyone tonight, much easier than a blind date. I saunter to my wardrobe, giving the odd backward glance to the mirror just to check I've not dreamt it. Yes, it's definitely there, an almost Susie-like mane of hair!

Clicking through the hangers, rummaging through drawers, I'm looking for a fun, stylish, outfit. Girls night out, this will be fun. I laugh out loud waking Ferdy, he opens an eye to check my sanity and just in case that noise is a possible call to his food bowl!

Now let me see, something I can dance in, something swishy……..my hands close round one of my favourite little dresses. It's a Miss Selfridges bargain, nabbed it in the summer sales. I leave the designer names to Suse. Labels don't bother me unless mine's hanging out, blowing in the breeze for all to see…….. River Island, size 14, really doesn't have the same impact as, Vivienne Westwood, London. It's a special little dress though and makes me feel great. Soft, black and flowing, with a ruffle of fabric down the low-ish neckline and round the hem, the best bit being the embroidery. Small purple and red flowers amongst green leaves cascade down the fitted bodice and just a couple more spill out onto the lovely, very swishy skirt, which is not too short. I then root around to find my classy 1940's black bow front, suede peep-toe sling backs.

Finally, with minutes to spare before the taxi arrives, (I had no choice in the matter, Susie insisted on organising the transport.) I quickly fasten my three-tier black glass bead necklace, matching dangly earrings, grab my small black bag, (with one red rose only!) and black frill backed jacket. As I pass the mirror for the last time, I'm so pleased with myself I even do a little victory dance towards the door! I quickly remove my specs and I'm away!

"Wahay! Who are you trying to impress?" Bina shouts from the taxi window, as they watch me get in.

"Only myself, for a change." I say smiling. "Anyway, you two look as fabulous as ever, are we picking up Paula next?"

"No, she told me a neighbour was dropping her off in town as he's going to the Connick Hotel for a chess championship, Harold I think she said his name was."

Bina smiles. "I think it's that little old, bloke next door. I know Paula looks older than she is, but I hope he isn't getting any ideas!" We all shudder……

"Ooo err, no thanks, you wouldn't get me getting fruity with an oldy." Says Suse in all innocence as we stare back!

"Ahem, I realise you've found Mr Perfect with enough dosh to lull you into the life you'd like to become accustomed, but all this meaningful relationship stuff has obviously caused you a serious memory lapse!" Susie looks a little affronted then stares ahead between the two of us.

"Yes, OK, I may have succumbed to the charms of a gentleman a *little* older than myself, but it was only a couple of dates and when I found out his exact age, I was off like a shot!"

"Oh! Of course you were! That's after you'd gone for that three-week cruise round the Med with Saga holidays, as his carer! He was sixty-eight and you were twenty-five for God's sake!" Bina and I started to laugh.

"You're a wicked pair of bitches!" Suse said sharply, then started to snigger.

"I was a bit naughty, wasn't I? I did make an old man very happy though! I only had to put me little blue tunic dress on and help him to a sun-bed and he was done for the day! It was a mutually satisfying companionship! He got to gaze at me in a tiny bikini and have me on his arm at the swanky dinner parties. I got a fantastic holiday and a couple of little trinkets!" She looked a little guilty. "Anyway, that's all way in the past now, it was just a bit of fun."

"*Exactly!*" I say, realising Susie was only too aware that some of her choices in men hadn't always been well thought out. "We've all had our fair share of the…Mr Incompatibles! But tonight, we're not even going to acknowledge the male fraternity, (Morry and Roger don't count, insisting on referring to themselves as, 'us girls') we'll just have a good gossip and more importantly, a good dance!"

The taxi pulls up, as we get out carefully, straightening ourselves up, we spot a large dark blue car pull up behind, with Paula in the passenger seat.

Driving the car is a male who looks a rather rugged forty something, pale shirt and dark tie. He quickly jumps out from behind the wheel and opens the door for Paula. We stand there, expectantly over smiling, desperate for Paula to introduce us.

"Penny, Bina, Susie, this is Harold Sinclair, Harry to his friends." Paula says proudly.

"Very pleased to meet you!" We all say in a rather over enthusiastic chorus!

"It's very nice to meet you too, ladies. I'm sorry I can't be more sociable, but I've got my first match at eight and I'm really in need of a warm-up!"

I know, at this moment all of us, without exception, were desperately wanting to offer him a warm-up of his choice, but Paula saw we had the same expression as her and quickly said. "Come on girls, hurry up, let Harry get to his games and we'll get to ours!" Was Paula being flirty and flippant there, surely not.

As the car drove away, we all turned to Paula. "Er…I think you've got some explaining to do, we thought Harold was the old bloke next door!" Paula knows she's going to end up frozen outside the Cromwell Arms if she doesn't just hurry and come up with the goods and tell us everything!

"Right, well…..old Mr Miller, also called Harold, had been up and down health-wise, not coping very well, so reluctantly the family decided to move him. He's gone to live with his sister, Ethel in Norfolk. Harry is Ethel's son, Mr Miller's nephew. He's sorting out the house, even considering buying it…. If I'll help him with the décor." She says very casually.

"*Oh… my… God…..*We have all dreamed, nay wished away all our wishes, hoped beyond hope, to one day have a dishy, solvent, single male move in next door, talk about jam, whipped cream and a cherry on top! Do you not realise how lucky you are Paula?" I say trying to get through to her.

Paula shrugs. "I didn't say he was solvent…… or single."

We all look totally crestfallen. "Nooooo!" We all say in a now hopelessly sympathetic chorus, as if she's just missed out on winning on the lottery!

"But he is, he's a bachelor and an architect!" She says with a wicked twinkle in her eye as she turns, making a dash for the bar door! We all race in after her, squealing like sixteen-year-olds pursuing Robbie Williams. A frightening sight for anyone on the other side of the door!

By ten Morry and Roger have caught up with us, (Morry having plied Roger with cocktails and removed his watch!) Chaplin's is buzzing and we've already been on the dance floor…. twice! (Fortunately, I haven't got a Rolf to compete with this time.)

Morry and Roger had spent most of their evening in Hepburn's bar and are delighted to have found Aubrey and Brett, (Brett Boden & Aubrey Sangs, stylists extraordinaire!) to join them.

As the DJ starts playing some oldies, the scene is then set. Adam & the Ants 'Prince Charming' comes on and there they are……the Queens of Princes, giving it their all on the dance floor, all the movements well-rehearsed, not an inhibition in sight!

"Come on girls, we'll show you all the moves!" Morry shouts, strutting his stuff.

"That'll be a first!" Shouts Susie as we all leap onto the dance floor. Morry is undeterred.

"Adam Ant, what happened to the man, he was bloody gorgeous and a genius, that look....and he had the cutest, tightest......!"

"*Morry!* That's what I love about coming out with you and yours.... always thinking exactly the same as us! Yes, Adam Ant...couldn't you just...!" I say thinking back to his posters on my wall and the mouth faded from being kissed every night without fail. My disco daydreams are cruelly cut short as I catch sight of someone I really do not want to see at this moment in time, I squint hoping my dodgy eyesight is deceiving me, but no! (Sorry, Grandma and Granddad) Damn and blast!! It is him.

I desperately hoped I was having a drink fuelled vision, but sadly, it wasn't Adam Ant, Jason Durr, or Charlie. I'd have even been more than thankful for a Mr Funny at this moment!

Sauntering in with his handpicked, usable entourage…it was……Todd Storm, (known as 'Windy' by ex-band members!) Mr Rockstar himself making his entrance.

I turned quickly to try and get Morry's attention before Suse caught sight of him, but she was doing her Diana Dors Fairy Godmother impression with Morry and Roger who were, 'burn baby burning it' as the Ugly Sisters! I danced up to Morry, trying to get him to turn round to see who was now closing in towards the dance floor, but it was too late, Suse did her final magic wand swish, turned and……poof! (No, not Morry sadly) Suse and Todd locked eyes at that very same moment, as the last drum beats of Prince Charming rang out.

Todd removed his pretentious cowboy hat, ran his hand through his shoulder length, raven black hair and smiled at her.

That was all it took, she was at his side like a shot, looking small and vulnerable, just how he liked his women.

"Bloody hell, not that Bastard back again, surely not." Spat Paula as she caught sight of Todd. I was shocked it was her speaking, I'd never heard her swear and not with such venom. She looked shocked at herself and added. "He is just so bad for her and just when she's met such a great new fella, we can't let this happen can we?"

We backed Paula to the hilt, as we saw Todd take her to a table in the corner and one of his minions, groupies, hopeful hangers on, rush to the bar and came back with glasses and a bottle of Moet.

"The smarmy, two-faced git! I can't believe he's just waltzed back in here like this, how many years is it? Wonder what crap he'll be telling her this time."

What could we do, we couldn't make a scene, we had to just let her talk for now, but there was absolutely no way any of us were going to let her leave this club with him. I'd drag her off and lock her in the 'Ladies' if I had to!

We'd both done some regrettable things in our lives so far, but as her best friend I was not going to see her give up Simon Forbes for this two-bit waste of space. Rockstar…Rockpool more like (shallow and murky.) We were all determined not to let it ruin our night and took it in turns to go over, pretend to be friendly, break up the conversation and take Suse off for a dance, as often as was realistically possible.

During one of these planned manoeuvres, I rushed over,

"It's your fave Susie, come and have a boogie, are you coming Todd?" I asked politely knowing full well that, 'Rockstars don't dance?!' When up on the dance floor Susie asked.

"Have you got a problem with me talking to Todd?"

She looked at me with suspicion. "Oh God no Suse, just it's supposed to be a girl's night out, we don't want you to miss anything!" I manage to say convincingly.

"I'll be back with you soon, Pen, honest, I'm just catching up. Todd's been all over the place, he's doing really well." She says, her eyes lighting up.

"Well, he could have sent you a couple of postcards over the last year or so, if he'd got so much to tell you. Just think on, you have got a 'boyfriend' now, Simon Forbes… remember?" I say, almost instantly regretting my sarcasm.

"Yes, thanks Penny, I do know what I've got in my life at present, I've met an old friend and I'm just catching up, I'm not about to elope! And before you say it, yes, I do remember Stonehenge okay!" With that she turns on her heels and goes off back to him. "Yes well, as long as news is all he's thinking of catching up on." I say under my breath protectively.

Todd finally gets up from the table, we suddenly look like a bunch of complete 'off beaters' as we dance inanely trying to get to the edge of the floor, just in case he persuades Suse to leave with him and we have to jump him and charge his ankles. We're then bobbing up and down stupidly, straining to see through the other dancers.

He leans in and whispers something in Susie's ear, then cups her face in his hands and kisses her, slowly, holding her gaze, he disappears into the crowd, his fawning ensemble rushing after him.

"Bastard," we all chorus in frustration. Then realise we're getting some strange looks from the surrounding revellers.

"B A Bastard, he's a New York rapper, we'd all been trying

to remember his name, we must be psychic!" Bina says, very unconvincingly, to anyone who hasn't moved away from us with embarrassment!

Susie then re-joins us, saying nothing more about Todd Storm. Somehow, I don't quite think we've seen the last of him. He knew he was on to something good with her, I really wished Simon wasn't away on business. I had to trust her, he had to trust her. Surely, she would see through Todd's lies this time...... we really hoped so.

Todd gone, a dancefloor reprieve, we threw ourselves into some serious, 'round the handbag' dancing, forgetting about the unwanted interruption. We did some over friendly group hugging to, 'I'll Be There For You' by the Rembrandts, then some very dodgy 'vogueing' and posing to...…'Drop Dead Gorgeous' by Republica. Also, some very funky lunging, that only the over thirties can get away with, to 'Freed from Desire' Gala and 'Star People' by George Michael……we were on fire!

Hot Gossip had nothing on us!! Then came the over the top, heartfelt lip synching to 'Love Won't Wait' by Gary Barlow, with a crescendo, finale of, 'As Long As You Love Me' by Backstreet Boys. Morry always feels 'I Will Survive' by Gloria Gaynor is a little too obvious and God forbid anyone accuse Morry of being too obvious!

Sometime later, I'm pushed, over helpfully, from the taxi and stagger into my hallway at 2am!

As I rush to relieve my weakened, over full bladder, trying to remove my clothes at the same time, I can see something through, fortunately spectacle-less, blurred vision. It resembles some old, sweaty night club singer who's spent the last twenty years giving her all after the pie and pea supper down at the workingman's club on Stranton Street.

Who was that beautifully coiffured and presentable woman that left this house earlier, she's been replaced by a river dredged Hilda Baker!

Even though I could have slept where I sat, (it was the thought of the round, red toilet seat marks on my tired backside that made me move) I wandered sleepily to my lotions and potions, removed the residue of make-up that hadn't slid from my face already. Brushing out the tin of lacquer from my hair was the difficult bit. Rubbing in copious amounts of Oil of Ulay I slide into my welcoming bed.

I know there is not a dream buddy I can think of that doesn't want me to drift off…yawn…and join him.… looking fresh, radiant, natural and alluring.… Jason, Robbie, is that Charlie? Oh, I see Adam has joined us this evening.……I know boys, I'm later than usual.…that means we'll have to make up for lost time……dream on…!

My 'Sandmen' beckon…….

Chapter 8

The week gets off to a 'great' start! Monday and Suse has managed to get us 7pm '**showing**', a most apt word for 'The Full Monty'! We both came out of the cinema with a rosy glow! Didn't even need to fasten our coats, just a mass of flushing, smiling faces singing a chorus of…'you can leave your hat on!' We were all, 'Well Women' after a dose of…… 'The Full Monty'!

I do now feel a bit guilty by the time Suse and I sit down to tea and cakes in Parker's on Tuesday after work, as I've been sitting on my backside for the best part of seventy-two hours, now I'm going to stuff my face with cream cakes. Susie reads my mind as I eye up the table and sigh.

"Oh! Come on Pen, I don't think a Tuna & sweetcorn bap and one chocolate éclair is going to suddenly balloon you into Demis Roussos proportions." She says encouragingly.

"You're right Suse, I also think I'd have to develop an awful lot of facial hair to resemble Demis, but I know where you're coming from."

As we laugh, chatter, gossip, sip tea and thoroughly enjoy ourselves and Suse diplomatically cuts the last éclair in half, so neither of us should feel *too* guilty!

She doesn't mention Todd Storm, but gushes warmly about Simon's phone call on Sunday night. But I know Susie too well, the reason she isn't saying anything about Todd is because she doesn't want my opinion…yet. There is no way he is not going to want to see her again, I just hope that her phone calls from Simon will make her think twice before considering seeing that, 'rogue of rock' again.

By Wednesday I'm feeling more up-beat, very much, 'at one with my world.' The family are thrilled at me making a surprise visit, including mum and dads over excitable Jack Russells, Eric and Ernie! (Dad's a big fan, we're just grateful it wasn't Bardot and Welch.) Mum tells me my brother Mike was about to pop round, but his head gaskets gone and he's off to Freddie's garage. "He's keeping it open especially for him!" She says proudly. "Well, being his brother, I don't think it's too much to ask Mum."

"Have you got a love life yet dear?" She says out of nowhere, as if I'm buying one from over the counter, or signing papers for permission to have one!

"Er, no mum, but I've had a few blind dates recently, Morry sorted out a couple for me."

She looks excited. "Now I like Maurice, he's so polite, now you could do worse than have a man like him, he's right under your nose and you just don't seem to see it, you get on so well together too."

I take a deep breath, "Morry is *gay* mum, I've explained this to you before, he lives with Roger." She looks undeterred. "Well, just because they live together and have retro wallpaper, tropical fish and a pink fridge, I think you could point the finger at half the male population if that were the case! Some men get dumped by their women and that's all they're left with. I think it's a little bit, 'sour grapes' on your part Penelope that you assume all men living together are gay!"

Here we go……."Mum I never said *all* men living together are gay, just Maurice and Roger, I told you last week they'd gone out to buy some new silk sheets…king size….for *their* bed…… just the *one* bed!"

Mum raises her eyebrows, knowing full well what I mean, tuts and says. "Now in my day the only thing you got, 'King size, was your cigarettes and a large white sliced!……..It is a shame though that he's crossed over to the other side."

"He's gay mum, not dead!" With that she gives me a wry smile and we take the tureens through to the table. As I sat down, Dad was already at the head of the table, Eric and Ernie either side, gazing up with crinkle topped, pleading eyes, knowing this was 'treat-time.'

"Any sign of a love life yet Penny?" Dad says totally unaware of the kitchen conversation.

I sigh, "I think ones coming into port Friday dad, oh no it's sailed off into the sunset without me again!" I say tiredly.

"Oh, sorry love, didn't mean to pry, just remember I've got the double ladders ready for him when he comes a calling!"

It was the same amusing dad jokes every time. "It's okay dad I'll make sure I bag a rich one, so it costs you nothing. Anyway, what's the point of having the ladders ready, I don't live here anymore, so, I can't elope from *your* upstairs window anyway, can I?" (Think I've got him this time.)

"Aha!" Says dad with a twinkle in his eye, "but you'll have sold your house to pay for the wedding, so you'll be holed up in the guest room with the black and white portable, so you'll be wanting to get off up to Gretna sharpish!"

"Oh dad! You never stop do you?" I look at his warm smiley eyes and mum laughing with him, then he stops and pulls himself up. "I know we joke on love, but I do know there wouldn't be a prouder dad than me to be standing next to you on your wedding day... or civil ceremony day... or partnership declaration day...or...."

"Yes, thanks dad, I think I've got the message! I'll give Donald a ring nearer the time. Anyway...." I say, neatly changing the subject. "Where are Donald and Molly at present. I rang last week and left a message, nothing heard, I know they were moving, did it all go ahead okay?"

"Your sister Molly says they've got a lovely parish, in Ely. The roads are so flat, Donald did his rounds on his bike today."

"His rounds! They've only just got there, haven't they heard of unpacking and settling in?"

My younger sister Molly is six years my junior, has three under-fives, Jerome four, Felicity two, and little Kezia at six months old. A vicar's wife, does the church paperwork, masses for charity and keeps the vicarage like a show house. Her excuse for being so organised, 'well you never know who could call', I suspect she hopes for heavenly approval.

She also, sickeningly, always manages to look like she's just stepped out of the pages of Harpers & Queen, effortlessly stylish. I don't know how she does it, I would be jealous, if I weren't so in awe. To top it all she is a wonderful sister. I do hope she thinks I have some redeeming features, I've hardly been the big sister who led by example, to be looked up to.

She's a strong and dynamic soul, I don't visit as often as I should, selfish reasons, she just makes me feel so inadequate! She's well-travelled, speaks French, German and Spanish. She was working for an overseas medical aid firm when she met Donald who was doing his missionary bit, (Molly says he's still doing his 'missionary bit'…that's why she keeps getting pregnant!) They never stop! Working and playing, I get exhausted just listening to her on the phone! They celebrated their fifth Wedding Anniversary by doing a sponsored charity bike ride. Thirty miles there and back, had a candlelight dinner, had too much communion wine and decided to make love in the church pews! (They felt God would have approved of their beautiful union!) She said through fits of giggles that Donald had put his cassock on, just in case they were disturbed by a late visitor. She'd said, in hindsight, that had someone caught him in his robes, with her naked and prostrate amongst the kneelers they'd probably have been hauled off to the ducking stool as worshippers of the Satanic darkness! It did look a bit kinky she said, but they had done every room in the house so what choice did they have? Indeed, maybe that's why they've moved again!

   I got up to go home around eight thirty. I fussed Eric and Ernie at the door and gave mum and dad a big hug.

   "Don't forget where we are love, keep working hard at that job of yours, but make sure you get out and have some fun! It'll soon be Christmas, all those office parties, eh?" Dad says encouragingly.

   "Honestly dad, I'm not a hermit. Anyway, I'm taken, mum has got me married off to Morry, you know, my gay friend?" I say looking at mum knowing her expression.

   "Well, you know your mother Penny, ever practical, at least he'll do the ironing and you'll enjoy shopping for his Christmas presents. *He's* not going to make do with a pack of spark plugs, a pair of musical socks and a tin of Quality Street, is he?"

Mum gives him a dig. "Geoffrey Wiseman, if you'd prefer a baby blue expresso maker, a pink cashmere sweater and leather chaps you just let me know!"

"Wahay! Lizzie my darling, if you want me to serve you coffee in that outfit, you just say the word…." Mum blushes.

"Oh! Penelope, isn't he a one?"

"I'm thinking not mum, but I'll leave you to continue indulging in your Christmas shopping fantasies in the privacy of your own home!"

They're both waving madly as if I'm going off up Everest for six months. I love them to bits and really should visit more often. They are totally un-judgmental and have seen me through some really crappy times. Family is everything when your world looks bleak and even more valuable when you have something special to share. I was suddenly feeling very content with my lot. I have a wonderful family, some incredibly loyal friends, a little house with a little cat to go home to, not the same as a special man I know, but at least I don't have to fight Ferdy for the remote.

I have a good job, it isn't mind expanding, or even that exciting, but it pays the bills, with enough left over for some little treats. I'd never known over blown luxury, what you don't know you don't miss and let's be honest, if you really want something there is *always* a way of getting it, (legally of course.) So……the big question is, do I really want a man in my life?

Yes, I do! Then, get off your well-rounded derriere and find one, they're hardly hammering at your door, (unless you count double glazing salesmen, or Mormons, the fact that they wear suits being the only thing in their favour. If I want windows, or religion, I'll go to the nearest showroom or church. I want to be preached at when I'm good and ready, not when I'm standing there with thirty minutes worth of Ruby Glow dye on my hair and the smell of over cooked chicken emanating from the kitchen!)

I was quite excited by Thursday. Suse would be coming round to sort me out an outfit for Friday. It was the turn of, Angus, he did sound a little less daunting….. hopefully. I'm sure he'd appreciate the difficult situation of dating past your twenties, he'll maybe be a little subdued, being divorced, I won't pick anything too colourful.

Suse arrived dead on seven, clutching a bottle of sweet white and a large bag of pretzels. She was wearing her bootleg jeans and a little roll-neck mohair jumper, her hair was pinned up loosely with only a touch of make-up, but she could have walked into any pub or club and still turned heads.

"Oh! I see you've started without me, half your wardrobes already out here!" She says, rooting through the mound of clothes strewn on the bed.

"I'm determined to get it right tomorrow Suse, I want to make a good first impression, do you think that's possible?" She looks me up and down, then smiles. "Anything's possible babe!"

"Thanks, I'm not *quite* a lost cause then?" I say plonking a large, flowered hat on my head.

"You will be if you wear that on your next date that's for certain!" She pulls it off, throwing it across the room. "Pen you've got some gorgeous stuff here, pour us a glass and we'll get started."

Two glasses of wine later and I was getting the hang of this accent and accessory lark! I stood there in long black, high-waisted, streamlined trousers, my legs looking surprisingly long with only a two-inch heel suede ankle boot. A pale green, frilly collared blouse, not *too* many buttons undone.

My black frilled back jacket with a large cascade of roses brooch on the lapel, large-stoned bracelet and matching necklace to make it less office-like. Suse pinned my hair up like hers with just some little loose tendrils, making it less stern.

"That looks really good Pen, smart but still very feminine." I did feel good and felt chuffed that Suse thought the same. "You are such a brilliant mate Suse, all your help and advice, I am so lucky having such a fantastic friend."

She suddenly looked uncomfortable. "Must be the wine talking. Maybe you'll change your mind in a minute." I looked nervous. "What do you mean Suse?"

"Oh Pen! I'm sorry. Todd rang last night. We had a long chat and I'm seeing him tomorrow night." She looked down waiting for my reaction. I stayed silent until she eventually looked up again.

"Well, I'm hoping that's *definitely* the wine talking, but sadly I doubt it. I don't know which I'm more surprised at…Todd having a 'long chat', as conversation was never his forte, or the fact that you've agreed to see him again!"

"Penny, look I know you hate the ground he walks on. I know what you think of him, but he's changed so much!" She sees my look of disbelief.

"He's done really well for himself, he's got a recording contract, had some great gigs in Europe, they love him in Holland and he's got a little place in the south of France."

"Come on Suse, wake up! The only reason they like him in Holland is because he reeks of cannabis! And *if*.…..and it's a big if, he has got a recording contract and a 'little place in the south of France' you can bet your life he's used and trodden on several poor sods on his journey to get there! I know I'm stating the obvious here but, *leopards don't change their spots!* Just to ram it home once again, in desperation and hope that you might just change your mind, you already have an incredibly gorgeous, devoted, honest, decent, hardworking leopard, sitting in France at this very moment! Just take a minute to consider which leopard you'd rather be curled up next to in your French chateaux love nest."

"Look I'm sorry Pen, I'm just not you. I can't settle for the first decent prospect that walks into my life. I want something more exciting than that. Todd has changed, I just want to talk to him again, just to talk. If you don't like what I'm doing then fine, it's my life, my mistakes. I'd better go, we'll have to agree to differ on this one." With that she quickly grabbed her coat from the hall and left. She knew I wanted to say more, she knew I would try anything to persuade her not to go. It wasn't her I doubted. I trusted that she would just talk to him, but Todd Storm wasn't a talker. He was a manipulative charmer, a liar, but what could I do, I was her friend, not her conscience.

Now I'd be worried sick all tomorrow, how could I keep my mind on *my* date when Suse was about to be……'Stormed' by Mr Rockstar!

As I removed and hung up carefully, my outfit for tomorrow night, I kept going over what we'd both said. I felt guilty for being so judgmental on the one hand, but angry that she was being so blinkered after what happened last time.

I poured it all out to Morry Friday morning. "Should I ring her?" I say, feeling I might have gone a little too far in my candid description of Mr Rockstar.

"Noooo, don't you dare! You were being cruel to be kind, it'll sink in, she'll see sense." He says reassuringly. "You know Suse, you've been friends too long. Remember that time she got miffed, accused you of being PC Perfect, cos you got me as the, 'the gay friend' and then you introduced her to Bina. Scared of losing your friendship, bit jealous remember? She went off in a huff. Four days later you rang her and she says she's got a date with Harry Wong, owner of the Chinese restaurant in Broad Street! Following week there she is in, Chaplin's getting jiggy on the dance floor with Hector Boras, that hunky, Nigerian doctor, from Radcliffes Hospital. We all ended up in hysterics when he told us he was bi-sexual! You went over and said, she'd beaten you into a cocked-hat and Hector had said….. 'Sounds great, can I bring a friend and watch'. You will always be friends."

"Oh, I don't know Morry, this isn't the same, there's no jealousy. That git has some sort of hold over her. She just doesn't seem to see what others see. She's got to get him out of her system without me interfering." I say sighing, resigned to the awful possibility I may end up losing her friendship for good this time. Morry can sense what I'm thinking, he gives me a hug. I finally look up.

"Now listen lady, you have another date tonight, both of you are grown women who have to make choices good or bad. Leave Suse to make hers, you just enjoy your date, forget about the situation. Don't worry, it'll work out. Just a… Todd Storm in a tea-cup!" He says, trying to stay in serious mode, then breaks into giggles.

"Trust you, you big jester, to see the funny side, but you're right…yet again, I should just leave her to it, she'll be in touch if she needs to talk." But, of course as the day went on, my thoughts kept going over our conversation, I mulled it over on repeat, again and again. What if Mr Rockstar tried to persuade her to go off to France with him, I couldn't bare it. Surely she wouldn't say yes.

Later, as I put on the outfit Suse and I had had such fun getting together the previous evening, I tried desperately not to start snivelling and spoiling the face I'd just spent the last thirty minutes applying! I then got angry with myself. Ferdy watched with a puzzled expression as I began throwing handbags about, (we never got to handbags, Susie had left by then!) I was chuntering to myself in childish frustration.

Anna had left a note on my desk before she left the office. It gave instructions to meet Angus at 'Minty's Diner' for a six o'clock. I was slightly puzzled at the early time slot and the venue, not exactly the first place I'd put on my list to meet for a date. Minty's was a bright family friendly place. Durham's answer to the Hard Rock Café' it was not! In Minty's the only autographed photos they had on the wall were, Mike & Bernie Winters, David Bellamy and the Krankies! It's hardly…… Schwarzenegger, Stallone and Willis, … (that's Bruce, not Freeman, Hardy!)

I just wasn't in the right frame of mind to make this a success tonight, or maybe disinterest and sarcasm would be something he was used to and we'd hit it off.

Who knows?!

Chapter 9

As I walk into Minty's Diner I gazed round hoping that someone would stand up and wave me over, before the waitress arrived and I'd have to describe the complete stranger I'm meeting. She will then loudly point out several possible lone males, before I can sculk off in embarrassment towards the right table.

I feel a tug at the bottom of my jacket, looking down I see two large dark eyes looking up at me from a round, rosy-cheeked face. "Are you Penny the date lady, my name's Humfy, my daddy is over there." A little chubby hand grabs my left thumb and pulls me towards a table. A dark-haired male stands up, next to him another young boy also gets up quickly. I approach the table with three sets of huge dark eyes gazing at me in expectation!

This is not what I was expecting at all. I take a deep breath.

"Well, this is a nice surprise, an evening meal with three lovely men instead of one!" Angus looks anxious but relieved.

"I just felt that the boys, being the most important thing to me, should be here, after all there is a possibility of a mum for them, as well as a partner for me?"

I resisted the instinctive urge to grab my coat and run, partly because I was still being held onto by 'Humfy' and partly because I was rooted to the spot with fear!

His hand gestures towards the boys. "This is Humphrey, he's nearly four, loves Postman Pat, Sugar Puffs and doesn't like peas, or having his hair washed. This is Jarvis who is seven, loves Lego and chocolate ice-cream and doesn't like spinach, wasps and girls!"

"Oh, right then, well, I'm Penny, I'm a little older than seven, I love cats and chocolate eclairs, I don't like olives, escalators and spiders....and you?" I look towards Angus.

"I think you'll find, according to......*their mother'*, I like too much beer, football, don't like showing my emotions, being romantic and DIY." He states flatly.

I squirm slightly, the boys seem oblivious to their dads open bitterness and cutting remarks. (Hell fire, and I thought I was going to be the sarcastic one!)

"Right boys, lets order some food now that Miss Wiseman has very kindly joined us for tea tonight.....shall we have her boiled, roast, or fried?"

They all laugh, (surely the 3year old doesn't understand that?) I start to feel quite uncomfortable. (Good job the place is not licensed, if he'd ordered a bottle of Chianti I'd be up and running for the door!) "*We* are having a large ham and pineapple pizza, garlic bread, potato wedges, tomato dip and large colas...... *'their mother'* was always on a diet, so she'd always have the salad....*you?*" He says, in a challenging manner.

I feel I really have to get through this evening without reducing....*'his boys'* to tears by letting them know in no uncertain terms, how right......*'their mother'* was all along. I take a deep breath and commit the first sin of dating...... lie through your teeth if it saves the situation!

"Ha! How can anyone be on a diet, when there is all this lovely food to choose from, I think I'll join you in the a......
then we can all be half baked!" He raises an eyebrow at me, wrong move, I tried to match his amusing cannibal joke. To say I ate very slowly was an understatement…The pizza dough was hard to chew and digest, with added dips of, *'their mother'* comments, as a relish and constant accompaniment.

Humphrey suddenly, without warning, clambered up onto my knee and asked if I would cut up his pizza, his father told me to take no notice and that….*'his mother'* does it to keep him like a baby, she spoils and pampers him.

But he was a baby, not even four, with the cuddliest little body and sweetest face. I held him tight as his lip quivered, his large trusting eyes gazing at me.

I compromised, by pulling off small pieces and pretending to share with him. Angus tutted and Jarvis just stared. I wouldn't be defeated.

"So, Jarvis, what subjects do you like at school, I used to love writing stories and drawing?" He looks at me with disdain.

"Stories and writing are for girls, I hate girls. I like numeracy and history, we're doing about the Egyptians, they wrapped their women in bandages and buried them in caskets, in tombs, in pyramids."

"I think you'll find Tutankhamen was a man, they did bury men that way too." He looks at me strangely.

"Do you think any of the women were alive when they were buried?" I turn quickly to Angus.

"Children eh! They seem to have such vivid imaginations. He'll have nightmares with that lot on his mind when he goes to bed."

"They've had a lot more nightmares about....'*their mother*' walking out on them, she only takes them twice a month, thinks she's going to get custody. She disappeared to Wales with a car salesman. He turned her head with his Land Rover, talk of renovating a small holding in the Welsh hills together. She thinks when the boys stay there with them, and a load of chickens and other mucky animals they'll be okay. My boys need their football, they need discipline and routine...they need..."

This was one sad and bitter man. I quickly interrupted seeing Humphrey's face crumple and Jarvis's eyes misting over.

"To be honest I think I know what you *all* need, yes I do!.... Some very large, ice-creams, with plenty of chocolate on yours Jarvis? What do you think dad?"

I smiled my best, 'let's change the subject and just enjoy the evening,' smile! As we tucked into oversized desserts with everything on it, (hell, I was going to have to live on cabbage soup and prunes for the next fortnight!) Angus suddenly sighed and leaned towards me. I was a little worried about what was coming, but he surprised me.

"Look, I'm really sorry for giving you a hard time, it's just....it still feels so raw. If I'm perfectly honest, the boys are everything to me, but I can't cope with them and I'm not doing them any favours, showing my resentment am I?" I actually found myself relaxing for the first time that evening. This is where I could offer the shoulder, make him see that not all women were wanton witches (not even his ex-wife) and that there *was* a light at the end of that tunnel.

"I'm certainly no expert, all I can give you is my opinion if I was in your situation, or your ex-wife's even." His face begins to soften, he wants to listen.

"Obviously, I don't know all the details, but as a woman, I know she must have felt very hurt and lost to walk out on her own children and the guilt she feels is probably tearing her apart. From what you say, you are now two very different people, but with only one common bond, two lovely boys."

His face softened, so I continued. "You've started dating again, so you know in your heart of hearts that you can move on and find a special someone who loves football, likes going to pubs and clubs and the city life you so enjoy. Agree to differ, (that sounds familiar!) Think of the boys, Humfy, sorry…… Humphrey, he's *only* three, he needs cuddles, he feels more than you realise. And Jarvis, he shouldn't have to listen to you referring to his mummy, (bandaged, or otherwise!) as…... '*their mother*'. He is so vulnerable and he's trying to make sense of it all and getting it so very, very wrong. They need both of you, now more than ever, you have to put your own feelings of anger and bitterness aside." He's listening intently. I feel I have to finish the therapy session and hit home.

"You loved each other once, you could still be friends, or at least civil, for the sake of the boys. No one wins by denying them animals to see, countryside to run around in, let them enjoy the contrast, make the most of their choices. Don't brainwash them and blinker them, use them as pawns, to relieve your own hurt. Both you and your ex-wife have started again, grasp it all with both hands, enjoy it! Most importantly make sure your sons enjoy it all too."

Angus looks down. I was desperately willing him not to shout, or worse, burst into tears. Jarvis is gazing at his dad, much too much worry in a face so young. Angus then lifts his head slowly, then smiles broadly at his boys, reaching over he tousles Jarvis's hair. "Don't look so worried Jarvy, your dad was just having a good old think there." He stroked his finger round Humphrey's face and touched the little boy's nose lightly making him giggle. Then he looked at me.......

"Do you know something, everyone else has just agreed with me, placated me, for fear I'd go and do something stupid. Not one of my friends, or family, have said as much as you, a complete stranger, and made total sense. I've been so wrapped up in my own dented ego that I just couldn't see how straight forward it could all be....and just how amicable it all *should* be. I felt so bad that I wasn't coping with the boys, but I was determined not to let...'*their*'....Shirley....mummy....see what a total hash I was making of it all. In fact, I can't quite believe how unfair and awkward I've been."

He sighs loudly. "We did grow apart, we do want very different things in life, but we do still have two fantastic sons who need us both, to show them love, fun and give them lots of very different experiences and happy times."

Now his eyes were beginning to water and I wasn't far behind him, I was willing him to say something else, fortunately he did.

"Right! Decision made. I think I've got a phone call to make." He says looking warmly at his boys. "I think we should call, 'mummy' and tell her what a good day we've had and I think we should ask her if daddy can take you down to her house with the lovely chickens a little more often, what do we say to that then boys?" Jarvis's face beamed, his worried frown gone, he got hold of Humphrey's little hand, waving it frantically.

"Yeah! We're going to see the cluck, clucks Humfy! We're going to see mummy!"

"Thank you so much, Penny, I've been such a fool and so selfish."

Angus grabbed hold of my hand and kissed it. I was quite taken aback.

"Hey, I thought Shirley said you weren't romantic?" We both laughed, he looked awkward.

"I feel terrible, I don't know anything about you, except what Anna has told me and here you are solving all my problems on our first date. Anna says you've been single for a while, you like strange fashion, cats, dancing and walking into sunsets." (This is when you wish if people *have* to ear-wig your conversation they'd get it right, Anna!) "Actually, I like *watching* sunsets in the countryside."

He looks a little crestfallen. "Ah! So, you're a country bumpkin too at heart, are you?" I raise an eyebrow.

"Afraid so, I've never been sporty, I couldn't name you a football player past the seventies and that's only because we fancied them, not because of their, 'beautiful game' sorry. Anyway, I think making friends is probably more important at the moment, romance will come and find you when you least expect it. I've convinced myself of that, so I may as well try and convince you too!" I give him a reassuring smile as Humphrey slips down from my knee and puts his arms out to daddy for a hug.

"Look, you've got a phone call to make and two over excited boys to get to bed, I've got a skirt to iron and an over excited cat to feed, so I'll say good night, okay." Angus got up, holding Humphrey, he tried to lean forward to give me a kiss on the cheek, but Humphrey got there first, we all giggled. Jarvis also hugged me and gave me his two left over jelly sweets from his ice-cream which he'd been saving for later!

"You see, you must be romantic, where else would Jarvis get a gesture like that from? Sticky, fluffy, jelly sweets, way to a girl's heart, works every time!"

I left where I came in, three sets of large, dark eyes gazing at me in expectation! Never mind wicked witches.....I think I had just obtained my, Fairy Godmother badge.

And with a woosh of her wand, she was gone... off into the sunset, yet again!

Saturday became a day of purging, of deep philosophical therapy, a cathartic cleanse-fest! I spent the whole day totally alone, (except for Ferdy, who retreated to the airing cupboard at the sound of the trunked monster, I dragged around the floor!) I spent several hours in guilt ridden cleaning frenzy! I still hadn't heard from Susie, I wrestled with my conscience and then with the duvet cover.

Mr Rockstar's face became the toilet bowl, as I rammed the loo brush triumphantly up his left nostril! Then poured bleach on what I, oh so wished could be his shrivelling privates!

There was no corner left unclean, by the time I was onto the second load of washing and ironing, the woodwork shone and the smell of Wheelers Traditional Beeswax had been breathed in a little too enthusiastically, so I was beginning to feel a little giddy but a little calmer! But still wished the phone would ring.

I had to stay positive, keep my mind occupied. I managed this till about 3.30 then made a large mug of tea and searched the cupboards for a comfort snack, found a bag of pork scratchings and a lone Jaffa cake……needs must, needs must!

I'd decided to do my catch-up notelets to unseen friends and relatives, well I'd made a fine start last night with the, 'good deeds', it was such a boost to have made such a difference to Angus and his boys. I felt I could appease a little more by continuing my feelgood activities. But as I was about to put pen to notelet, the phone rang and my heart nearly stopped! Trying to stay calm, I picked up the receiver willing it to be Susie.

"Oooohooo! Only me, how did last nights liaison go then?"

It was Morry, obviously hopeful, no news was good news!

"Er, not exactly, 'Sleepless in Seattle.' Partly because he brought his children along and partly because all he needs at present is, a kick up the backside, a bit of pointing in the right direction and a healthy eating guide." I say, relieved that this isn't a screen phone and Morry can't see me wiping the pork scratching crumbs from the front of my jumper!

"It was certainly different as dates go" I continued.

"But I think you can safely say we weren't compatible, although Humphrey and Jarvis were lovely little boys, made me feel quite maternal."

Morry's voice goes up and octave. "Humphrey and Jarvis, what sort of names are they to give a baby for God's sake, they sound like a pair of balding, old men's outfitters?" I laugh, trust Morry. "Probably came from the same baby names book that your mum read when she gazed at her tiny bundles and thought, Maurice, Alma and Phyllis! Pot, kettle, black, I'm thinking here Maurice!"

He retorts quickly. "At least ours don't sound as if we've stepped out of a children's nursery rhyme, Penny, Freddie,

Molly and Mike, Freddie went bump and fell off his bike!" Morry is on fine form today.

"Are you sure you've rung the right number Morry? I thought our, 'bitching' conversation night was Monday?" He laughs. "Ooooh get you! Sorry, got carried away, I'll get to why I've really rung."

I sank back in my chair and got comfortable. I felt this was going to be good. "I think you might like what I've got to tell you." I was all ears.

"What is it Morry, love it when you've got a good bit of gossip to share, I always know it's going to be something worth hearing." He took a deep breath. "Well...My Rojere was in Spirals menswear this morning and who should walk in?"

I feel I have to play the game. "Jason Durr...Adam Ant with the tight little...?" He snorts. "We should be so bloody lucky! No, it was...Benny 'The Bass' Bentham!" Confused, I say tentatively. "Your Rojere's not got himself mixed up with gangsters, has he?" He snorts again.

"Where are you, we're not in London's East End, the bloody thirties docklands! Benny Bentham! He was the bass player with 'Tempest'...Todd Storm's band, remember?" It suddenly clicks. Morry continues. "Well.... Rojere knows him and Joe Trent the drummer, they go way back. Years ago, Benny was up in the air about his sexuality. I think all the unisex, glam rock, New Romantic club scene and soft rock stuff threw him. He was getting a bit worried he'd got rather attached to his lip gloss and eye liner, thought he was on the turn. Anyway, my Rojere introduced him to a female trucker called Priscilla and he's never looked back, think he's got all options covered."

I'm champing at the bit now and Morry's gone off at a tangent.

"Get to the point Morry…pleeease!"

"Keep yer frizzy wig on miss! Anyway, they were catching up on a bit of news. Benny and Joe have been away doing some backing tracks for another singer." I heard him take a sip of something, it was after three on a Saturday, probably be a Gin and It. He continued in a loud gossipy whisper.

"Well, the conversation then got round to, 'you know who' and how bitter they are about, 'Windy' dumping them when he got a sniff at that record deal, suddenly deciding he wanted to go solo so he could get *his* name only, on everything!"

I was starting to feel a little excited. "What else did they say, do they know something?" Morry's voice lowered, not easy for him mid juicy gossip.

"Well, put it this way, the ex-band members have a very good solicitor suing our friend Windy over breach of contract and… Todd Storm no more owns a villa in France than I have a yacht moored in the Caribbean. What's more…. the place he's been staying at in the South of France is owned by a woman called Germaine Franks. She's that over-priced, second-rate fraudster, oh sorry, 'Therapist' to the has-beens, oops sorry again, C list stars? Seems he's in hiding there, only reason he's over here is to see a couple of contacts and try and get some easy money, he needs it quickly!" Morry finally came up for air.

"I knew it, I just knew it! I bet he's trying to wangle a loan from someone not a million miles from us. The devious bastard!" I was angry, but also worried, how could we let Suse know.

"Susie isn't going to listen to me if I tell her. She'll just think I'm saying stuff to get rid, what can we do Morry?"

"I don't think *we* should do anything Penny. Think about the situation. Susie knows exactly what you think of him, but deep down she does trust you. I think she's just giving him one last chance to try and redeem himself, hoping that he may just be the exciting charmer he was when she first met him. Honestly Pen, I think when he gives her a line, the sob story to try and get a loan and let's face it he's not going to be subtle, he's desperate for cash! She is going to smell that dirty great rat and I'm not talking James Cagney!" I'm now imagining gangsters again as Morry continues. "Remember, she plays at being vulnerable and girly, but when she's made a fool of, especially twice, he's not going to know what's hit him!" I sigh loudly, slightly unconvinced.

"Oh God, I do hope so Morry, so what now, do we just sit tight and wait?"

"Look, you've got that next date on Tuesday, keep your mind focused on that for now. Give her space to think and make up her own mind. When she rings and she will, just let her talk. Don't forget, Simon is due back next weekend, she has to make a decision before then, it's not long, you'll cope."

I seriously doubted it, especially if Mr Rockstar didn't make his move and she made the wrong decision. "Okay Morry, I'll keep me mind occupied reading up on organic fruit and veg production for my date with Ben!" He laughs loudly.

"Wahay! That sounds like a recipe for a wild night! Don't forget, if he offers to show you his courgettes, you're onto a winner! Bet he knows his onions. Let me know if he gets 'fruity'!"

"Yes, yes, thanks Morry, as long as he minds his, 'Peas' and 'Quinces' we'll be fine, fancy playing gooseberry?" I smile at the thought of Morry sitting between us making continuous fruit and veg innuendoes.

"No, I do not lady! You wouldn't stand a chance of a second date with me there. If he's a tousled-haired, healthy hunk, in checked shirt and dungarees, he's mine for the taking girl!"
He giggles uncontrollably.

"Don't get me started Morry, you can't turn straight men gay anymore than me wafting in on your Rojere in silk shirt and little else is going to turn him heterosexual. Anyway, that's quite enough of our dodgy fantasy scenarios, I'm off to finish me housework before the Ugly sisters get back and turn me into a pumpkin!"

Morry is now high-pitched and giggling. "Ooo, as long as it's an *organic* one, eh?"

"Right Morry, see you Monday and watch where you put your Kumquats!"

Four hours later I had finally finished my housework! A very satisfying day! Who needs visits to the gym when you can do the weekly top to bottom housework regime. Arms, biceps, triceps, dragging an old fashioned hoover round seven rooms. I must have walked a couple of miles round the house, up and down stairs with washing, ironing, duster and polish, at least 30 times.

My face now actually resembles a pumpkin! Translucent, rosy and glowing, my hair is frizzy and clinging in strands to my forehead, my T-shirt is damp and sweaty and my old, baggy tracky bottoms are stuck in the most inappropriate places!

This of course is that time when the doorbell will ring and the man of your dreams will be standing there, in a suit and wafting of Fendi aftershave, clutching roses, saying he just wanted to surprise you and do you fancy supper at, 'Juliennes'?

I rush to lock the door not willing to risk that rare possibility. I run a bath, while consuming a lump of Edam cheese and half a French loaf, (I think mum says you get cramp if you bathe after eating...or is that swimming?) Sod it, it's worth a bout of cramp as I open a small box of chocolates, I'd put away in my, 'gift drawer'. (They were a three for two offer, so of course, I'm only eating the free ones.)

I light a couple of candles, sprinkle, scatter and pour a bit of everything into the running water, so the bathroom smells like a perfume emporium....... wonderful. To lie in suspended, weightless, heated, peaceful, comfort, going over the trials of the day. A cuppa nearby, (glass of wine optional, fear of drunken drowning steers me clear of this one) and a couple of treats within reach. (I did try the chocolate éclair once, but with eyes closed, mistook it for the soap!?!......Of course had the 'man of my dreams' been there, who knows...... might have taken on a whole new slant to the saying, have your cake and eat it?)

As a huge smile drifts across my face, I sink into the soft, enveloping bubbles and my imagination wanders and it has absolutely nothing to do with soggy eclairs...

Chapter 10

The next couple of days were a bit of a blur. Monday morning was only made memorable due to, Anna lunging at me. She ensnared me in a big bear hug, rendering me almost breathless! She thanked me for…..'sorting out the… Bottomley Boys!' (Gangsters came to mind yet again!) She then enthused at how much happier Angus, Jarvis and Humphrey were when they came round for Sunday tea! She said Angus talked non-stop about the evening and appeared quite smitten.

Panic rising, I quickly put her right on that one, without dampening her enthusiasm too much, but on the latest revelation of learning his surname, there was no way….no way…..I was going to become……..Mrs P Bottomley.

I know it shouldn't matter and if you truly love someone. But it would take an awful lot for me to become a Mrs Smelly, Mrs Willy, or …Mrs Bottom…anything posterior related! Bottomley, Sidebottom, Higginbottom. I'd like to forget I have one without being named after it.

I think my humour could just about run to Mrs Farthing…… as in, Penny Farthing. I could live with that. Although I'm sure Morry would take great delight in comments like, 'the old village bike' and 'is that you Mrs Fart-hing'?

June of course was also in hot pursuit, for most of Tuesday. (There are only so many times you can allow your boss to find you skulking on all fours in the large records cupboard, before he wonders if you're a total inadequate, or you're timing your file searches with his visits! (The leery look on Mr Preece's face when he caught me in there for the third time said his mind had settled on the latter!)

It was a difficult manoeuvre getting myself and a large file box through the door with Mr Preece determined to stay put in the doorway and let me squeeze past. He winced as the corner of the box jarred his groin, sharply! (That'll have dampened his ardour, hopefully!)

June caught me finally, taking refuge by the photocopier.

It seemed Ben was already staying with them, apparently, he'd brought them down another bee-hive, with Scottish bees, she'd said enthusiastically. I pictured them tartan, instead of striped, with small sporrans for nectar and making, 'och ay buzz' noises. I kept this visual amusement to myself fearing June would not only find it, 'not funny' but possibly insulting to the insect world in general! He'd also brought six jars of pickled marrow and a bottle of rhubarb wine? What could I say, this man certainly knew how to please.

She rambled on about Ben's practical prowess, how he'd mended the leaking sheds, done in a day what it would have taken Barry a month to do, (poor Barry, probably feeling even more inadequate than usual.) Anyway, by the time I left the office, Ben was just about everything a girl could wish for, according to June, (which was slightly worrying because in her eyes that probably meant a bit geeky, with no sense of humour, so that was me in for another interesting evening.) I shook my head slowly in disbelief that I was continuing this endless torture! We were, apparently meeting outside, 'Elliots'.

It's the only, *totally* organic restaurant in the city, so June had booked it saying *we*, (meaning Ben) couldn't possibly eat anywhere else! I'd try anything once, within reason. I certainly wasn't averse to healthy food. Full of nutrients, vitamins and no chemicals. It would certainly make a change from the contents of *my* fridge.

What I did object to in these places was the fact that you always got half a portion for twice the price. (Then again, maybe half a portion was all you really wanted of wood pigeon stuffed with nettle and kohlrabi in a wax bean sauce!)

The evening started with a difficult couple of hours before I even left the house. Lost without
my reassurance from Suse. I really missed her friendship and I *really* missed her fashion advice.

I sat there for ages, trying to get my face together, as I looked in the mirror, I imagined her sitting behind me. Laughing about the shape of my over plucked eyebrows, telling me which shade of lipstick to wear and to watch the blusher, or I'll end up looking like Charlie Caroli! I smiled, but my eyes filled with tears. I was being silly, I know. She wasn't me and she was right, she'd always wanted excitement and exciting people like…Todd Storm? Maybe it wasn't just exciting men she wanted in her life. Maybe she wanted exciting friends too, maybe she had finally outgrown me. It was too much, I put my head in my hands and sobbed…...and sobbed   ……the tears just came.

By the time I'd got a hold of myself, poor Ferdy was rubbing round my legs, purring in concerned confusion at the noise coming from his, 'house person'. It was now seven twenty and

I had to be out of the door by seven forty. Oh hell, what *was* I doing? I had to pull myself together. I had to get a grip and get this evening over with, just make the best of yet another unsuitable date.

Ben……Mr Organic. Well, apparently, he liked natural things, fresh with no chemicals, or additives. Could I do it, could I be brave enough? What had I got to lose, the chance not to date a stranger, or if he didn't like what he saw, the chance to date yet another………stranger.

I scrubbed my face of foundation, blusher and lipstick. I scrubbed so hard I was left with a rather ruddy glow, hmm very outdoorsy, he'll like that. No make-up? Not sure, I'm thinking, my eyes look like winkles in the sand, he'll think I'm ill.

Maybe I can do the English rose look…....pale and interesting? In the rose world I'd like to be a…….'Buff Beauty,' pale apricot, fragrant with attractive foliage and an outstanding autumn display! Sadly, I think I'm more an 'Alberic Barbier, a pale, old rambler, flourishes under poor conditions and can last well through winter but prone to mildew! Harry Wheatcroft and my Grandad have a lot to answer for!

With Vaseline on finger and thumb I give my eyelashes a natural shine, the same on my lips. I then brush out every ounce of, 'extra firm hold' hair lacquer from my tangled mane and plait it, one behind each ear, very country lass, no ribbons, better to leave that to the schoolgirl hen nights!

What to wear, I rummage madly…cream sweater, thick cord buttoned jodhpurs, brilliant! It was either the land army look, or I was auditioning for 'Haircut 100'!

It was nearly December, it was cold out, he was practical and earthy, I'm sure he'll like it. Too late now, I grabbed my brown coat, the one that Susie always said looked like some students, dodgy duffel! I was past caring, I hated being late.

I found a parking space just round the corner from 'Elliots.' I pulled nervously at my plaits, as I walked quickly from the car. I hoped this place wasn't too up market, I'd feel like a builder trying to go into Harvey Nics for a bacon bap. There was no one at the entrance, but I heard a chirpy, lilting voice behind me.

"My favourite pin-up, the…..'Dig for Victory' girl… how lucky am I?"

I turned quickly, trying not to over smile at my instant hit, in case it was some old duffer in a flat cap on his way to the British Legion, who was still having flashbacks from 1945 and thought I was a Vera Lynn tribute act. No, this was definitely *not* an old duffer! But……he was wearing a flat cap! Must admit, not my favourite headgear, unless you're over sixty, or Terry Thomas driving a natty little red MG out of Elstree studios, but what was underneath the cap made me forgive and forget instantly. He quickly removed the said tweed item, ruffling his thick blonde hair.

I tried my best to hide my obvious amusement, not just at the hat, but the fact that he was standing there in…thick brown cords, thick cream cable-knit sweater and was also wearing….a duffel coat! He instantly looks just as amused saying,

"I know I told June to tell you a wee bit about me, but I didn't know she was going through the finer details of my wardrobe!"

I feel slightly embarrassed, what if he thinks I actually asked what he was going to wear, then copied it? I realise it's the sincerest form of flattery, but to a stranger, it looks just plain weird!

"No, honestly, June said nothing about your clothes, I was running late, it's a cold night. I would have worn a dress… but…well…"

"Hey, no, look, I'm not being critical, it's a great look, suits you……very earthy, very fresh. I'm not really comfortable with the 'painted lady' look on a girl to be honest, we can leave that to the butterflies." He smiled a lovely broad smile, very fresh, *very*……..earthy!

As we sat down at a little table, by the window, I noticed the surrounding tables were displaying an awful lot of Fair-Isle. It was a bit like a grand seventies knitting convention, with an awful lot of clashing colours and patchwork jumpers.

There were some obvious keen, 'Good Life' fans who'd watched the early episode where Tom and Barbara got a loom to home knit and had obviously followed suit and…….*made* their suits, it appeared.

I wasn't knocking it. It's 1997, the veggie, wholefood thing is still seen as a bit sixties hippy dippy and unusual in a country full of fast food and fried everything. This place had a very, 'retro' feel…a colourful cosiness to it. Although there was the odd suspicious looking old hippy throwback, a wispy bearded male, who was no doubt trying to persuade his pretty, nubile twenty-something companion the advantages of living in a commune! The advantages all being Mr Beardie Weirdies, as he gets to have sex with a young woman that wouldn't have normally given him handbag, (sorry crocheted tote-bag!) room otherwise! I shudder at the thought. Ben notices.

"Are you cold? You'll have to come round here and squeeze in next to me!" Ben beams.

"It's ok, think I'll wait till I'm onto the decaff, hand-churned goats cheese and boysenberry biscuits before I get that intimate, but thanks for the offer!" Ben still beaming.

"Och, no, sorry, I wasn't making a pass, there's a radiator behind me." Then trying to ease my obvious embarrassment he kindly adds. "But I'm open to offers after the Apple mint jelly and organic clotted cream."

I smile, giving him my best, flirtatious, Vaseline lashed flutter, it would have looked so much more seductive had they been, a set of breeze producing false two inchers, (still talking lashes here!) but I did my best. He was literally, a breath of fresh air. He talked about the organic plant production, with so much enthusiasm. It was quite obvious that I didn't understand all the technical terms he was using, or some of the plant names, but he made it so interesting and he was more than easy on the eye to watch and listen to.

I did know some of the fruits and veg Ben mentioned. I'd loved gardening with my dad and grandad years ago and still potted up a few herbs and flowers for my small back garden.

But Ben was into it on a much larger scale, selling to hotels, cafes, restaurants and some local shops in and around Fife. I listened as his story unfolded. He had a lovely voice, that melodic Scottish brogue.

He told me he'd moved up to Scotland with his father, after June's mum refused his proposals of marriage for the last time. June had told me she and her mum never got over her father's death, June was only little, but she'd stood and watched her mother clutching his body, sobbing, distraught that she hadn't been there to help him. Even knowing he was dead, she'd sat cradling him for over two hours.

It was a heart attack and at four years old, it was June that called the ambulance…....maybe I should forgive her not having much of a sense of humour.

Ben continued. "My dad met June's mum about twenty years ago, he'd been left to look after me when my mum decided to go off and 'find herself' with some long-haired, bearded hippy to a kibbutz in Israel, some ten years earlier." (So glad I hadn't commented out loud on my, 'beardy weirdy' observations earlier. That would have put an unsubtle damper on the evening.)

"I was only five at the time, I don't remember much about her, but my dad gave up his city job in London, we moved to Yorkshire, then onto Northumbria, he took on a loan and a smallholding. He was determined to get back to his ancestors love of the soil and gave me a fantastic childhood. He met June's mum, Nesta on an organic agricultural growers course. She and June we're trying to be independent and self-sufficient. She wouldn't let Cam, my dad, do anything to help at first, but he kept on calling. I was turning into a confused teenager at the time and meeting June who was then seventeen going on forty, she nearly put me off girls for life!"

I laughed. "She is a bit old before her time, but God love her, with what happened you can see why she grew up fast. Anyway, what happened next?" I willed him to keep talking, I was thoroughly enjoying just listening to him talk and it kept my mind off the food! Mmmmm……Dill and pecan mash coming up. Literally.

"Well, dad tried his best, they moved in with us, Nesta loved the farm. We got more chickens, kept collecting peoples left over animals. A couple of hand weaned sheep, a runt pig, a donkey with bald legs, it went on. Dad put more of the field to use and we started selling the fruit and veg and eggs. On Nesta's birthday dad bought her, her very first bee-hive, both she and June love bees. He proposed....... she said no. It went on like that for the next six years! I went off to Agricultural College, by the time I returned in time for June and Barry's wedding, Nesta had decided she wanted to go home…to Laurence."

I looked puzzled… then shocked. "Oh, no she didn't…… join him." Seeing my expression, he put a reassuring hand on mine.

"No, no, even after all that time she still felt that Laurence was and always would be, the one person she truly loved. She felt she was betraying him by being with dad. She'd never sold the house, she'd just rented it out, so she went back." He sighed.

"She's still there. June visits when she can, she lives in the past and still talks to Laurence, it's all very sad. Not just for Nesta, but for June, who in a way, lost her mum, as well as her dad. That's why I've always kept in touch, I'm the brother she *should* have had. My dad truly loved them both." He bit his lip hard. "It broke my dad's heart. Being walked out on twice. You sometimes feel it's not good to get too attached to people, is it?"

And there it was. The reason why this handsome, intelligent, gentle human being was in his thirties and still alone. Not because he was throwing himself into the business and had no time to date, but because he was terrified of being walked out on, just like his poor dad.

Ben continued. "Sooo…that's when dad and I decided to move back up to Fife, it's where our family came from, it was *us*, 'going home.' Dad's brother Gregor was retiring and sold us the land, we've never looked back."

"My God…and I think I'm hard done to sometimes. You and your dad certainly haven't found success by the easy route, have you?" I say with a reassuring smile.

"Makes you more grateful for what you've achieved and gained if you've been round the houses and through the mill to get it. I'm just so proud of my dad. Bringing me up, for keeping going, he is my hero." I saw his strong jaw stiffen and he squeezed my hand. "Right, well that's my life in a nutshell, what's *your* story?"

"Hey! If that's your life in a nutshell, it's a rather large coconut and in comparison, mine which will be a rather small hazelnut. But nuts apart…..ouch! Oh dear, I promised Morry I wasn't going to make fruit and veg innuendos, I'd leave them to him!" Ben laughs and the weathered skin around his eyes creases. "Nuts aren't fruit and veg. Anyway who's Morry, is he a…'Melon man'?"

I start to laugh now. "Oh, nooo! Twisted or otherwise, Morry is more your two plums and a corguette man…if you get my drift! Do they have Morrys north of the border?"

"Och! Aye, yes, definitely! I'm not sure about as far up as Muckle Flugga in the Shetlands but we have two hoteliers in Crail and I know of a rather colourful transexual café owner in Auchtermuchty!"

"Oh, Morry will be pleased, he and Roger will be donning the tartan and storming the borders, threatening pink frilled sporrans, ginger lowlights and latte flavoured shortbread for all!"

We both sit chuckling at that visual delight conjured up. I am really enjoying this evening, but it's going far too fast, we're now on the lemon tea and lavender creams and we're getting on *really* well.

"So, June says you'll be taking over from dad, are you looking forward taking full control?" He leans back, looking serious, I want to keep him talking but I'm not sure if I should have asked him that one.

"To be perfectly honest I don't want it to happen, but dad really needs to ease up a bit. I want him to spend more time with Aggie." He's smiling again, raising his eyebrows.

"Aye! He did get there eventually… third time lucky! Aggie owns a B & B in Kirkcaldy. She buys her fruit and veg from us. She had to wait a while mind. He was understandably a wee bit stubborn in the romance department! I made sure I was always busy and that he *had* to deliver her order, she did the rest, she's so good for him. I'm a great believer in, all comes to those who wait."

Oh yes! I'm mentally cheering! So, hopefully his dad's experience hasn't put him off. He's just biding his time for the right person to come into his life, thank heavens for that. Wahay! It's lashes at the ready girl!

"Absolutely!" I say in enthusiastic agreement. "Nothing worse than rushing in, wishing your life away, you never know who, or what, is round the corner."

Flutter, flutter. I try to keep eye contact, but don't think he can see these un-mascaraed efforts, especially with only the one stingy candle on the table. I lean forward slightly and then try the Marilyn Monroe husky, breathy whisper.

"So, what do you see in your future?" In pronouncing the breathy 'f' I blow out the candle, and I'm sitting there looking like Madame Pluvierre in the middle of a mystic palm reading, as candle smokes swirls between us. As the waitress quickly rushes over with a taper to re-light the candle, Ben asks for the bill. Damn………. I've blown it, literally!

"Look it's been a great evening, but I really can't stay out much later, I promised June I'd be up
at dawn to help renovate the turkey house, she's got a friend for Christmas, called Eve, (what else!) coming next week and a dozen assorted chickens on their way. I'm away back up to Fife on Thursday, so I must get on, sorry."

"No, not a problem, you're obviously very busy, with the business and everything. It's that time of year for you, all those Christmas bookings coming up. Every eatery will be needing its seasonal fruit and veg." I tried to stay upbeat, I couldn't bring myself to be anymore forward, or to question the possibility of seeing him again.

As we left and the cold wind hit our faces, he took hold of the front of my duffel coat, pulling me towards him. He began to slowly do up my duffel togs, (had it been anywhere else, or slightly warmer, I'd have possibly wished he was undoing them!)

"Penny, this is a bit awkward for me, I feel I've really enjoyed your company tonight and in different circumstances I'd be asking if I could see you again, but I feel that might be a little unfair." What was he on about, June definitely said he was single, there's no chance she'd allow her step-brother to philander, what on earth was he trying to tell me?

"Er, I don't really understand what you're trying to say Ben?"

"Look it's my fault, I've misled you slightly, in normal circumstances I'd have asked if you'd
like to come up to Scotland after Christmas, when we're quiet. You know, celebrate Burn's Night or something, share a haggis."

"Sounds good to me!" I beamed. "June hasn't told you I've got a turnip allergy or something has she?" He smiled at the same time pulling me closer, which was a nice feeling.

"Och noo, it's not June's fault at all, I didn't tell her till today. I'm going away after Christmas. I'm taking ten months out to travel Italy and Spain. I'm going out to visit organic producers there, we're having trouble with our, Foeniculum vulgare!"

I stare in surprise. "Oo er, that sounds horrible, what is it?" I ask, dreading the reply.

"Fennel! I think we're not getting our poly tunnels to the right temperature we have a lot of soggy bottoms." He says seriously. (I know the feeling in this weather.)

"I talked to dad, he knows we need to get a better range for the restaurants, so he and Gregor are going to re-do some of the hot houses, rest some of our land for a year, before I finally take over"

"So, what you're actually saying is you're going to Europe… for nearly a year?"

Ben looks awkward, but those blue eyes are now staring straight into mine, making it very difficult to feel annoyed with him. "Look, you're more than welcome to come out there at some point, you know, when I've found a base and settled, just pop over."

"Well, I do have, (did have?) a best friend in the travel business, you never know." I say flippantly, trying to disguise my disappointment of not having the opportunity of spending Christmas with this man and his organic Brussel Sprouts.

"Look, just have a think about it, I know it's not much to offer in the way of a second date, but maybe memory of this and the Italian sunshine may go some way to persuading you it could be possible." As the last word left his lips, he'd found mine. Softly and very gently his hand cupped my face, sliding to the back of my head as his kiss became much firmer, I closed my eyes and let him continue....Had this been 'Pride and Prejudice', it was my moment to swoon.

It had been so long since I'd felt a kiss like this. It wasn't quite as intense and spine tingling as Charlies, but by heck, it was a damn close second!

As his face moved away, he released his hold and I staggered slightly, feeling a little foolish I said.

"God, that Rhubarb wine has a lot to answer for!"

"Well, tell you what. I'll send you a postcard and if you decide to pop over, I'll scour those Italian markets for rhubarb and try and have a couple of bottles on ice for your arrival." His smile and the look in his eyes was so very hard to resist.

"Sounds good to me, look forward to your postcard." He then began to walk slowly backwards, keeping eye contact. Still smiling he said. "You never know, I may send you Christmas card before then, which do you prefer, Scottie dogs sitting on a tartan rug, or Grouse in fields of heather?"

"You mean I can't have grey kittens with tartan bows sitting in a heather sprigged basket?" And as he waved and turned the corner, he shouted. "Aye, for you Penny, my sweet friend, anything!"

And I sort of knew from that last line, that's exactly what he would be, a sweet friend. Had I been twenty-five possibly waiting a year to see whether you're going to be a couple is acceptable, but sadly at thirty-seven, it was risky. But I was not going to dismiss Ben altogether, and as I took in how bright the city's Christmas lights seemed to have become, I suddenly acquired a little spring in my step and bounced back to my car!

I re-lived the evening, in my mind several times over as I made a cuppa, sank into a bath and lay there, gazing at the ceiling.

Then just as my eyes began to close, just as my consciousness was drifting off and trying to rid my whirring brain of the thought that I was still going to be… in the words of that oh so depressing seasonal hit by Mud ……...'Lonely This Christmas' ….the doorbell rang!

Chapter 11

My heart raced as I jumped from the bath, dripping I grabbed my dressing gown. Oh hell! Maybe it was Ben? Maybe he'd changed his mind, decided not to go to the sunny climbs of Italy, decided the lure of me and a cold February was too much for him! Fat chance!

I seem to remember, I couldn't even get Warren to swap a windswept weekend in Kendal with his mate, drippy Dave, so what pray made me think Ben was suddenly giving up a year in Europe with organic Fennell, for my affections.

It was nearly midnight. My mind was now switching to the horrible possibility of two Police officers at the door with news I just didn't want to hear.

The bell rang again, several times in succession, whoever was there needed me to answer urgently. Thinking of my safety at a time like this, I shouted out as I got nearer to the door. "Who's there? Who is it please?" I could hear a faint moaning, a slight whimper. Probably some drunk staggered up the wrong path, I put the chain on the door and peered through the gap like some old spinster. "Pen....er...Penny...I am *so* sorry." And there she stood, pale, dark bags under her eyes, which were red rimmed from crying. "Oh, my good God! Susie?"

I opened the door as quick as I could and pulled her in, she fell into my arms sobbing, her whole body shaking, as she tried to get the words out.

"Susie, don't talk, its ok, just come and sit down, here I'll put the fire on, you look frozen, hang on I'll make a cuppa." I tried to get as many comforting anomalies into the one phrase, to get her calm enough to speak. I rushed from the fire, to the kitchen, removing her coat and hat in between squeezing her hand. I watched her distressed sobs. Oh bloody hell! It'll be something to do with that bastard, I know it will. Think of the worst of the worst scenarios.

Oh, bugger! Maybe she's pregnant!

Waited all these years and she ends up with the spawn of the devil....and it's probably twins, triplets or......a whole band. No, she can't be, he only saw her Friday.

I sat down, put the cups on the tiny coffee table next to her, then took her hands, she couldn't bring herself to look at me. "Susie... Suse, whatever's happened, I'm here for you, *whatever it is.*" It made the tears gush even more, I reached for the large, 'soppy movie' sized box of tissues and handed her two. She took a deep breath, then looked straight at me.

"I am truly sorry Penny..... for treating you the way I did and for saying all those things...." I shrugged and smiled. "You had your reasons."

"No, let me finish, don't make excuses for me. Where that man is concerned...I not only seem to have been blind to his faults, but also deaf, dumb and positively prostrate with tunnel vision! I couldn't have been anymore narrow sighted if I'd been wearing carthorse blinkers."

I interrupted. "Well, not unless they came in green satin with matching fur bridle of course?" She tried to smile through her tears, then hugged me.

"Why aren't you in a huff, why don't you get angry and give me a hard time?"

"Hey! The only reason you got off lightly is because the small wax effigy I have of you in my airing cupboard is now tarred, feathered and has a large hat pin up its bum. Oh no sorry that one's Todds! I love you to bits Suse. You're me best friend, we both realise that on certain things, we just differ, getting mad at each other over stuff just mars our friendship. I value that and you, too much."

She began wiping her tear-stained face. "Now you're just making me feel even more guilty than I did before I plucked up courage to come round." She sniffed loudly as I passed her tea, she always liked the cup with the big ginger tabby cat on it which said, 'I'm the Cat's Meow.' She was and always would be.

"Well, I hate to draw attention to the fact that it's after midnight, I'll be turning into a pumpkin and you've turned up looking like the ghost of Jacob Marley. You've got tear stains on me sofa, you're drinking me tea and you still haven't told me what happened? And please, choose your words wisely, me teeth are grinding already with the thought of what that feckless toss-pot may have come up with this time. I hope to God you haven't been through another dodgy marriage ceremony and he's dragged you to Blackpool, Las Vegas amusements, with some Elvis impersonator in a black quiffed wig, singing Heartbreak Hotel, and two chalet maids as witnesses?"

"Well, if you bloody well let me get a word in!" Suse tries a smile.

She wipes her eyes, sips her tea, straightens herself up and sighs loudly.

"Todd took me out on Friday, to some grotty little bar off the beaten track. He said he was hoping an old friend of his would be there, said it was the blokes local. Most of the evening he just talked non-stop about his, apparent 'champagne lifestyle'. About his place on the Riveria, how he had at least ten gigs coming up in Europe and his British comeback" (Comeback! Didn't think anyone had noticed he was here in the first place, deluded tit!)

Suse continued. "In between switching on the charm of course. Telling me I was so much more beautiful than he remembered." (Yeah! Well, in between his quota of dope and groupies, lucky that he actually recognised her at all.)

"Did he at any point actually ask anything about *your* life, whether you were married, had a boyfriend, or did he assume you had just waited for his prophet like return?" She looked skywards.

"He asked nothing about me Pen, it was as if days, not years had passed between us. I stupidly saw him again on Sunday, we ended up in the 24-hour services at Leeming Bar! He said two of his roadies had some paperwork he had to sign so he'd better hang on…… I ended up drinking three cappuccinos and chewing on a stale cheese roll, I was fuming! He then asked if I was still working at Farriers, when I said yes, he asked if I could possibly get him a cheap flight back to France next week." Her anger was starting to rise, like mercury in a thermometer.

"Bloody cheek! *Then*, he asked if I'd ever decided to spend that money I was saving, that old Uncle Herby had left me. I thought, now that is strange, fancy *him* remembering that!" (Yeah. Fancy?!) She sipped her tea and relaxed a little.

"Anyway, when I realised, he was probably moving on again next week, I agreed to see him again tonight. I knew in my heart of hearts that I didn't want him anymore and nothing was going to happen." She smiled as she saw me visibly sigh with relief.

"Simon rings most days, when he gets a bit of time between conferences, sales meetings and wine tastings. He describes all the wines to me, the bouquet, the colour, the beautiful places they come from, all in such a lovely eloquent way. He really wished I was there, at the hotel for him to come back to. It would have made his time there so much more pleasurable, rather than just financially lucrative. He says how much he misses me and I miss him and I know now Pen, which person I *really* want to be with."

"Thank the heavens for that". I sank back into the chair smiling. "So tonight, you told Todd Storm to go forth and multiply then?"

"Well, I did try. He kept saying I'd led him on, said he'd come back to renew his 'partnership' with me, our souls were irreversibly entwined. (He should certainly be irreversibly entwined and how.) He reckons it was all he ever wanted, us to be together, sharing *everything* we have." I grabbed her hand and squeezed it tightly.

"Presumably, by everything, he meant he'd be sharing Uncle Herby's money and you'd be sharing him with…well, basically anything in a skirt that has breasts. Well, all I can say is, you don't know what a near miss you've had. I'll tell you the latest news, from the cart-horse's mouth, so to speak."

Susie's expression then turned from sadness to real anger, as I told her about, 'Windy' and his phoney lifestyle and the list of obvious untruths, that Roger had uncovered and told Morry, all from the ex-band members. "That cheap lump of...I can't believe I almost fell for that bull-shit! So, he was taking me to all those shit-holes because he didn't want to be recognised, or seen by the lads. What an absolute......*port*-hole!" I could tell when Susie was really angry. She never normally allowed the 'lady' in her to use 'hole' words, particularly two in one sitting.

"He *had* the bloody cheek to tell me *I* had led *him* on! Right, that's it Pen, we need closure......no, we *need* revenge!"

"Now that sounds quite appropriate under the circumstances. But look, it's nearly ten to one, my brains addled and in need of sleep closure at the moment! I've got to be up at six thirty! Do you want to kip here?" Susie got up quickly, grabbing her coat.

"No, Pen...I really want to get home, Coco and Chanel, (her semi-human Siamese!) they'll be waiting up, to be honest my mind's buzzing. I'm going to get a few plan notes jotted down, I'm on flexi this week, so I'm not in till ten tomorrow, sorry today!" We hugged each other with relief and with love. "God Suse, it's such a relief to know if I ever *do* get another date, I might now end up wearing the right shade of lipstick this time."

"Oh, sorry Pen, I've been so wrapped up in my own misery and self-importance. You've had two dates and...and....I know nuuuurrrthing!" I laugh at her attempt at Manuel from Fawlty Towers!

"Sorry can't possibly tell you all the gory details in ten minutes, so you're going to have to meet me in Parkers tomorrow at two. Now this slap on head.....you bugger off, comprende?" As I lovingly push her towards the door doing my best Basil Fawlty impression!

"Don't forget to bring a notebook Pen, we have to get this right, we've got a couple of scores to settle with the great... *the late*....Todd Storm."

As I closed the door after one last hug, I was tired but jubilant to think that Todd Storm was about to get the wind up. Yes, let's hope our plans would just, blow him away......permanently. We realised murder was out of the question, you can't kill the son of darkness. But a spot of ritual humiliation and removing his sunglasses before dawn should do it!

"Morry, you look as if you're catching flies!" I laugh, in between telling him about my date with Ben, my midnight visitor and our plans for revenge. His jaw got slacker and slacker as he sat there agog.

"Me emotions are wrecked! That romantic kiss, the love that could be, wrenched from your dry and over-buffed fingers. Then the fear...the not knowing......who or what, was at your door. The laughable possibility that it could have been, the organic man of your dreams. Then......poor Susie! The drama and eventual realisation that the man she trusted contained more garbage than Seaton Carew's land-fill. Hell! What a night love. Bet that was one for the diary?" He put his hand to his head in mock concern and steps backwards.

"Yes, thanks for reducing me life to am-dram proportions Morry. I realise to you we're just one big soap opera. Look, tell you what, to keep your excitement on a Drama Queen high, I'm meeting Susie at Parkers at one, can you make it? I think I've got a bit of an idea for teaching old, Todd Storm a lesson and you can help. Fancy being in on this Morry?"

"Oh! You try and stop me lady. I definitely want in on this! All girls together! Do you want me to get me Foxy Fay outfit on and seduce him? It would be a struggle but I could force meself, in the name of revenge?" I look startled.

"Much as that would be a wondrous sight to behold Morry, I think with the amount of stuff he smokes and drinks he's probably been with a 'Foxy Fay' already and not even noticed. You're on the right lines though, but we need something that assaults *all* his senses, that crushes that ego of his and sends him back under the stone he crawled out from under."

"Oh, Penelope, Penelope...a word." It was June. This sounded ominous, was I going to get berated for not using my charms to make Ben stay and not disappear to Europe for months on end.

"Oh, June....yes, I was going to come over and have a natter."

"You know me Penelope, I haven't got time for frivolous, coffee time banter." Oh gosh no, heaven forbids! I bit my lip so as not to say it out loud.

"I just wanted to say, thank you, for spending the evening with Ben after he told you about his immanent travels. It can't have been easy, knowing this wonderful man was now not available to you." I looked a little put out at her finality of the situation.

"Well, actually June, we had a lovely evening, he didn't spoil it, he left it till our farewell embrace." I could see her visibly stiffen at the word…...'embrace'. "Told me his plans and gave me an open invitation to join him out there in Italy, when he's settled."

"Oh…..Oh I see…Not quite what he told me Penelope, but you know men, they don't like to hurt anyones feelings. Barry and I got an invite too. I'll let you know when we're going over, maybe you could travel with us, we've got a large camper!"

"Ooohoo! me too!" Shouts Morry, "He's called Rojere, there is nothing that man can't do with a sheet of nylon, eight tent pegs and a pound of Cumberland sausage!" Thank God for Morry. Stopped me having to promise June I'd bunk up with her and Barry in their big yellow van. I could feel a Kenneth Williams moment coming on…..ooo err, carry on camping!

Morry and I reached Parkers windswept and still giggling at the prospect of camping with Barry and June. Then, I caught sight of Susie, she was looking as beautiful as ever. It was only twelve hours earlier she'd looked like the wreck of the Hesprith, said she'd only managed four hours sleep and there she was, Audrey Hepburn on a caffeine high.

"Suse, hope you don't mind Morry being here, I've had a bit of an idea and I think he can help." She grinned, quickly pouring teas as we huddled round the table.

"No, of course not, in fact, we may be thinking on the same lines. Are we set? Notebooks out, let's synchronise pencils and watches." (My, she was taking this seriously, she definitely meant business.)

She began riffling through her handbag. "What about this then, for starters? I have here a rather fetching photo of, 'the real' Todd Storm. I think we may be able to use this, don't you?"

"Oooo! I think that will certainly give him the following you may be after, what do you think ladies?" Morry had a wicked glint in his eye.

There we were like the three witches, cooking up potions and plots that would certainly turn Todd Storm into something his rock comeback hadn't quite allowed for.

"Right then Pen, can you sort out photocopying and the distribution of the posters? Morry, could you sort out the venue and a suitable audience? I think club 'Peacocks' would be just perfect. He won't have a clue that it took over from, 'Flames' six months ago, will Theo mind, it's short notice I know?"

"Leave it to me babe, Theo will love this, a bit of pressure, bit of theatre, he'll be in his element, he'll make sure the right people are there don't you fret." Susie leant back in her chair, a real Cheshire cat smile on her face.

"Okey dokey then, cakes all round before we get this plan into action. By the way, I've already rung the man in question and arranged for him to meet me outside 'Peacocks'. Eight o'clock tomorrow night, so we *have* to make this work." I looked startled. "How did you manage that, I thought you'd already said your good-byes, hadn't you?" Susie looked sideways giving a very naughty wink.

"Let's just say, I may have given him the impression of a record producer in the vicinity, if he sings a couple of numbers at the club tomorrow. Also the possibility of a bit of Uncle Herby's cash for a 'loan'……..*and* the added incentive, as if the other two could fail…the possibility of …'farewell sex' with me!" Morry and I gawped in disbelief.

"It's alright." Reassured Susie, back to her confident self.

"I didn't make any promises, he's a desperate man, a user and loser, he'd sell his granny for a tenner and green shield stamp if he thought it would get him a sniff at fame and fortune."

I looked aghast! "Well, you've certainly changed your tune. I thought he was Mr Rockstar, Mr Exciting?"

Susie pulled herself up and sighed.

"It took nearly losing *our* friendship Pen and nearly cheating on the best man to walk into my life, to make me think very seriously about *my* future. And to realise after years of being treated like a piece of fluff, an acquisition, that I was actually, a grown up. And that I deserved respect, love, commitment, romance, protection, honesty, deep understanding and most importantly, some good, slow, sensual, mind-blowing sex!" Morry and I chorused. "Oh yes! Hallelujah to that one girl!"

"Oh, I know it's early days with me and Simon, but I've missed him this past two weeks and I know he's missed me. This is as normal as I've ever felt, I don't want to lose this man and certainly not to someone like Todd Storm or, as his birth certificate shows…Dudley Crabshaw." Morry clamped his hand over his mouth in hysterical disbelief.

"DUDLEY…CRABSHAW! Oh…my…God.…...You could not have wished for better in the revenge stakes could you, what was poor Mrs Crabshaw thinking?"

We all just fell about. This was perfect…just perfect. As we, 'ladies did lunch' for the rest of the hour, Susie insisted on being updated on my men, lack of and any other interesting gossip going that she'd missed out on. Among the update, I told Suse I'd spoken to Paula on Monday. She and Harold had been out to choose some cream, eggshell paint, tiles and vertical blinds. She was being very practical in her assistance to Harold, but I could tell, even over the phone, that she was blushing when she said he'd asked what colours she'd prefer in the master bedroom. Which word made her blush more I asked, master or bedroom? She nearly choked on her tea, but you could tell, she was secretly loving every minute of actually being wooed by this man.

Susie seemed really pleased for Paula, but thought, maybe I should have got in first, as he was quite a catch. I reassured her that even the more than lightly prospect of me being on my own for, yet another Christmas, did not warrant the tactics of stealing a friend's man. But I did reassure her, that of course I could have, had I *really* wanted to.

And as we dispersed from Parkers into a dismal December afternoon, the wheels of revenge and closure were put in motion. Phone calls were made, scenes were set, props were found. This was a stage debut, Todd Storm, alias Dudley Crabshaw, was not about to forget. This was going to be a memorable night for *all* concerned.

Back at my desk, I carefully got the wording right and photo set. I managed a few extra photocopies with each file. (The guilt made me put an extra £1 in the tea tin.) I didn't enjoy being this sneaky, but, mine was a small part to play, but an important one.

Later, I rushed quickly up and down North Road, lobbed a copy into the bars and onto available lamp-posts, bus-stops near 'Peacocks'. Morry had spoken to Theo, who had rung a friend who was a reporter. The press involved! This was getting better by the minute.

Suse rang me later, to check all was under way. She'd also had a call from Morry, about the venue and press being there. We couldn't believe we were actually going to go through with this, but we'd gone too far to back out now.

Anyway, we felt Todd Storm should get his crack at fame once again, a bit of well-deserved publicity. What fading rockstar didn't want a second chance of a comeback, a real boost to the never-ending ego? This was going to be….'banging man'!

Chapter 12

My mind wasn't on work. I rang Morry for reassurance, watching the clock as Thursday slowly ticked by.

"Are you sure we're doing the right thing?" I knew his conscience was much more at peace than mine.

"For heavens sake Penny! The blokes a complete tart! You don't want him sniffing round Susie and spoiling her chance with the Simon, now do you? He's a lying creep, he deserves a lot more if you ask me, I think we're being very kind, considering."

I relaxed, my moral standing and the slight pangs of guilt began to slide away, as I heard myself saying enthusiastically.

"You're right Morry. He's lucky we're not plying him with alcohol, shaving his eyebrows and dressing him in inappropriate clothing before the press photos." Morry laughs wickedly.

"That *can* be arranged, you just say the word girl."

Panic rises again. Why am I so worried? Susie wants revenge. She wants rid, we are getting rid! I threw myself into work as the angel and devil of my conscience fought above me. The wicked twinkle in the eye and the horns just showing above my hairline by the end of the day seemed to show who was winning.

After a *very* light tea, (I kept feeling quite nauseous at the thought of the look that would appear on Todd's face this evening.) I searched my wardrobe and drawers for a suitably colourful outfit. 'Peacocks' by name and 'Peacocks' by nature.

I wasn't going for a classic female gay look tonight, although I secretly loved the power suit, shoulder pads, mans shirt and hair tied back, side parted and slicked in good old fashioned, vogue styly, so cool.

It would be far too crushing for me to be propositioned by gay men, thinking I was a gay *man*, instead of girly lesbians thinking I was a hunky lesbian female. Go on, which is worse? Even as a heterosexual, it matters.

I pulled on my purple glittery trousers, squeezed everything in, then caught sight of my backside in the mirror, it looked like a large bruised plum. What the hell, I was hardly thinking of potential boyfriend material tonight.

I slid on a white T-shirt with the jewelled words, 'The Cat's Whiskers'. I felt it was safer than, 'Oi-Feelya, (Ophelia?) Queen of the Fairies', 'Bend Me, Shape Me, Anyway You Want Me' or 'Two's Company Three's an Orgy'! This is the sort of souvenir attire you have to put up with when you have Morry as a friend. I was lucky with the last one, he was torn between the one I can actually wear or, 'People who live in glass houses, shouldn't have sex!'

I quickly back combed my hair, hooked in some large earrings, grabbed my faux fur collared jacket and gloves. I was past the age of queuing at club doors in what resembled, little more than underwear, arms folded firmly across your chest so that the doorman couldn't measure the size of your nipples as to whether they'd let you jump the queue……or them, to get in.

To be honest, I never actually wore *that* little. In my twenties I had the slightly rock chic look, so I had the excuse to wear seventy denier tights, knee high DM boots, layered tops and waistcoats...

I was of the opinion, that it added to the air of mystery? It was probably the reason why I was never the sort pushed into a corner with the full-on charm offensive, for a quicky behind the club. They only had to take one look at the layers of armour to know by the time they'd reached anything of interest, we'd both be freezing, stone cold sober and have politely exchanged first names and fake phone numbers.

I smiled at the thought of my lack of armour on *that* night with Charlie…..and the… *genuine* phone number…..I wished I'd called earlier….what if…. I pulled myself back to reality, no time for being maudlin, things to do, people to see and revenge to wreak! I fed Ferdy and gave him a quick cuddle, which I then realised gave me a rather attractive hairy chested look. Now what an earth was I going to attract in 'Peacocks'? Too late to change, I had to go, Todd so needed his groupies tonight.

I was allowed straight into the club, as Theo had given the doormen our names. They'd also been primed to be over enthusiastic at the arrival of the, *one and only*, Todd Storm. I was inside the club well before his arrival. I caught sight of one of the posters, now up all over the area, I was wickedly pleased with myself, (the devil's horns were really starting to show now.)

There was a photo of Todd, that had obviously been taken by Suse in a moment of intimate madness and had Windy doing his… 'Am I not a rock God of amazing proportions?'…Standing there in a rather nose wrinkling, cringe making, leopard skin, posing pouch! (Remember Susie's man judging? The posing pouch analogy? 'You know exactly what I've got, so no point hiding this much of a good thing'.) Susie had decided it was time that as many people as possible got the chance to peruse his……..'good thing.'

The bouncers had removed any obvious posters from outside by seven-thirty. Just in case Todd was more sober than normal in the quest to get his hands on the cash, or Susie for his, 'farewell sex.' But I laughed as I read the poster again…..

FOR ONE NIGHT ONLY – DUDLEY CRABSHAW…..
Alias TODD STORM former singer of rock band,
TEMPEST.
Singing at PEACOCKS – autographs and press photography allowed.
Thursday 4th December, 8pm onwards.
COME AND JOIN 'WINDY' FOR A 'BANGING' GOOD NIGHT!

And right in the middle of the poster, a *very* much enlarged version, of *that* photo.

Morry and Roger were in their element, this was their turf. They rushed over with several equally colourful males.

"Ooohoo! Penny love! Meet the gang. My Rojere you obviously know, but this is…Rupert, Patti, Eddie and Eugene."

Lots of hand gesturing, catwalk preening and air kissing followed. "Look luvvy, Theo says Susie's just rung, they're on their way. Windy, it seems rang her to say he wanted to make a good impression with the record producer, he's hired a car, asked if she'd share it, so they'll *both* be here any minute. Theo's going to get the stage ready, I'm going to mingle, don't look so worried sweets."

Before I could reply, the doors opened, the girls turned and started to scream with delight. There he stood, in the doorway, right on cue, Mr Rockstar. He looked a little taken aback at the reception, but got over that pretty quickly, then decided to go for it, just milk it.

Keeping the door open so the cold wind blew his black locks forward, his cowboy hat in place and of course the dark, dark sunglasses. Looking like a Spaghetti Western Heathcliff. He posed there in head-to-toe black leather, which of course, made *this* crowd go even wilder!

Theo, his gorgeous, big black torso vying with the sight of this, equally imposing stranger, began to speak from the stage area, in his rich, low, but commanding voice over the near hysterics, which was now taking over the club.

"Theo Blake would like to welcome, to 'Peacocks' a singer who has been, in our opinion, grossly overlooked in the music business. We would like to give......... Dudley Crabshaw, alias Todd Storm, the welcome and the audience, he so deserves."

At the mention of his real name Todd visibly winced and turned to Susie, but she was gazing at him, urging him on, smiling innocently as she waved her hand across the crowd mouthing. "Isn't this fantastic, they're all here, just for you." She then rushed forward, pushing him firmly towards the stage and he, taken up with the attention and the importance suddenly bestowed on him, began to stride in macho like fashion through his *very* touchy-feely audience towards the stage. He even huskily managed a......... "Thank you babe." To a vibrant redhead who grabbed his right buttock and squealed, "Oooer girls, that's a bit lush!" Susie quickly passed the stage-hand Todd's backing tape, before whispering sexily into Mr Rockstar's ear, (for the last time, hopefully?)

"Go on, show this crowd the real Todd Storm.... give 'em cock. Ooops! Sorry, rock!"

Todd looked at her over his sunglasses with slight, rising panic. Too late....his intro came booming over the speakers as he walked to centre stage. Theo looked him up and down, raised his eyebrows, then shouted over the microphone. "Let's hear it for the amazing, rugged, rock star that was, Todd Storm. Who has come out, in every way this evening, as the even more amazing, Dudley Crabshaw! Let's give him a firm clap on his entrance ladies!" And with that the place erupted.

Todd by now was looking a little uneasy but it soon past, with the thought of a possible record deal beckoning and a contact in the audience, he couldn't have wished for a better reaction, regardless of what name they were using.

As he began to sing, throatily throwing the sexier lines at the colourful groupies in the front row, he suddenly realised someone had come on the stage behind him. Two male dancers, in long black, leather coats and cowboy hats, with their backs to the audience had appeared. Todd kept on singing, but as the music started really rocking the dancers began moving, both then swinging round to reveal the rather fetching attire under their coats. Leopard skin posing pouches, with black leather cowboy chaps, studded belts, braces and bare chests.

Mr Rockstar fluffed a couple of lines in shock, he was more used to girlies in little animal print pants, gyrating round him. He moved across the stage, looking down towards Susie, she just cheered with encouragement... "You rock baby...go for it, you big freak!" She knew he couldn't hear her over the noise, he just pouted and strutted off, with apparent reassurance from his, 'lovestruck' and usable groupie. He kept on singing, even when the male dancers thrust their leopard skin rolled up socks at him, he looked a little worried, but turned towards the vibrant redhead who had grabbed him earlier, she was now blowing him kisses and shouting……

"I love you Dudley, I want you babe!" which was giving his ego enough of a boost to keep him going. Then the flash from the crowd, then another, he could see a couple of blokes at the back with long lensed cameras. The second song was now coming to an end. By this time, Todd had all but forgotten the male dancers and had been singing solely to the sexy redhead.

Suse looked on in disdain, incredulous that even with the thought of cash and sex with her, he was still so full of his own self-importance and ego he assumed he could have the lot.

So that's exactly what he did get…*the lot*! As the song came to an end, the male dancers pressed themselves against him, he tried to move, but both were too strong for his lanky frame. As they held onto him, the vibrant redhead bounced onto the stage, wrapped herself round him, clutching one of the posters, which he then caught site of. As he removed his sunglasses in shock the 'girl' kissed him full on the lips, tilting her head back just far enough for her long red wig to slide from her head, revealing very short, dark hair.

"It's a bloke for fucks sake!" He shouted, but before he could untangle himself from the groping hands the cameras had flashed again. As the lights came on and Todd suddenly took in the crowd properly, his jaw dropped as he surveyed his groupies, most of whom looked stunning, but all had Adams apples and some, just a touch too much make-up.

Theo grabbed his shoulder before he could get off stage and booming across the club said.

"We'd like to thank you for giving us an…amazing and *very* sexy performance and whipping this crowd into a frenzy!

You have got yourself many new admirers on our, 'Peacocks Tranny Night.' Thursdays will never be quite the same without a hunk in leather to admire. Let's hear it for Dudley Crabshaw!"

And with that our…….Todd Storm's wind was well and truly blown from its sails.

He staggered off stage covered in bright lipstick kisses from some overzealous groupies, who were grabbing their chance and anything else they could get their hands on, before he managed to escape. His lips narrowed as he came straight over towards Susie. Morry, Theo and I kept close just in case he lost it.

"What the fuck do you think you were doing you crazy bitch? Where's the record producer? If you've ruined my chances of a deal bringing me to a place like this, you won't have heard the last of me you vindictive cow!"

Just as he stepped a little close for comfort, a smartly dressed male walked from the crowd.

"Hello, I'm Eugene Dalton of Sniarbon Records, really liked your performance on stage tonight, Dudley, that voice has potential. But I wasn't too pleased with your attitude to your fans, you're not homophobic are you, Mr Crabshaw?"

"Er, Christ no. By the way the name is Todd Storm. I have no prejudice where my fans are concerned, it was just, I didn't realise the venue was…was a…"

"A gay club Mr Crabshaw? Think of the pink pound. If you want to make it in this business think, Elton John, George Michael, Alice Cooper." Todd then smirks. "Alice Cooper isn't gay!" Eugene stiffens. "He has a girls name, wears an awful lot of make-up, and has shown an awful lot of drag queens the way forward. If you want to rock, you have to shock, Mr Crabshaw!"

"Well, you can stick it Mr Dalton, this is a bloody circus and the names Todd Storm, *alright!"* He says leaning towards Eugene, anger rising.

The crowd parts slightly, he looks up quickly as two men step from the crowd towards him, handing him a large brown envelope. "On behalf of our solicitor we would like to hand you this, which you will accept in the presence of *several* witnesses. It's a court summons, for breach of contract." Todd stares at the set faces of Benny 'the Bass' Bentham and Joe Trent.

He tries to soften his expression quickly. "Hey, fellas…it wasn't what it seemed. I just went off for a little break in Europe, exhaustion…. you know how it is?"

Benny stepped forward, keeping constant eye contact.

"No actually, we don't know how it is. You left us high and dry. We had to find session work where we could, Joe's wife was pregnant, you selfish bastard, you knew that when you left the band. They're living in some shitty little two up, two down with a youngster. While you…....you were off round Europe, staying in flash hotels, shagging groupies and smoking and drinking yerself into oblivion on money which should have been ours! Yeah, must have been *really* exhausting for you!" Joe couldn't bring himself to speak, he just stared ahead, his eyes watering. Susie then stepped in between them but turned towards Todd.

"Now *you* know how it feels to be used, lied to, duped, cornered and crapped upon from a great height." She leaned her face close to his, so he could feel her anger. "I think you should leave this club, in fact leave this country, get back to your fake life in France. See how long they'll put up with a parasite like you over there!"

With his beast of darkness tail well and truly wedged between his legs, he began to push his way through the crowd.

"You'll regret losing me Susan Parks"

"Like a hole in the head babe! By the way you should have taken that record contract it was just the ticket!" He slowed up, turning slightly.

"Oh yeah and why is that then, because you realise what you're losing if I go?" Susie, looking gorgeous, pulled herself up, she let her long coat fall open to reveal the *sexiest* and *tightest* of lemon-yellow cat-suits, thrusting her perfect cleavage forward, licking her lips, she purred.

"Sorry darling, the only person losing out tonight is you. 'Sniarbon Records' spelt backwards is, 'no brains' which suits you *perfectly*. Afraid you've lost a lot more than me babe…. Bye-bye……*Mr Rockstar,* bye-bye."

And as Todd Storm walked away from the crowd and out into the cold, dark street he became once again just plain old, Dudley Crabshaw. What a shame, eh?

"Ooooweep! Ooooweep! Come on ladies! Now we've got rid of that old tart!………

Mr No-more Rockstar, let's get this party started!" Morry shouted, looking like a hyper calypso dancer. He then grabs me and Susie, pulling us in to the psychedelic, light flashing, whistle blowing, hand waving, colourful world that is……. 'tranny night' at Peacocks! As we bobbed up and down, a sea of flamboyant, 'gaiety' I hugged Eugene and thanked him for playing the Record Producer at such short notice. He said it was no problem, he was in the Chester-Le-Street Theatre Group and was playing,

Lady Bracknell in 'The Importance of Being Ernest', so it made a change to be in trousers! Always pleased to help a thespian!

We had a fantastic night, even got up on stage with, all of 'the girls'. There was Suse, myself, Morry, Patti, (now devoid of red cascading wig from her frenzied fan appearance earlier.). Also, Eddie and Eugene, while Roger looked on, tutting as *his* Morry became the ring-leader.

We began with a version of the bump, then into a rather wayward interpretation of sixties go-go dancing! We ended up looking like Lulu and the Second-Generation dancers on a bad day at rehearsals. But what the hell, we were having a ball! I found muscles where I didn't know muscles could be.

My legs ached *so* much I could barely press the clutch pedal on my journey home. I dropped Susie off at her place. She lived the other side of town. We tried to talk but our ears were ringing. But we knew exactly what each other was thinking, occasionally we'd just laugh out loud and screech. "The look on his face! Oh! Priceless……absolutely priceless!"

I pulled up outside her stylish Victorian terrace off Clay Path. We hugged. Then she turned to me as she went to slide out sedately from the passenger seat.

"Oh, I don't know what I'd do without you Pen, you really are the very best friend anyone could ever have." I squeezed her hand. "Is that the Martinis talking? Anyway, you mean… 'bestest' friend, don't you?" She grinned, then putting on a slurred voice said. "Penn..ee...lope Wiiiis…mann, you are my estest…. bestest … fwend…ever….in the whole wide world….no, in the *univerrrrrse*!" And with that she did our favourite Dick Emery trip and staggered to her door.

I wound down the window and called in a loud whisper. "Hey Suse, the neighbours will be twitching the nets, it'll be all round the street, the drunken floosy at number six has been out on the tiles again."

She turned giggling. "I really must endeavour to have sex with Simon on the front steps when he returns. One doesn't want people to remember one for *just* being drunk, does one?" We both stifled snorts of laughter as she put her key in the door and I drove off home.

Both Susie and I had put in a half-day for Friday so we could get to Parker's for one thirty, hopefully clutching the first edition of the Durham Gazette.

Morry and I could barely concentrate, but forced ourselves to produce some decent work, as New Year assessments were due. Mr Preece had done his monthly hand-clasped strut around the office first thing this morning. He told us, he felt at least two staff would have to go in January, due to expenditure and falling profits. (Wonder if his middle name is 'Ebenezer'?)

We knew this was usually scare tactics to make everyone keep their minds on work instead of Christmas parties at this time of year. But of course, we couldn't take the risk, that possibly this year, it could be genuine. Having said that our Christmas party arrangements had been well on the way since mid October!

Friday the 19th December was the date in question and that seemed to be possibly my final chance of finding anyone to date over Christmas. I have to say though, work colleagues are not my ideal relationship material. Especially when you've only just agreed to a second date and it's all round the building that you're loved up and inseparable!

It had happened once, some years ago. He wasn't someone I'd seen much of in the building, or really noticed, but he made a beeline for me and caught me under the mistletoe. A few shared vol-au-vents later and some flirtatious conversation and we appeared to be seeing each other!

The initial catching site of each other in the corridors, making the heart flutter, the snatched moments of touching hands as he helps you at the coffee machine. Or when he suddenly appears at the file room door and there's no one else around. Your heart is thumping, you quickly check for privacy, then the quick, but...

...oh so passionate kiss. Your senses are so heightened at the thought of being caught, as you cling to each other wishing you had the guts to lock the door, click off the light, throw caution to the wind and just go for it! Of course, I had never actually been that sexually liberated, (well apparently, not without two Martinis and a hotel room, I was later to discover!)

But it seemed Cindy Giles *was* that liberated! Two weeks later, I caught her and my apparent, 'office romance' Nick Clarke, going at it with *their*, 'heightened senses' over two large file boxes! I don't know who was more shocked, them or me. Nick quickly did the line, "Penny, I can explain!" Which seemed rather laughable in the circumstances, I didn't think explanations were really necessary.

Needless to say, things were a little strained as Nick decided to work a months' notice, before moving onto better things? (Possibly somewhere where file room keys are not available to all members of staff?) He ignored me for the full four weeks, which was rich seeing as he was the one guilty of file-andering! Or maybe it was something to do with the fact that everyone became aware that Cindy Giles wore a peep-hole bra and crotchless pants under her pinstripe suit and Nick had a tattoo of Mickey Mouse on his nether regions! Goodness me, how on earth did everyone find that out? (Ooops! The horns were showing again.)

As my mind wandered wickedly, I shoved several files back onto the shelves in *that* room. Strange how, after that file room incident, Mr Jenkins decided on re-shelving and insisted that all file boxes were to be reduced in size to fit the shelves. (Surely as us women know, if you're going to find yourself straddled across a couple of boxes…size does matter!)

I caught up with Morry. He was just rushing off to meet Roger for a bit of lunchtime Christmas shopping, we chatted and giggled non-stop about last night until we parted company on the corner of Silver Street. "See yer Monday, have a good weekend chuck. Ring me if there's any goss, I won't forget to get a paper, bye luvvy." With that he was rushing over to greet Roger who was waiting patiently by the bank.

I rushed down to the newsagents. Oh, Lordy, lordy and there it was, the local paper with the headline…'Spennymoor's Aging Rockstar Shows His True Colours at Peacocks.'

The picture of course was the one complete with Patti clinging to Todd, poster in hand and *that* look on his face. I tried to read and walk, desperate to find out what the article revealed. They referred to him as, 'local lad Dudley Crabshaw,' only using the name Todd Storm as a reference to his days in the band. There were several quotes from Benny and Joe, about lost earnings and their surprise at him turning up at a gay club, after being such a womaniser. Theo also had a ball, putting in his two penneth, after all it was good publicity for him and his club.

I caught sight of Susie, clutching the paper, she looked upset, she kept wiping her eye and screwing up her face, she broke into a panic-stricken run as she saw me. Oh please, tell me he hasn't been round to see her, conned her with more lies, or hurt her in some way. Maybe she regrets the revenge, maybe she feels we went too far.

"Pen.... oh bugger! I've only gone and lost one of me contact lenses. I was laughing so much reading this, tears streaming from me eyes, I rubbed too hard, now one of me precious greens has gone. I look like an obsessive David Bowie fan!"

I was so relieved, I started to laugh with her. "Haven't you got a spare, you're usually so efficient, don't you keep one of everything in that handbag of yours?"

As we sat down, she rummaged madly through her bag.

"Well, that's the problem...*one* of everything. Oh yes, I've got a spare, but it's amber! I'll look like one of those dodgy, cock-eyed, old moggies I always want to bring home when I visit the cats refuge. I'm gonna have to put it in regardless, I can't keep squinting like this." I ordered the tea and sandwiches, trying to sympathise without sniggering too much. Suse then rushed off to the ladies, returning with said odd lenses in place.

"It's just a bit quirky Suse. If you're that bothered, you'll have to look at people sideways, that'll probably worry them more than resembling an alien reptile" She shot me a look.

"Are you saying I look like an alien reptile? Right, that's it I'm off to the nearest optician, I can't go round the town like this, I'll have to go home."

"Will you stop panicking, with the two-foot lashes, red pout and cascade of shining hair who's going to notice the colour of your eyes?" She then looked hurt instead of pleased.

"You mean I spent nearly £400 on different coloured lenses and no one even notices?" I raise my eyebrows in disbelief. I really couldn't win, could I?

"Right, get pouring the tea, let's just have another laugh at old Dudley. What a story! Couldn't have been better if we'd written it ourselves. Do you reckon he's speeding across the channel as we speak?" Susie leans back, smiles and sighs.

"Oh, I hope so…...I *really* do hope so."

Chapter 13

I tried to do a bit of Christmas shopping Friday afternoon with Suse, but she insisted the most important item we had to concentrate on was, a new dress for tonight, as.... Simon was due home today. He was going to ring her as soon as he got back to his house in St Johns Chapel.

He was looking forward to getting home, then to taking her out on the town, to catch up on all
he'd missed. (Obviously certain newspapers would be well hidden and 'catch up' would be the heavily edited version!) So, of course a new dress was a must, to keep his mind on other things.

She ended up with a stunning cobalt blue dress, with a sash waist and beading along the shoulders and neckline. (She decided she could also wear it for her family's Christmas Do, so that was settled.) I got myself a new bobble hat, thermal socks and a rather nice roll neck sweater from the reduced rail. (My family wouldn't expect me to be wearing anything else at our Christmas pile in!)

I then made the foolish mistake of coming out into the melee again today. The Saturday stampede, (what possessed me?) I was under the deep-seated illusion that I may still get a social life and a man over the festive season. So, I felt, if I got all the Christmas shopping out of the way early,

I'd have that free time to pamper myself, sort my wardrobe and be ready for all those fantastic festive invitations to come flooding in? Yeah, right!

I could feel my anger rising and my patience waning after just an hour and a half. (How do these people 'make a day of it'… as if it's a pleasurable thing!) My feet had been trampled on and I had several large cumbersome, finger numbing carrier bags weighing me down.

As I waited, in yet another queue of at least ten people, to pay for items I wasn't even sure of, I finally found myself behind a dithering male who hadn't the cash for the bottle of £9.99 perfume he'd just spent two minutes choosing. (Oh! Happy Christmas *Mrs* Dithering Male.) He then produced a credit card. Oh no, here we go!

The young assistant, (who looks about twelve) can't remember what to do with credit cards, she rummages under the counter blankly then rings the bell.

"I only work the Saturdays over Christmas, sorry!" The manager finally appears. By then I'm seriously wondering whether to put the items back. But then I'd have to come out again and find something else and it'll be just as bad in every other shop! I grit my teeth, trying not to sigh too heavily.

I turn slightly and catch sight of another bad-tempered shopper, looking even more disgruntled, back hunched, mouth pursed like a hen's bottom, frown lines like ploughed furrows. Oh my God! It's a mirror……and it's me! I suddenly feel guilty, I'm turning into a grumpy, female Ebenezer Scrooge. I'll probably end up being cornered at the Christmas party by Mr Preece as he eyes up a like-minded soul.

I pull myself up quickly in shock. Never mind the visit from the three ghosts, let's just skip to buying the huge goose and waving the old festive stick quickly.

This city is festooned with twinkling lights, every shop has the old Christmas faves blasting out
in the background. How can I feel so un-festive to the strains of Slade's Merry Christmas Everybody, Aled's Walking in the Air, not to mention traditional carols, Silent Night, The Holly and The Ivy.......

I finally pay for my items, the poor assistant looks as harassed as I feel, I thank her and make the effort to give her a big, cheery smile, which she returns. "Merry Christmas!" We both say in unison.

I come away feeling a little better and quickly pop into the nearest café, where I can see a spare seat, I have twenty minutes with a reviving cuppa and a small eclair. Then it's off, elbows akimbo, back into the milling throng.

With so many nephews and nieces, as well as Bina and Denzel's two to buy for, I have a good excuse to spend time in all the best toy shops. This, of course, is where the real Christmas action is!

Try before you buy? You can spend hours just pressing buttons on musical toys and fun speaking games, you can repeatedly squidge and maul all soft toys that come to hand and more importantly watch the latest Disney releases on the kids' corner screen, preferably sitting on a small plastic toadstool sucking a free lolly! Magic! Where's that old Ebenezer now, eh?

But something, always seems to pull me in a certain direction, I just can't help myself. I've done it every Christmas now for the past five years. I sidle, slowly to the, Baby Department. Gently running my fingers across the tops of prams and picking up tiny baby-gros, wondering if I'll ever get the chance of producing something that will fit this adorable, little garment.

As I gaze at other women, usually years younger than me, cooing over their little miracles, spending time carefully choosing fluffy little coats and hats and brightly coloured toys to make their baby's eyes shine and their little faces light up with delight, I breath a heavy sigh.

I can't help but look in the direction of a beautiful girl, with masses of raven-hair, her tum fully rounded with their next baby. She touches her other child's head and the young boy cuddles into her bump. Her partner glows with pride, as he carries several large bags of baby accessories and Christmas presents. All three cuddle in as far as the bump will allow, blissfully unaware of the stranger gazing at them with tear pricked eyes and a sense of deep envy and uncontrollable sadness.

I turn away quickly. I don't know why I put myself through this. Or, maybe this is one of my visiting Christmas ghosts, but which....not past.....not present.....but hopefully, *hopefully*....of things yet to come?

I wipe my eyes quickly with a tissue then smile at a little face peering at me from a pushchair. I move swiftly off to find the, 'five to ten-year-olds section', for presents to please some of my more, 'style conscious' nephews and nieces.

Why can't the colourful patent leather shoes and boots with cats, bees, flowers and rainbows on, come in adult sizes? Why can't *we* have coats in bright pink with ballet dancers on, or orange and red striped trousers. You become an adult and unless you're deemed eccentric, or Morry, bright colours are a no-no all of a sudden.

You get past thirty and its…...'Sorry Madam, unfortunately you're old enough to know better, so this one comes in beige and taupe only.'…Oh great… thanks!

Finally, after three solid finger and foot numbing hours, I stagger home, more than satisfied with my efforts. Two thirds of my Christmas list sorted and it is only December 6th! (Stick that in yer grate and burn it Mr Scrooge!)

Ferdy rushes from the lounge windowsill towards the kitchen, as he sees his 'human bowl filler' arrive home. As I enter the hall, he greets me tail aloft, whiskers forward, in full appealing hungry seal mode. Not a cat to understand patience, he walks in front of me several times, weaving round my legs, nearly tripping me up, risking being crushed under several bags of festive fayre.

"If I fall now, I can't open a tin of cat food, can I you daft fur-ball, now shift before you do us both an injury!" He then sits abruptly, nearly sending me headfirst into the sink! I decide, possibly easier just feed him first, then I can unpack in peace and safety.

As I sort out the bags and carefully label them all with names and contents, I feel quite smug at my sudden burst of efficiency. Sadly, it doesn't last long, as Bina rings asking if we can, synchronise filo-faxes for the festive season? I scurry round trying to find my diary and a pen, trying to convince Bina that I'd mislaid it under *all* the Christmas shopping I'd got while out today. She tells me she has all her dates organised, (and I believe her!) Seems they're spending Christmas in Ireland with Denzel's family, as they were with hers last year. They're going on the seventeenth, midweek, so it's not too last minute and crowded on the ferry, as they'll be packing the car to the gunnels and trying to make the journey as enjoyable as possible for the children.

So…...she asks slowly, (giving me a chance to open my diary at the right page) if can I come to their pre-Christmas drinks and nibbles on the fifteenth……it's a Monday?

I tell her, yes, I can just squeeze her in. Who am I trying to kid, I've got the annual invite from Morry and Roger to their, 'Christmas shindig', on the thirteenth and an unconfirmed yes, to a carol concert with mum and dad on the eighteenth! Could Christmas get any wilder? (I really do hope so!)

Bina tells me she's had a definite, 'yes' from everyone else. Paula is going to be there with Harold. Susie will also be there, (my usual ally), but of course this year she has the gorgeous Simon Forbes on her arm.

As if sensing my awkward singleness, Bina quickly reassures me that there will be, loads of people there, plenty to have a natter with…...maybe more?

I thank her for the invite and say that I'm quite happy with a natter, I couldn't imagine anyone appreciating me doing, 'maybe more' at a family and friends' wine and nibbles night.

I was still mulling over my disappointment at my lack of Christmas invites as I walked into the office on Monday. I noticed Anna and June, each clutching an envelope and looking really excited. Anna bounced over, beaming. "Check you're 'IN' tray Penny, go on, check it!" The sheer explosion of obvious glee was instantly infectious and I found myself bounding over to my desk like an over-excited child. I could see a very stylish cream envelope with gold trim lying there. Was it a Christmas card from Ben? Well, June would have one, but why would Anna?

Was it a big Christmas Bonus? Mr Harkass always used expensive envelopes. I carefully used my paperknife, slowly running it across the top to keep the suspense. Bit by bit I pulled out the large gold embossed card....

TIFFANY & JASPER WOULD LIKE TO INVITE YOU TO....
OUR CHRISTMAS SOIREE,
FRIDAY THE TWELFTH OF DECEMBER.
EVENING DRESS REQUIRED.
WE LOOK FORWARD TO THE DELIGHT OF YOUR COMPANY! RSVP

(Mmmm…...that sounded sincere?) I felt just a touch less eager than Anna as I put the envelope back in my tray.

"We're so excited Penny, it'll be so stylish, so classy, can you believe she's invited us?" I look slightly bemused at Anna, who obviously equates Tiffany with Royalty.

"Well, they have to invite some plebs, just to make themselves feel even more superior than they do already." Anna and June tut at my Royal faux pas.

"I think that's a little, 'chip on shoulder' on your part Penelope. I think it's a wonderful festive gesture from Tiffany. Is it possibly the fact that you don't have a, 'man friend' to take you, that makes you sound just little bitter and hostile?" Ouch! That was a bit below the belt, even for June. Hadn't she tried to push her, stepbrother Ben at me as a possible 'man friend'?

"Oh, sorry June, I didn't realise it was requisite that all women *had* to have a, 'man friend' to be allowed to accept a party invite." I step behind my desk just in case she runs at me with the stapler!

"I'm actually quite happy to go to a 'do' on my own. Anyway, I'm quite sure Ben would have jumped at the chance to take me, had he not been so busy." June huffed loudly. To stop the possibility of another caustic comment, Anna cut in quickly.

"Well, seeing as this *fantastic* invite has got us well and truly into the festive season, let's get the 'deccies' up. Put a bit of Christmas glitter into our dull little office. Come on June, help me get the tree and the tinsel from the stock cupboard."

I saw Morry, moving crab-like along the corridor windows, he peeps round the door. "Is it safe to come in? I couldn't help but overhear, I see June is doing her usual, 'Mood of Many Colours' at this time of year." Morry gives me a reassuring hug.

"Oh, I know she finds Christmas difficult, what with her poor mum. It must be so sad to hear her say the same thing every year, telling her they'll get a proper tree when her dad gets home. I know it's not easy for her, I should be more patient. But surely after all we've said, she does know we're here for her and we do care." Morry hands me a cuppa from the tray.

"You know the old saying love, 'you always take it out on those closest to you.' So, start feeling sorry for poor old Barry. Imagine? I bet he spends most of his festive season hiding in the turkey house!" Morry then leans in. "But it's not a bad party invite, is it? Even I've got one, me and Rojere are the token gays." I look surprised at his assumption.

"Surely in her circles, thespians, stylists, the camper the better, isn't it the done thing to have the classic gay entourage amongst her high-class friends?" Morry laughs loudly, then snorts.

"It's not her, seems Jasper and buddies would like to see all homosexuals hunted down and burnt at the stake! Apparently, he was propositioned at boarding school ……

.......assumes we are all testosterone seeking missiles that stop at nothing in our pursuit of turning straight men gay! Tiffany told me the only reason he's allowed *me* to come is because I have a, 'long term partner', so obviously me and Rojere are going to have to walk round like Siamese twins in case we worry the host." My turn to give *him* a big reassuring hug, but we're already giggling.

"I'm sure you'll have a great time regardless, it's hardly the first time you've had opposition?" Morry winks. "Opposition or proposition? Oh, don't you worry about me babe, I've never been one to let a dose of homophobia ruin a night out, each to his own I say! I wouldn't miss this for the world, I'll be having a good old nose round their posh gaff anyway, see what us….. 'plebs' are missing."

My week went quickly, there was piles of work to get out of the way before the Christmas break. I buried my head in files, spreadsheets, legal documents and a few colourful choccies that seems to crop up here and there! (Christmas time has its pluses, Jesus born in a stable to Mary and Joseph, and we get Quality Street in abundance to celebrate his birthday, praise the Lord!).

I made the effort to pop my head round Tiffany's door to thank her for the invite and return the acceptance. Fortunately, as I was *so* busy, I couldn't stop to talk, shame!

She said she was, 'thrilled' I could come, but made sure she got in that the reason it was such short notice was that the caterers couldn't alter their menus and three couples were taking a last-minute break to St Lucia, so she needed numbers.

I felt like, 'The Prisoner.' 'I'm not a number, I'm a human being,' or was that the Elephant Man? She went on to tell me, we were lucky to get an invite as it was going to be the party of the year. God, she was so modest! She of course, had to ask if I had a suitable dress, I answered enthusiastically, that I had plenty of evening dresses in *my* wardrobe.

She looked at me with that slightly sympathetic, demeaning expression…I'd show her! (Wishing I was a size ten like Suse, then at least I could have borrowed one of her fab creations.)

By Thursday lunchtime I was starting to panic a little, I rushed up Saddler Street looking in all the clothes shops. The only two dresses I'd seen that were anything near suitable, were way out of *my* price bracket. There was no way I was paying over the odds for a full-length evening gown I'd be lucky to wear twice.

I shot down a side street across the town to another dress shop I knew, when my eye caught a flash of red. There in the window of a……charity shop was a stunning full-length evening dress. It was draped on a tall slim mannequin it looked far too small for me but it was definitely worth a look. I hurriedly went in, trying to see if there was an assistant who could tell me the size. Two elderly ladies smiled cheerfully, both stepping forward to offer assistance. The taller of the two spoke first.

"Hello dear, can we help?" Her wrinkled face caked in powder and a touch too much rouge, making her look slightly doll-like.

"Yes, the lovely red dress in the window caught my eye, it looks a small size, could you check the label for me please." They both bustled round each other.

"Here Phyllis, this is your forte, you can get up that window step can't you, you know my old knees won't make it." She gives her companion a playful shove.

"Oh, me again, doing all the clambering about. Never mind your knees Beatty Featherstone, funny how you can always manage the stairs when there's a cup of tea and a digestive biscuit in the offing!" They both set off towards the window, continuing their playful banter.

"It's got clips in the back dear, to pull it tight on the dummy, it hasn't got a size on but Beatty thinks it's probably around a modern-day size fourteen, would that be any good for you luvvy?" I smile broadly.

"Yes, that should be fine, could I be a nuisance and try it on?" They both help each other to remove the dress from the window.

"We're not really supposed to dismantle the window display, Mrs Hargreaves will have our guts for garters!" I feel a little guilty.

"Oh, sorry, am I ruining your hard work, it's just it's perfect for a party I'm going to on Friday." They both usher me and the dress towards the changing room.

"Ooooo! Don't you worry pet, we'll get a hat and pants on that dummy before she gets back." They both giggle naughtily.

"Anyway, we can't lose a possible sale, it's all for a good cause." I felt slightly embarrassed then, I hadn't actually noticed which charity shop I'd come into, but as they handed me the dress I caught sight of the large card label.......'Help The Aged.' Oh, how very apt! I was paying to help old people and the dress was assisting an old bag to look presentable in her hour of need, perfect!

I carefully undid the tiny buttons down the back and slid the soft, layered red chiffon fabric over my head, this was a beautiful dress, vintage quality, made me feel every inch a lady, fitted well and I looked, dare I say it ...quite glamorous. Even Suse would have been proud of this creation.

"Need any help with all those buttons dear?" I opened the curtain slightly. "Yes please, this is a bit of a vintage classic, we're so used to having zips nowadays." The younger lady helped me with the buttons as the other looked on. Her eyes appeared to water a little, then she spoke.

"Oh, you look beautiful dear, can I tell you a little secret......that dress was mine....I wore it over fifty years ago. My husband saved up for a year to buy me that dress with a little bracelet and dinner at the Ritz. It was our tenth wedding anniversary, it's a bit special." I gaze at myself in the mirror, in a dress so full of memories, it *was* a bit special. Well, if it was good enough for Beatty Featherstone and the Ritz it was good enough for me at Tiffany and Jasper's Christmas Soiree.

"I'll have it, it's perfect and I *will* take good care of it." I say, with a reassuring smile towards Mrs Featherstone.

"I'll probably be back in next week, I've got a few Christmas events coming up, (I had to convince someone!) You seem to have upstaged the best clothes shops I've been in so far. And you really can't beat paying only £15 for such a stunning dress."

I left the shop as if clutching the crown jewels, so proud of my find. Roll on Friday, at least I knew I wasn't going to bump into anyone else at the party in the same dress. (Even Susie's great Aunt Winnie who dressed in the designer labels of her day..... a couture Molyneux, Dior, Balenciaga or Schiaparelli, would surely agree this dress had history and was unique.)

I didn't see Morry till Friday morning. He'd got a half day, so he could take his mum and dad to the coach station. They are spending Christmas and New Year in Scarborough with his Aunt Nelly who has a hotel there. I caught him bouncing up the stairs. I had to tell him about *the* dress.

"Oh, Morry, it's just so elegant, so sophisticated." I knew what was coming even as I said it. "So why on earth are *you* wearing it then!" He squeals at his witty reply.

"Yeah, thanks sweety! Love you too. Honestly, as long as I can get my hair right and walk in heels, I'll feel so good, so classy." He shares my obvious excitement.

"Oh, and this is coming from the woman that wasn't that bothered about going, now suddenly you're Cinderella, pushing the ugly sisters out the way and rushing off to the ball."

We both start sniggering. "Can we hazard a guess at the ugly sisters?" I shove Morry playfully. "Shhhh, don't make me laugh someone's coming." Mr Harkass has caught us being frivolous in the corridors again.

"Remember, Wiseman and Wild, January cometh... think on."

We skulk away like a pair of Bob Cratchits, having to resist the strong temptation to bow low, walking backwards while, ingratiatingly tugging our forelocks.

I end up clock watching and scramble for my coat dead on five. I'm out the door and away in minutes. Within an hour I'm lying soaking in a deep scented bubble bath, it then crosses my mind that maybe it *is* going to be a good Christmas after all. With another party invite and still another couple of weeks to go…...anything could happen….. absolutely anything!

I padded into my room, rooted out some, 'reasonably sophisticated' underwear. I felt I had to honour Mrs Featherstone and this dress and make a real effort. I had absolutely no doubt that no one but me would see this underwear, but it had to be elegant and feminine. Orange cotton tangas with a black cat on the front were *not* going to cut it. I had a matching set of lingerie in red, which would be perfect under this beautiful gown, it also pulled the wrong bits in and thrust the right bits out. I then tried to remember Susie's advice about pinning my hair up, leaving little tendrils loose, keep it soft looking. By the time I'd struggled with my hair my arms were aching and my face was pink and flushed. Fortunately, I had the necessary hours to get myself in any semblance of order. Being a, highbrow 'soiree' it didn't start till eight, with champagne cocktails, buffet at nine, then dancing till dawn, apparently. Kippers and scrambled eggs were being served to all who could stay the course. I find kippers repeat on me, so hopefully I can surreptitiously leave my glass slipper within eyeline of some, handsome Prince and politely leave by midnight.

Well, well…though I say it myself, I do look damn well near Cinderella-ish! I scrub up well for an older gal. The dress looks the part. I go straight to the bottom of my old oak wardrobe and pull out a large, watermarked box. Carefully removing the layers of tissue, I lay eyes on Grandma's mohair jacket, black with jet beads adorning the tiny stand-up collar.

It was seven thirty-five and I was in the car and on my way. Tiffany and Jasper had just bought a rambling, 'cottage' (six bedrooms and two reception rooms the size of tennis courts,) on the outskirts of Lanchester village. They of course weren't like the rest of us, who would have dossed in basic squalor and two tons of brick dust till we'd saved up and paid for, alterations and work needed. They on the other hand, stayed in comfort at, Mummy and Daddy's residence, a large, sprawling pile, on the outskirts of Wolsingham. The builders, painters, interior designer, stayed in situ until it was completed.

They moved in two weeks ago when everything was in place and ready, apparently the 'cosmetics and aesthetics' *only,* came to £24,000!

I paid so much less than that for my whole house ten years ago. It was another world. And I was....... amazingly and in around twenty minutes, about to step into it.

Chapter 14

I suddenly felt a little nervous as I pulled up to see several waist-coated males politely taking car keys to park guest's vehicles. Just as I switched off the engine, a tall, slick, dark-haired young man opened my door. He held out his hand to assist me from the vehicle. I tried hard to be ladylike, willing myself not to get a heel caught in my long gown, or step into a grate, or something equally embarrassing.

"Excuse me madam, may I have your car keys?" I handed him the keys to my rather scruffy, (I knew I should have gone through the carwash yesterday.) Fiat Panda. He smiled as he took my keys with several colourful fobs dangling, including a fat black cat, a pink fairy and a tag that said, 'If found by a hunky male please feel free to resuscitate owner with mouth to mouth.' (Now that *was* embarrassing.)

I pulled myself up, gathered the bottom of my dress, adjusted my jacket and slowly and regally walked up the path towards the huge door festooned with a very large, expensive, hand-made wreath. Several reproduction Victorian lamps lined the walkway, it was all very stylish and tasteful and I felt a slight pang of envy. Just how lucky was Tiffany, having all this at twenty-eight years old. But as the door was thrown open by a rather over simpering Jasper proffering a hand, the envy soon disappeared.

"Oh, it's the lovely Penelope Wiseman, do come in, you gorgeous creature you."

He grabbed my hand, (his was rather cold and clammy), then propelled me towards Tiffany who is looking like Princess Margaret in her hay-day, complete with tiara.

"Oh, Penelope, good of you to come, you look, *absolutely...* er...smashing." She then grabs my shoulders and air kisses me like I'm someone she adores. This is all very insincere and a little disconcerting, hope they're not all like this. I quickly thrust the small house-warming gift at her and wish her and Jasper a great first Christmas in their..... humble abode?

She thanks me profusely then goes all girly on me.

"Oh, Penelope it's all so wonderful, it's just like a magical fairy-tale. I have found my handsome Prince and we're to live happily ever after....Am I not the luckiest little Princess ever?" That'll be the reason for the tiara then. I thought it was just me in Cinderella mode. My eyes dart about in sheer panic, please let there be someone else here I know, *please*! Too late, she spins me round quickly.

"Do let me get you a drink" With that she clicks her fingers under the nose of an approaching waiter, he stops dead in his tracks proffering the tray of glasses.

"Champagne cocktail, do help yourself darling." I try not to let her see me wince at her obvious, 'hostess with the mostest' talk and carefully take a glass. Sipping as elegantly as I can, I sigh deeply as I look round at the high-class crowd...hells teeth, what on earth am I doing here?

It was an invite for two, I wished Susie could have come, but she was spending the week, making up for lost time, appeasing her guilt with Simon. Not a bad way to be punished in my book. Go on then spoil me, do your worst with, chocolates, presents and passion. I *will* repent…*eventually.* Lucky, lucky Suse, I bet she's not thinking of me at this moment, well I hope not.

Finally, I see June, heading straight towards me through the be-suited and be-jewelled crowd, I'm obviously the first person she recognises, she's got the same slightly panic-stricken expression I had two minutes ago……she's also alone. I smile broadly, hope she's forgiven me for not feeling so bum-kissingly grateful at getting the, Quinn & Mills 'Royal' invite.

"Are you okay June, where's Barry? You've not sentenced him to solitary confinement in the turkey house, have you? You've not left him cleaning out beehives with no supper." (I hoped she would find just a little humour in there somewhere. I couldn't help but keep trying for a break-through.) June looks skywards, but then smiles.

"I have done no such thing, he is doing what he does best, he's taken my coat to the cloakroom and is getting me a drink." I put my arm round her shoulder and hug her…..very carefully.

"Oh, well done you, a house-trained man, that's what I like to see. Keep it up, it's going to be a long evening, you may need him more than you think." Although I was sure once Anna and Mark appeared she would be fine.

Canapes, Hors d'oeuvres, (or horses doovries as Morry so qaintly puts it) by the tray full, suddenly appear everywhere you turn. The buffet table was like the feeding of the five thousand. Only they wouldn't have had Salmon en'croute, or assiette anglaise, chanterelle vol-au-vents, foie gras and sesame ficelles, followed by Cointreau conde, Crème gaufres or Tarte aux pommes with Sabayon! (Apparently, it's not done, in certain circles, to eat in English anymore. Bon appetite.)

Morry and Roger eventually made their entrance…late and loud. You could see the look of slight panic in Jasper's eyes as he rushed to Tiffany's side, kissing her quickly and grabbing her hand as they welcomed the dynamic duo. He stuck to Tiffany like glue just so that….'the gays' were well aware that he was *all* man and totally, absolutely unmistakably, heterosexual.

Of course, Morry being Morry, feigned the macho bit almost convincing Jasper, after shaking his hand firmly, but then quickly pulled him forward and chuckled.

"Oh, now I do like a man with a firm grip." Jasper was just starting to perspire, but looked slightly relieved as Morry added.

"Oh yes, I bet you can wow 'em down on the golf course with a hold like that?" But it didn't last, he almost put poor Jasper into a state of hyperventilation by adding.

"My Rojere's got a handicap of twenty-seven and two left feet if you ever want to, 'play a round' with him, he'll be yours for the asking!" He just couldn't help himself. I rushed over and shot Morry a look that said, I think that's enough, but Tiffany who had had several champagne cocktails by now guffawed with laughter.

"You little tinker Maurice, I knew you'd tease my Jasper, but let me just say there is only one dish on *his* menu and if he's a very good boy tonight he may just get a nibble of my…… chausson aux pommes de vacherin!" Morry and I looked at each other and winced. As she giggled hysterically, several people went quiet, obviously like me, racking their brains gathering what little left of their school-day French and rather confusingly coming up with…... apple turnover, a large meringue, fresh cream and fruit? The mind boggles. Poor Jasper's face was a picture as Morry gave him a wink and wished him luck.

By ten, as if by magic, the lights dimmed and the music got louder and everyone made their way towards the dance room, (the second reception room, complete with DJ and dance floor!) this was obviously to try and wear off the contents of the buffet table we had all just devoured.

I was beginning to feel a bit of a, groseille (gooseberry?) when I saw Morry rushing over. I assumed he was going to drag me off to dance so was surprised when he grabbed me and turned me round towards the wall. He did his usual unsubtle whisper.

"When you turn back round check out the bloke at 9 o'clock." I looked puzzled.

"It's just gone ten past ten, what you on about?" He looks skywards and tuts.

"There's a bloke to your left as you turn, he's been watching you, he can't take his eyes off you…I think you've pulled girl."

I felt myself flushing as I turned slowly, trying hard to stay casual and hope the whole room isn't aware of my thumping heart. That can't be him, surely….

"Morry, you don't mean the tall, gorgeous looking bloke in the designer suit?"

"I most certainly do! This is your big chance girl. Look at you, in that dress, why wouldn't he be bedazzled, you look stunning." I squeeze Morry's hand. Pulling myself up, took a deep breath and turned my head towards the handsome stranger and smiled.

But as he returns the smile, Tiffany catches him looking at me and squeals with delight.

"Oooo, I saw you Fraser Grant you big flirt you…….like the look of our…'lady' Penelope?…. Well, why wouldn't you! She looks just lovely in that sexy dress doesn't she…. doesn't she Fraser? Come on darling let me introduce you!"

Morry leaves me standing. "Sorry babe, you're on yer own for this one." Tiffany not only drags poor, Fraser over but has two equally, 'one cocktail too many' girls with her.... this is going to be so mortifying. I cringe as they all descend on me giggling.

"Penelope daarrling! Firstly, let me introduce you… to my…. good fwends… hic… oops!… This is, Jocasta Ferring-Read and this silly filly is, Dodie Olivier-Barnham."

It brought back memories of one of our favourite name names. …'Boarding School Names'. Pick your first family pet name and first stately home you ever visited. It never fails to tickle. I was Trixie Castle-Howard and Susie was Jinty Pierrepont-Hall….. Okay yah!

I was quickly brought back into focus as they all guffawed and pushed poor Fraser towards me.

"And this handsome catch is Fraser Grant….and I think he's got his eye on you Penelope." He offered his hand, taking mine, he kissed the back of it softly. (This is the second gentlemanly hand kiss this month!) The girls continued giggling, but to our mutual relief they disappeared towards the dance room.

"I'm sorry about that introduction, but at least the ice is well and truly broken, but not to Titanic proportions, hopefully?" He keeps constant eye contact.

"And can I just say, you look *truly* beautiful and fill that dress to perfection." I feel myself blushing as he steps back and gazes up and down my body. My heart is thumping, maybe he's noticed it thumping too as I see his eyes linger on my chest.

"Er, thank you, it's just a little something I threw on, I've had it ages." (Why do we say that? To make out we never buy anything new, careful with money, or to give the impression no matter when he calls, we'll be wafting around in a chiffon number. All pretty laughable really.)

"So, tell me all about yourself, I haven't seen you at any of Tiff and Jass's dos before?" (Please, don't ever let me get close enough to call them Tiff and Jass.)

"Well, there's not a lot to tell really, I work with 'Tiff'. How about you, what do you do, how do you know…Tiff and Jass?" (Oh God, I hope he's worth it.)

He quickly whisks a couple of glasses from a passing tray and hands me the fuller of the two, as he does so I get a waft of expensive aftershave and breath in deeply. He smiles again. His tanned skin is glowing, he has that clean, toned look. Very like Simon, takes pride in his appearance, but not too fussy. Fresh and manicured, it gives him an edge, makes him seem precise and controlled.

"I'm a D.S." (Dishy Sod? Desirable Sexgod? Dream Stud….. .my mind is wandering.)

"Was up at Ponteland, doing a stint in the training department, but to be honest I like to be where the action is." My mind still wandering, I reply. "Oh yes, me too." He then grins. "Really?" I look embarrassed.

"No sorry, I mean I'd rather be in something with variety than too much routine." (Yeah! Harkass, Jenkins & Preece that's where the action is, who am I kidding?) "So, where are you now?" I ask trying hard to concentrate on the conversation and not what a gorgeous shade of blue his eyes are.

"I'm in Durham CID…you know…Crime Investigation Department. I really like getting my teeth into a bit of serious crime detection." (Wow, I'm talking to a Detective Sergeant, they find all those clues and information, interview all those suspects and deal with all those horrible crime scenes.)

"It must be such interesting work, all those fascinating cases, bet you've seen and heard some incredible and probably pretty awful things in your line of work?" He leans forward, his aftershave now almost overpowering.

"Sorry, can't divulge details of cases, I've signed the Official Secrets Act, have to be careful what we say and who to." I raise my eyebrows slightly.

"It's okay, I'm not a reporter, press, or anything, you're quite safe with me." He slides his arm round my chiffoned waist, pulls me closer then whispers.

"I have no doubt I'm safe with you Penelope, but I've known women who get quite turned on by gruesome details, it's quite *amazing* what turns some people on." I look startled.

"Ugh! The thought of dead bodies and gory case details is definitely not my bag, I'm not some weirdo into haemophilia.... no, no I'd never...." He looks equally startled.

"Hey Princess, I wasn't suggesting for one minute that you would....I was just saying that's sometimes a reason why some women have a thing for Police officers...By the way I think you may have meant, necrophilia?" He now has an amused look in his eye.

"Sorry, it's just I've never met a Police officer before...well not in a social capacity.... Only when my car was...oh...I'll just shut up, the hole I'm digging is getting big enough to fall into now." He laughs and slowly runs a finger down my cheek.

"I have to say, I think I gave you a bit of help with the digging, don't be too hard on yourself. We're nothing special, just....

...ordinary men and women trying our best to uphold the moral majority and the laws of the land."

His jaw was set as he spoke and I found it difficult not to feel very proud and just a little in awe. He also appears to think I'm worth gazing at and talking to. And we do talk, laugh and even dance. Which he enjoys, he appears adept at most things so far. We just seem relaxed, having fun and getting on brilliantly... maybe, Cinderella *will* get a chance to leave her glass slipper after all?

I make an excuse to find a bathroom for a quick breather.

"Oh! Isn't he dishy Pen?" Anna had bounced up behind me in the corridor. "Has he asked you out on a date yet? He should, you look just gorgeous in that dress, it wouldn't go anywhere near me, you're so lucky being so petite." Petite! I could have kissed her. Having said that it was all comparative. She was wearing a rather tight black dress with a little too much lace stretched across her ample bosom, resembling two bald men sharing a hairnet. I then felt a little guilty when she could sense a possible critical eye.

"I look just bloody awful in this, don't I? It's the only party dress I could get anywhere near me, the weight just piles on, suppose I will have to make that New Year Resolution... yet again!"

"Rubbish, you always look great Anna. I bet Mark loves you in that dress." Her eyes sparkle naughtily.

"Well, he prefers me out of it actually!"

"You see! That's what matters, at least you've got someone who loves you to bits and your bits! He's patient, loving and makes you feel happy and you make him feel the same, that's a big plus in my book."

She nudges me gently. "Well, judging by the attention that hunk of man out there is giving you, maybe you have found the same?" She looks at me questioningly.

"His names Fraser Grant, he's a DS and he is just so…nice… *really* nice."

She gasps. "Nice! … Really nice?" I find the bathroom and as I turn to close the door I add.

"Well, alright Anna, he's absolutely … gorgeous…but you know my luck, been there before, I'm not holding my breath."
I close the door with Anna tutting back down the landing.

"Huh! I don't know, *some people*, wouldn't know magnetism, even if it were pinning them to the fridge door."

I sit awhile, contemplating my last hour or so. We are getting on really well…could this be him. A Detective Sergeant…well…mum and dad would approve.

Just think, Mrs Penelope Grant…..(admit it, we all do it?)…. Suse would be thrilled I was seeing someone, so….so…Simon? Right, pull yourself together, we won't be planning the wedding just yet. I'd be happy with just a date, I'd be happy with the… magnetism…. especially if it meant being pinned up against a fridge door!

As I walk back along the landing, I look over the balustrade and see him in the hall chatting to several people, he looks so confident, but not full of himself, he caught sight of me as I descend the stairs. "You look like a movie star coming down her staircase to greet her adoring crowd. Maybe it was fate that brought us together this evening. I hope that doesn't sound too corny. It's just my work hours are so erratic, I nearly didn't make it tonight, when I think of what I could have missed."
I felt myself go quite weak.

"It does seem strange. I might not have been here either. I was a last-minute invite, to make up numbers, maybe it is fate, our destiny planned for us to meet?" I said, giving him one of my best eyelash flutters.

"Yes, well, I'm sorry to spoil the moment, but it's getting late for me, I'm on the early shift tomorrow." (The eyelash flutter fails again. I really will have to revise that move.) I sigh a little too obviously. "But it's Saturday tomorrow?"

He smiles that smile. "Yes, I know.... No rest when dealing with the wicked. Sadly, criminals don't take the weekend off either, so I don't have a lot of choice."

He then gently takes my hand. "Look I don't want you to get a chill out there, but would you mind just walking to the porch with me? It would be nice to say goodbye with a little privacy." My heart was racing. I caught Morry in the corner of my eye, biting his knuckles in realisation of what the next few moments might hold. This is all his fault, he pointed him out. (I'll bear-hug him later!) We go into the colder, but much quieter, porch area. He gently pulls me towards him.

"Before I say goodnight, can I just ask, are you married, seeing anyone?" (Strange, I thought we covered everything as we chatted earlier.... relationships, well mine, not his.)

"No, no...I'm not married, look, no wedding rings." He laughs.

"You could have removed them?" I look at him making sure he makes eye contact before I continue.

"I'm not that sort of woman, I wouldn't have affairs and I wouldn't two-time." He pulls me closer.

"Just what I wanted to hear. Footloose and fancy free, a fun-loving girl, with no ties."

Before I had time to reply his mouth covered mine and his arms wrapped around me, as I tiptoed to keep my neck from cricking. His aftershave swept over me, strong and powerful and his kiss was the same. But it felt so good, I couldn't quite believe tonight was happening. He released his hold slightly and said huskily.

"I just can't believe how lucky I am to have met you tonight, that someone so stunning hasn't been swept off her feet years ago. Look, I'd love to take you to dinner, get to know you better, can I tempt you to a table at, 'The Straw House'?" (Someone pinch me, I must be dreaming! No don't, if I am dreaming, I don't want to wake up!)

"The...'The Straw House', is that possible so near Christmas, it's so exclusive, it'll be fully booked surely? Yes, I would love to go to dinner with you." He grins then pulls out a long black diary, with the Durham Constabulary Police crest on the front and flicks through it quickly.

"I am working some awkward hours but us single guys try to give the, 'marrieds' some family time at Christmas." I gaze at him in awe again.

"Oh, that's so thoughtful ...you don't have anyone special then?" He continues looking over his diary pages.

"No, no one special, my wife and I have separated. It takes a very patient lady to put up with the long hours and stresses that our job entails. Could you?" He catches me off guard with that one.

"Er....I have a few hobbies that could keep me occupied while you're not around." He then winks, raising his eyebrows.

"I bet you have Princess, you look the sort of woman that can keep herself entertained." (What does that mean?!)

He could see my puzzled expression. "Don't worry that gorgeous head of yours, frowns are so ageing and I don't want to see perfection spoilt." He drew me close and kissed me again.

"Look, let me take your number. I've got some nightshifts to work, but shall we say the twenty-second, it's a Monday. I know the owner of 'The Straw House', he owes me a favour. I'll ring you to confirm, or in case a runner comes up. May just ring you anyway, might find it difficult to wait ten days not seeing you in this beautiful dress and hearing your voice." Phew! What could I say, I nearly succumbed to a Jane Austin swoon.

"Thank you…honestly, that's a really nice….no a lovely…thing to say, thanks." He gently cups my chin and gives me one final kiss. He turns as he opens the front door.

"Here's to fairy tales….. Princess." With that he kissed the back of my hand again and was gone into the night.

Well not quite, I stayed in the porch long enough to see one of the waist-coated males drive round in a silver BMW, (not quite a white charger and certainly not a classic motorcycle, but it'll do.)

I rushed back into the now chaotic throng, the music had been put up a notch and people were dancing….they were absolutely everywhere, a sozzled throng, bouncing up and down.

Morry and Roger rushed at me desperate to get every detail of the last fifteen minutes. "Did you kiss?! No tongues, I hope! Was it toe-curlingly sensual?"

"It definitely reached my toes, but not quite all the way up the back of the neck." I said with a big ear to ear grin.

"Right, that's it, you're making us jealous, get on the end of that conga line and let's see you make a fool of yourself with the rest of us worse for wear party people."

So off we went, through every room, till the DJ put on some back-to-back, seventies glam rock. Slade, Sweet, T-Rex. Everyone started rocking, singing like there was no tomorrow, absolutely full of every type of festive spirit. I knew my feet would pay the price, but youthful memories took over and we strutted our stuff into the early hours.

This girl was too happy and having too much fun to leave at midnight!

Chapter 15

I tried to wake myself very slowly just in case it had all been a dream. I turned to see my red dress hanging up on the back of the bedroom door. My mohair jacket was draped next to me on the pillow, I leaned over, breathing in deeply and there it was, the smell of his expensive aftershave, left like a clue to his existence. Definitely not a dream then?

My aching bones needed recuperation so I spent nearly an hour in the bath after feeding Ferdy, who thought it was his birthday, as with my mind elsewhere, I opened a tin of minced steak and gravy, I didn't care, he got the lot, my little furry buddy, what the heck.

I then spent hours on the phone to anyone who'd listen. Making out I'd casually rung for a chat, then when asked how my evening had gone, they got the lot! Bina and Paula seemed thrilled, both with echoes of... 'about time... couldn't have happened to a nicer person......maybe this is the one... and he sounds just perfect.'

I tried my best not to be too full of myself, but I was really chuffed when I rang mum and dad. Mike and Freddie were both round there and Freddie came to the phone. "Hey, well done sis, fancy baggin' a bobby." He says proudly.

"You make him sound like first prize in fairground side-show, thanks though bruv, nice to know you approve."

He goes on to tell me how good the Police were when he had a break in at his garage in April. I vaguely remember it, but you never quite see them as people at the time, more uniformed robots, but they did get all his welding and spray paint gear back, which was pretty amazing.

He put mum back on the phone. "Oh, I can't wait to tell Mrs Gurney...*My* daughter going out with a policeman, not just a policeman, but a Detective Sergeant. Bring him round for a cup of tea and a mince pie dear. I can get out the Crown Ducal and I'll prime your dad not to ask his theories on the Tony Mancini case, or Jack the Ripper."

I stifle a laugh. "Mum, hold your horses, I haven't even been out on my own with him myself yet, never mind festive teas with the family, but I may broach the subject when we have dinner together." After I told her a little more, I could hear my dad mumbling in the background.

"Take no notice Penny love, your dad wants to know, if he's so good looking, dynamic and bright, why did his first wife leave him?" I feel a little uncomfortable, I realise dad is being ever over protective and practical and doesn't mean to hold a pin above my bubble.

"Well, you can tell dad I don't know, but then why is his apparently, beautiful, intelligent and witty daughter, still on the shelf at thirty-seven? It just happens. You can also tell him not to worry as I've inherited his pessimistic outlook. Fraser will be well and truly scrutinised before he's even halfway through his main course." Mum laughs.

"Oh, you know us dear, we just want our children to be happy. Anyway, we'll be seeing you on Thursday, won't we?" I'd clean forgotten about the Carol Concert.

"Oh, er, yes, of course mum, is everyone else coming?" Maybe if someone else is crying off I can make an excuse…...

"Oh, everyone dear, Molly, Donald and the children are arriving Tuesday but they've got to travel back Christmas Eve as Donald's doing his first midnight mass and carol service in his new post, it's all so exiting for them."

"Yes, okay, I'll be there mum, I'll bring their pressies too, see you then mum, love to all. Bye."

I tried not to dwell too much on dad's negativity and quickly made another cuppa and called Suse, she'd put me back on track.

"Oh! Pen, wow, he sounds fantastic babe, well done you! I wish I'd seen you in that dress, sounds fab." I was so glad that she sounded so thrilled.

"You will see me in it Suse, Roger took loads of photos throughout the evening, Morry insisted. He wanted some blackmail shots!" Susie squealed. "What, of you, what on earth were you doing?" I gave it a couple of seconds, I knew Suse would be champing at the bit.

"Well, I was actually looking demure and classical in the foreground, I was merely the stooge for his sneaky shots of Tiffany. The girl got so steaming, she tucked her evening dress into her undies, still wearing her tiara, which by now had slipped to a rakish angle over one eye. She then proceeded to climb onto an antique table and gyrate and wiggle her 'superior' bod to Gina G's, 'Ooh Aah Just A Little Bit'!" I could hear Susie now giggling uncontrollably.

"As if that wasn't *more* than enough, it was made just a tad more nose wrinklingly embarrassing, when Jasper and his equally quaffed up buddies, began to remove their ties and shirts to join her floor show!" I could hear Susie almost choking with laughter as I continued.

"Yes, I know! How do you think we felt? By then her mother was helping to serve coffee desperate to sober up the crowd. Morry nearly got a hot black Kenyan down one leg, which in normal circumstances would have been a lucky night, but she nearly scalded his prize Armanis!" Susie came up for air.

"Oh God Penny, how could you keep a straight face saying goodbye?"

"I couldn't, I didn't. By then they'd been force fed at least three black coffees each. Her tiara had been re-perched and she kept apologising that she hadn't mingled more. I told them both it had been one of the best, if not, *thee* best party I'd been to. Of course, she was thrilled. Drunk, but thrilled."

I didn't let on that my brilliant evening had had nothing to do with her lack of mingling, her one mingle had done the trick brilliantly, pairing me up with Fraser.

Suse sighed loudly. "Well Pen, this Fraser sounds just the ticket babe. I tell you what, with him knowing the owner of 'The Straw House', do you want Simon to suss him out, you know have a word with his brother, he's bound to know him working there, you know……if he's *so* well in?"

I ponder. "I don't know Suse, isn't that a bit sneaky, a bit untrustworthy… he is a Policeman?" Suse giggles. "Yes, I take your point, but he's also a man, you can't tell me as a bobby, he won't have done the odd little check on *you* already."

I sit up startled. "What! Checks, why, who, what for, why?"

Suse continues her teasing. "Come on Pen, he'll have that meticulous detective brain, reading between the lines, watching your body language……*the clues are there.!*" Now she's sounding like Lloyd Grossman on Through the Keyhole.

"Hey, I've got nothing to hide and hopefully neither has he……But, if Simon calls his brother maybe mention him, bit of background, maybe? Sorry Suse, have to go, promised Morry I'd ring him before three, you're coming to his do tonight aren't you?" I check my watch.

"Yes babe, of course. Shame Fraser isn't going to be there, I could give him the once over." I raise my eyebrows thinking that one through.

"Not such a good idea Suse, I want to be in with a fighting chance with this one, nothing personal."

She giggles. "Oh Pen, I am more than happy with my Simon. Anyway, I've never made a play for your men?" My turn to stifle the laugh.

"No, you didn't have to, one look at you and they were never going to be mine in the first place! Don't worry, I'm sure you did me many a favour there. See you tonight Suse."

I squeeze another cup from the teapot, I'm parched with all the talking. I pick up the still warm receiver.

"Morry, is everything okay at Chez Wild & Good? Do you want me to bring anything over tonight?"

"Just yourself sweets. My Rojere has got everything well and truly under control. You know what he's like babe, parties are his forte, it's military precision or nothing, he's like a whirlwind of Dior satin, he's been up since six, I'm exhausted just watching him." I picture the scene and stifle a giggle.

"Anyway, you little vamp you, has 'our Fraser' rung yet?"

"Give the poor bloke a chance, he was on an early shift,

he's probably at home… sleeping it off." My mind begins to wander as I picture a bed and his sleeping, tousle-haired torso.

"More like he hasn't been able to get through on the phone even if he wanted to, you'll have been telling the contents of your address book and anyone else who's willing to listen. Don't blame you though babe, the man is…*sex* on legs."
(I'm picturing that bed, that torso again, then by the silence, maybe Morry is too!)

"He'll ring when he has time, or something to say. I think I can trust this one Morry." I can hear him trying to suppress his laughter.

"What! You're all at it, what are you laughing at?"

He pulls himself together. Oh babe! Just remember, *everyone* has a vice and with their jobs, their stress levels, they have to release it somewhere, drinking, gambling, the gym, copious amounts of sex. I've known a couple of plods in my time."

"Morry! That's a terrible thing to say!"

"Oh, you're just such a push over lovey! I'm joshing, I'm sure he's one of the good guys, you can almost see the Colgate ping glinting off his teeth when he smiles. Could be that romantic Christmas you've always dreamed of chuck" I climbed down off my high horse.

"Oh, I know it seems daft Morry at my age, but I still want the romance, all the falling in love bit, meals by candlelight, talking in front of a big open fire, walking in the snow…..do you think I am just being daft?"

"Well, no babe, I don't think your being daft…just maybe a touch unrealistic. Just be careful the 'rose-tinteds' don't make you see what you want to see, rather than what's really there that's all. But so far, from a nosey, old spectators view, you've got a fella who thinks you're bloody gorgeous and you'll be one down, two to go, with your meal at 'The Straw House'…so just enjoy it babe."

"Ah thanks Morry, you're a love, I'll see you later, give Roj my love too. Bye."

I had a great bunch of friends. I smiled as I pulled down the attic ladder and went in search of Christmas tree and decorations. It was time to get well and truly festive. It would probably have taken slightly less than three hours had the lights worked first time. Of course, sentimental fool me, had insisted on keeping Gran and Gramp's tree lights, the screw fit ones, that when one bulb goes, they all go. You sit there for forty minutes, cross-legged, back aching, going through all of them with the last spare bulb you can find and it's always the last one you try, no matter which end you start!

Finally, it was lights, camera action….and that's exactly what I got. No sooner were the tree lights up and twinkling, when Ferdy spotted the tinsel and shiny baubles. I could see his eyes rolling, which to go for first? Off he shot leaping sideways, deftly flicking four small glass baubles at once, one hitting the wall and shattering, this in turn made him leap higher scattering some small round Santas.

He then rushed headlong into a mass of tinsel, rolling maniacally, clawing at the glittering strands. He stopped dead, I could see him pull back, hiding in the shiny mass, swaying slowly, he'd spotted the small, feathered tree Robins.

"Ferdy, don't you dare!" Too late, he pounced on the smallest one, grabbing it in his mouth and running off through the door and up the stairs. No point me following, he'll be under the bed, guarding it. I'll retrieve the remnants later. I'd just finished adding the pine-cones to the fireplace garland when the phone rang. My heart lurched, could it be him? It was only four, wouldn't he be sleeping?

"Hello, is that you Princess?" My heart was pounding so hard, good job he couldn't see me blushing. "Hi, Fraser, yes, I thought you'd be sleeping off your early shift?" I heard a loud roar, then he raised his voice slightly.

"It was a long day, a few in the cells, so I had to work over a few hours, I'm just on my way home now." The noise rushed past again. "Couldn't you have rung from home?" Sounded like heavy traffic in the background, I was straining to hear.

"Hey, Princess …didn't want to wait any longer to hear that sweet voice of yours. I'm in a phone box, I was just collecting a suit from the dry cleaners. Sorry about the noise. I would have used my mobile but it's my work one, no private calls, you know how it is. Anyway, I just didn't get time till now, I had a mountain of paperwork to finish, deadlines, had to be done Princess." There we go, caring, conscientious and he gets his suits dry-cleaned.

"Oh, it's no problem, nice to hear from you, hope you've enough hours to catch up on your sleep." The traffic becomes really loud. "Couple of lorries just going past Princess, look I'll call you again. Just to let you know all okay for the twenty-second."

"Great, I'm really looking forward to it." He laughs "I bet you are Princess. Don't forget you're mine this Christmas, no hunting for Princes at your friend's party tonight, mind you if they're all gay there won't be a lot of choice. Unless of course *you* swing both ways……..do you?"

I had told him about Morry's party in passing, he has got a good memory. Well, he's bound to have a retentive mind, it's all part of his job.

"Well, hope it's not too much of a disappointment that you can't picture me in a lesbian clinch, but I am straight. My gay friends do actually have friends and acquaintances of every persuasion, *even* Policemen! But thanks for letting me know I'm yours, does this mean we'll be swapping Christmas presents then?" I felt daft as soon as I'd said it, he took a while to answer.

"Sorry Princess, this traffic is awful, enjoy the party, don't worry I'm sure I'll find a little something to put in your stocking this Christmas. Look, I'll ring again before the twenty-second, be good." I was about to speak but the phone went dead.

I sat for several minutes, twiddling my hair, with a rather silly smile on my face going over his words, keeping the positive lines locked in my mind, then went on to finish putting up the decorations. I managed to get most of my Christmas cards written, ready for posting and have a quick tidy round, before catching sight of the clock. It was nearly six. I rushed upstairs to get ready. Morry had told us all, in no uncertain terms, Christmas colours only. Green, red, gold and silver. Plenty of festive glitter and sparkle. I had a rather fantastic silver, layered frilled blouse with sleeves that made me look like a festive calypso dancer. It was a good ten years since I'd worn it but it was well worth a second airing. I loved Morry and Roger's parties because it gave me an excuse to wear what I really liked, clothes I felt showed my wilder side. I'll continue to try and convince everyone I do have one, unleashed from time to time. (If only I'd got a signed statement from Charlie!) Clothes of my prime, they gave me a chance to be who I wanted to be and not the person I felt people expected me to be…at *my* age! So, out came the short red and green kilt, seventy denier black tights and my favourite knee-high D.M.s, which I tied with long gold laces and threaded in a small bell on each. I straightened my hair to make it look as long possible, put in a tiny ponytail at the top tied with red and green ribbon. Accessorised with gorgeous red and green earrings, matching choker necklace and bracelet. I felt great, full of fun and I knew that's exactly what Morry and Roger's party would be. I looked at myself in the mirror, *I liked* what I saw, but somehow, I don't think Fraser would have. I think he likes his ladies a little more elegant and restrained. Just as well he's not at tonights party!

Morry and Roger have the most fantastic house. One of Roger's design friends let him know about it some years ago, 'a good price and with potential'. They spent nearly a year getting it into a stunning showpiece of style and comfort. Just off Pimlico, on South Street, a beautiful town centre Georgian, three-story terrace. Not only overlooking the River Wear but also with stunning views of the Cathedral on the other side, it really is the envy of many. They of course know this and have dinner parties and get togethers at every opportunity to allow as many friends and acquaintances as possible to, 'ooo and aaah' over the rooms and of course the view. They are fantastic hosts and never precious over their belongings. Morry always jokes, 'we may be stylish, but we're not foolish, if you can get flash at half the cash, we're in.' So, if the odd arm waving dancer broke a vase, or ornament, they never flinched, but you can bet Roger had the dustpan and brush out within seconds, forgotten.

I squeezed my little car in next to Roger's sporty Mazda. Morry walked to work, over the other side of town to our offices in Old Elvet. (Only around the corner from the Police Station. Just think how close Fraser has actually been all this time?) My mind's wandering again. The door to Chez Good & Wild is flung open.

"Oooo, who's going to be the belle of the ball then." Squeals Morry looking me up and down and catching sight of the Christmas bells on my boots. "Sweetie! You look like a little tartan Morris dancer!" I laughed, well used to his jibes.

"Back at you, you fabulous festive shimmering elf! Green satin does suit you!" He blows me several air kisses. "Love you too darling...now get in before your nether regions get a chill in that kilt...or is it a tartan belt?" I do a pretend swat, then rush up the stairs with him in pursuit.

The kitchen and dining room are downstairs for everyday use, but the first floor has an incredible party room at the front of the house, which makes the most of their enviable view. Not that you can actually see a lot on a dark winter's night, but their summer party is legendary.

"Hasn't Rojere worked his magic yet again?" He says looking admiringly at his partner, waving his hand across the vibrant and festive room. A huge table laden with so much food it looks like the scene from 'A Christmas Carol', you'd expect to see the opulent velvet clad ghost of Christmas present holding his fruit laden horn of plenty .... but no it's Roger in red velvet jacket clutching a huge plate of chicken legs, complete with frills, (that's both the chicken and Roger.)

The room is awash with handmade holly wreaths and garlands of pine branches, cones, berries and red roses. "Those roses must have cost you a fortune at this time of year...." Roger looks very pleased at me noticing.

"Perks of knowing a florist! Paula let me take a handful after she'd given me an arranging lesson last night. I helped her get a big Christmas restaurant order done and she let me take the leftovers." He seemed thrilled.

"Paula, letting you take something for free. She must be in love again." Remembering some years back, when she let me have a pair of clogs from her collection and a rather quirky hat I'd always coveted. It was only because she'd been asked out by Ray Flowers, (what else was he going to become but a florist?). They met on an advanced floristry course, she was besotted for months, hoping she would eventually become ... Mrs Flowers. Sadly, he went off with a small, delicate thing called...Rose. Fortunately for me, she never did ask for the clogs and hat back.

Several more guests appeared at the door, including Suse and Simon. They looked so fantastic together. Simon had on a shiny, dark green suit, a blood red shirt and a gold tie, normally an ensemble like this would be a strange combination, but he was the male equivalent of Suse, he just looked good in anything. Suse of course went for the contrasting look, she was wearing a little red dress, halter-neck, slashed to the waist, matching red leather, high-heeled boots, green patterned tights, a fantastic ivy leaf necklace with matching earrings and a mass of gold bangles, she looked stunning.

She rushed over after hugging Morry and Roger. "Pen, you look brilliant, love that blouse...shame Fraser can't see you, you look so cute!" I smile broadly, but can't help feeling he'd probably be looking at her rather than me.

"Where do you get such fantastic jewellery from, don't tell

me, your friend Paul has just leant you a couple of trinkets for the evening?"

"He's an absolute darling, these are actually from a show they're doing in January, so I'm exclusive tonight. What do you think of Simon's outfit? Doesn't he just look the part...... like an expensive Christmas present…can't wait to get back to his place and unwrap him, very slowly."

"Eww! Best friend in ear shot thank you, T M I!" She giggles.

"Sorry Pen, I was forgetting, you haven't managed to get any yet have you." I look shocked.

"Excuse me Mrs Frisky Foreplay-Forbes, we're not all sex mad, some of us are still more than happy with the romance of it all." She snorts.

"Yes, like I said, you're not getting any! You never know, if this hunk Fraser is anything to go by, you may be getting more than you bargained for this Christmas."

I look confused. "What do you mean, if Fraser is anything to go by?" She leant out towards Simon who was still being cooed over by Morry and Roger.

"Simon…Simon, darling, tell Pen what you know about her new fella…she's dying to get the gen." Simon moved in next to me, he leant forward and kissed my cheek.

"Lovely to see you again Penny, don't look so worried, not all bad. Or maybe you like bad boys?" He winked and Suse giggled.

"No really, I didn't find out that much, just that my brother said he doesn't actually know the owner that well. Apparently, Fraser was the CID officer sent to deal with a couple of break-ins at the premises. My brother said Mr. Straw was so grateful to DS Grant for catching one of the offenders, he offered him a free meal for two."

I looked slightly deflated. "You mean I'm a free meal?" Simon hugged me, reassuringly.

"No, far from it. That meal was used up some months ago it seems. But he has continued to use 'The Straw House' as his chosen venue for…… romance?"

I feel a little flushed, but quickly go on the defensive.

"Well, he's a single bloke isn't he, it's a pretty impressive date. You were impressed weren't you Suse, when Simon said he was taking you there?" I look towards Suse for some back up.

"Of course, I was, but from what Simon's brother says, he's quite a regular." She can see I feel a little duped and crestfallen, so adds. "Having said that, like you say, he's single and if he wants to find someone special then why the hell shouldn't he take his dates to the best restaurant in town. Let's face it, you'd be more insulted if he was only taking you to the help-yourself buffet at 'The Mammoth'. Think yourself lucky babe and he does say you're his Princess, maybe for him the search is now over."

I smiled as Suse hugged me tightly. Yes, maybe this Prince and Princess were about to find *their*……happy ever after. (Actually, if I'm honest, I really liked the help-yourself buffet at 'The Mammoth', less pressure to use the *right* knife and fork.)

Morry and Roger began clapping their hands and shushing everyone. Morry spoke first.

"Right, my sparkling beautiful people, it is *so good* to see so many of you here and all looking as if the tinsel fairy has waved her magic wand in abundance! We want everyone to just have an absolute ball, but firstly let me pass you over to the twinkling star of the show…….my Rojere."

Roger shyly steps forward. "Just to repeat Morry's thanks

for such a lovely crowd tonight. Food is ready, please just eat, drink and be merry, leave nothing, because what you don't eat now we'll be putting it in your party bags later! We'll give you all forty minutes, then the tables will be cleared, moved and the games will begin. Oh, hang on, I think Morry is starting already."

Morry is now clutching a large garden trug with dozens of blank badges and pens.

"Right tonight we want everyone to add a little spice to the mingling, we're all going to use our…..Porn Star Names!"

There was a huge ripple, (or should that be nipple?) and a chorus of, '*oh no!*' As everyone passed Morry to get to the table, he continued. "You know what to do, think of your first pet, that's your Christian name and then the name of the street you were born on. Me First, me first!"

Another of our name games and naturally Morry's favourite. It never fails to amuse, especially the newbies to their party traditions. Morry was on a roll.

"Yes, sexy soul mates, you can call me………Butch Byker!"

Everyone guffaws with laughter as he goes on, aiming this at the new to this experience, that his first dog was a bulldog called Butch and he was born on Byker Street in the Walker area of Newcastle. Hard to believe, although he did say they moved to Sacriston when he was ten. I don't think he was ever comfortable as a, 'Byker boy'.

Inevitably, it became my turn……here we go. "Er, my very first pet was a hamster called Fluffy and I was born on Beaufront Avenue." Another roar of laughter, then Morry shrieks.

"You're Fluffy Beaufront! Loving it, *loving it!*" (He obviously knows my porn star name from our numerous previous parties, but just loved shouting the names out with total joy and renewed surprise!) And so it went on, Roger became, Prince Donkin, Suse became Ginger Folly, (But was grateful her parents hadn't got a house round the corner at Dyke Heads?)

Simon became Tootles Malone, obviously we weren't going to let him forget that in a hurry! There was also a Booby Stargate, a Rex Villier and I appeared to be cornered for far too long, by a long-haired male called, Chudley Broadmayne? I think he'd got his boarding school name by mistake, can't imagine anyone sitting down to watch...... 'Hot and Steamy' featuring the porn star.....Chudley Broadmayne.

Bina and Denzel, or should that be Baby Sheldon and Lucky Reagan arrived, followed by Paula and Harold, alias Perry Hylton and Bonzo Goldcrest, (now I *could* see that name on a film!) who were whisked away by Roger to gaze at the festive florals from Paula's emporium.

Harold seemed a lovely, polite and patient soul, very well suited to Paula, definitely an, 'opposites attract' situation there. She told everyone who would listen, just how busy the shop was and how well she was doing. When I finally got a word with Harold, he was full of admiration for her, but said she worked too hard and he was going to make sure she had a proper rest after Christmas and New Year. He told me to keep it secret, but he had tickets for a week in Paris late January. I squeezed his arm and said she would be thrilled. He looked very relieved. He was unsure as to whether this independent, practical woman would like romantic surprises. I assured him, *all* women like romantic surprises. (My turn soon, I hope? Not with Harold of course.)

Eventually after some general chatter, Bina and Denzel asked several questions about Fraser. With Bina being a Lawyer, even part-time, she had actually come into contact with DS Grant since his return from the Training Department. "He seems charming, very determined, well, at work anyway."

Said Bina, looking straight at me, eyebrows raised, waiting for a response.

"Oh, I think he's pretty similar out of work too." I smile sweetly. "I'm hoping to get to know him a lot better on our dinner date." Bina smiles broadly. "Well, I hope he's like my Denzel and just sweeps you off your feet." Denzel coughs loudly.

"Ur hum, if I remember rightly, I didn't get much chance to sweep you off your feet as you'd already knocked me off mine! You got your claws right in, I didn't stand a chance." All said with a roguish twinkle in his eye. She shot him the same look.

"....And you loved every minute of it you Celtic animal." She then grabs his mop of ginger hair and growls like a tigress. I left them in a passionate clinch and rushed off to mingle. The tables were cleared, the Persian mat rolled up carefully, then music started. Apart from endless and very manic dancing from many of us 'Disco Divas', Morry would stop the music every so often for us to play a silly game.

Matchboxes on noses, no hands, first team to get it to the end of the line. Hysterics ensued, Foo-foo Moncrieff with tweaked button nose could not retrieve the 'Baubles Team' matchbox from the large conk of, Tinker Lovaine. The 'Fairylights Team' won that one, but were let down later when Pippy Foxglove got their team spoon on a string stuck in her cleavage...needless to say there were plenty of 'canine' volunteers to retrieve it. Down Rex, down boy!

It was just a fantastic party and a great start to the social festive fortnight. We laughed so much we ached. We danced so much our legs went to jelly. We sang so much our voices went altogether. Fortunately, Morry and Roger have great neighbours who were all there, enjoying the endless fun along with us. It's not just food and drink and the people, I love just getting giddy on the atmosphere, the complete party package, being able to enjoy the company and the music, it was a great night.

I said my goodbyes around two. Bina told me, not to forget Monday night, Suse said she'd see me then too. Morry and Roger gave me a party bag full of gorgeous bath baubles and a box of food.

"Go on babe, it'll save you cooking anything tomorrow and Ferdy will thank you for the chicken, our old Toddy loves a bit of cold chicken." I look surprised. "Where was Toddy, did you leave him with Roger's mum and dad tonight?" They both laughed. "Toddy's as deaf as a post now. He's been fast asleep on his chaise-longue in the corner of our room all night, we love the furry old duffer, but he can't hear a thing."

I laughed and hugged them both. "Thanks for a fantastic time, see you Monday Morry."

Chapter 16

I hadn't set my alarm, I was allowing my body to recover, but Ferdy had other ideas and pounced on the bed, meowing as soon as I moved. I stretched my aching party bones and decided today was for pottering, a lazy day. There I was, upset at not getting enough Christmas invites, could I have coped with any more...well I'd give it a bloody good shot given half the chance!

A day like this has a real plus for the living alone. There is no one to say...'Are you going to slob about all day? Aren't you going to do something constructive? You're wasting a good twelve hours here.'

Not in my book! Everyone needs a day where they can do just what they want and if that means doing absolutely nothing, great. I can get up unashamedly late, wear my jim-jams till lunchtime, watch a movie, read a paper, or a book and just chill, without feeling any guilt whatsoever.

Mind you, wouldn't mind watching a movie curled up next to Fraser. I just might make an effort to change out of my jim-jams if he was popping round. He'd have to whistle for the wafting chiffon number though!

I did make a little effort later, to try and keep my ever-wandering mind on other things, I wrapped Jerome, Felicity and Kezia's presents, as I was seeing family on Thursday. I'd already wrapped Molly and Donald's 'communion wine'! I liked to make sure the children had the Disney paper and lots of bows and shiny stickers. It would be Kezia's first Christmas, she's at that lovely age where the paper is much more interesting than the contents!

    I'd done so little today, but still fell into bed just after ten after a long, skin wrinkling, soak in
the bath. My head hit the pillow and as I drifted off, my dreams took over……..I appeared to be dancing the night away in a large ballroom, which was apparently suspended over the River Wear. I appeared to have a queue of men, snaking into the distance, down a long marble staircase. All in brightly coloured suits, some I recognised.

    Jason D. in orange velvet, very tactile! Also, rather bizarrely, Chudley Broadmayne in yellow, Ben in red and Charlie in a rather fetching green satin, he quickly kissed my hand and told me to….'wait for him'….but I didn't wait. I danced past them all as Fraser appeared, wearing a bright blue suit and very dark sunglasses. I kept telling him I wanted to see his eyes, after the fifth time of asking, he removed his glasses, his eyes were lazer bright and the exact blue of his suit, but as he danced me away from the line of lovely men, he just kept saying, 'all the better to see you with'…… 'all the better to see you with'…

    Well dreams *are* supposed to be strange and subliminal……. aren't they?

    Last night I'd decided to set my clock twenty minutes earlier for Monday morning. I fancied the walk on a frosty, winters day, in the quiet early hours. I lived on Laburnum Avenue, in a cul-de-sac, a Victorian mid-terrace, nice and quiet with no through traffic. Perfect for Ferdy, who liked to wander across the road through the fence and disappear in the long grass around the old office buildings. It wasn't a long walk for me, but I decided to take an alternative route this morning. Going up Margery Lane, then Quarryheads, I peered down South Street in case it was worth calling on Morry, I looked at my watch, he'd be long gone. He liked to be early most days, said he needed to be on his second cup of coffee before he could get his brain in gear. I didn't believe that for a moment, he was incredible with figures, a brilliant accountant. I rushed down Church Street, then for some reason, (surprising? Not!) I strolled casually down New Elvet, right past the Police Station. Well, it's not as if I knew what shift he was on, I was on my way to work. I had every reason to be walking here, at this moment in time? My heart leapt as the door opened, two male officers in uniform appeared, one smiled and made a comment to his buddy, they walked towards a Panda car. I hovered, no one else appeared and I suddenly felt *really* silly and just a little bit juvenile. Bit like hanging around the youth club doors hoping the lad you fancy will come out. What would he say, what would *I* say? I scurried off to work feeling like some daft fifteen-year-old, but with no excuse, being an even dafter thirty-seven!

    I was happy to get to work, back in familiar territory, regaining some control. I pulled myself together and taking off my coat, quickly took a tea from the tray and rushed to my desk, sitting down with a big sigh of relief.

    It was always lovely being in the office at this time of year. Everyone seemed to be in a jolly, festive mood. Anna brought in *huge* tins of mince pies to share out, which made the morning cuppas a bit of a treat. We all worked hard but managed to chat endlessly about Christmas events, family, holidays and of course inevitably getting back to Friday night's party.

Tiffany, it seemed, was conspicuous by her absence. June said she'd told her not to disturb her office unless it was a real emergency, as she had so much work to get finished and some important documentation to sort out……

Wasn't anything to do with the envelope containing four photographs, left on her desk for when she arrived, with a note saying… 'Wiggle it, giggle it our very own Gina G-string' then?

Morry appeared late morning, squeezing in next to me behind my desk, biting his bottom lip. He showed me copies of the photos, carefully keeping them out of sight of the others in the office. I nearly choked on my tea as I stared at him, then at them, then at him again.

"I got them done in Boots yesterday, me and Rojere decided to have a stroll, what with all the shops being open. I can tell you Pen, I could barely look the assistant in the eye when she said, 'do you want to check the contents sir, make sure they're yours.' Embarrassed wasn't the word, it looks like some sort of sex party, I didn't know Roj had caught that, or that, he says pointing at the obvious!"

He's showing me a photo, it's of me looking oblivious in the foreground and Jasper, who along with his pals had finished their floor show and grabbed Tiffany to lift her off the table…fireman style! I'm standing in-front of what can only be described as six half naked men and Tiffany's delicately thonged, nay cheese-wired peachy bottom, in full view right behind my head!

I gasp. "Morry, I can't believe you let Roger take that!"

He quickly shoves the photos in his jacket pocket and leans in as the girls look up. "I didn't mean to, I kept saying, 'keep Pen to the right', he was so busy concentrating on you, trying to make it look as casual as possible. We thought she was still dancing, I never thought….." He bit his lip again, but it didn't work this time and he burst into fits of girly giggles, I couldn't help but follow. "Oh my God, is that why she won't come out of her office? You rotten sod, she'll be mortified, I would be… strewth, I think I'd have to leave my job!" He pulls himself together, now looking very guilty.

"It's OK. I'll give her till lunchtime, then I'll tell her I was taking your photo, caught the background by mistake, the note was just my little joke. I'll tell her no one else has seen the photos, I'll take her an extra Jaffa cake, she'll be fine. I'll put her mind at rest, that only this old poof has seen her backside in all its glory, she's got nothing to worry about. Now if it had been Jasper's, we might have got a few more viewers." I shot him a look. "Don't say that for God's sake, we'll *never* get another invite."

"Well, it's not like she needs to work here, if she feels that way." Morry tuts.

I did finally see Tiffany, it was late afternoon, I tried my best to speak to her without visualising *that* photo, it was definitely a leveller. Brilliant party Friday Tiffany, thanks again for the invite." She looks at me suspiciously.

"Seems Morry has some photos, have you seen them?" I clench my jaw as best I can. "Yes, he brought a few to show me at tea-break, I'm glad he got a couple of my dress, came out really well. I think you were somewhere on one or two, anyway everyone seemed to be having fun."

She held my gaze, fortunately I must have given her the impression I hadn't seen anything untoward. "I may not be at the office party this Friday, I think Jasper and I are going to friends at the weekend, I'll see how the week goes."

I actually felt a little bit sorry for her. "I'm sure it'll be a pre-break week, very festive, no big surprises, well unless we get a Christmas bonus from Mr Harkass." Tiffany sighed, then smiled, looking straight at me.

"I've always put you slightly above some of the others in this building Penelope. I don't have to put up with the jibes and underhand remarks. I work here because I *want* to, not because I *have* to, there are some people who just can't understand that ethos." With that she turns on her well-heeled court shoes and closes the door to her office behind her. Huh, wish I was working here because I wanted to, not because I had to. There's no way I would be couped up in this office that's for sure, I'd be combing out matted cat fur and walking dogs at some animal sanctuary, I certainly wouldn't be stuck behind a desk here.

Later, as I grabbed my coat and scarf and walked out into the cold evening air, I considered getting the bus, or jumping in a taxi, but decided to walk home again. This time I took my normal route through town, across and up Silver Street, through Allergate. I picked up a daily paper and a carton of milk on the way. Just as I clicked the kettle on and opened a tin of food for Ferdy the phone rang. Probably Suse, checking what time I'm going tonight.

"Is that my Princess in that sexy red dress?" I wasn't ready for that one.

"Er, no…it's your Princess in a pin-striped skirt and white cotton blouse." Silence, then he sighs. Bugger, have I said something flippant and stupid, so I add. "Sorry, I've just come in from work, I haven't got my home-head on yet."

"Hey, Princess, don't worry, I was actually just picturing that tight little pin-stripe skirt and that white cotton blouse, couple of buttons undone…nice" Was this actually Fraser, or a pervy phone call?

"Er, my skirt isn't that tight actually and my blouse…." He sighs again. "Princess, I was just joking, I've obviously called at a bad time, look I've just rung about the twenty-second." I knew it, he's going to cancel, he's changed his mind, I knew he would.

"Is there a problem?" I try to ask calmly. "No, no problem, Princess. I just wanted to pick you up myself that night, you know drive you there, save you the hassle, I haven't got your address." I was almost about to say, haven't you found it on your police computer yet, but I didn't want to tempt fate. I gave him my address quickly.

"Yeh, I know it, that's off Hawthorn, isn't it? We've had a couple of burglaries reported round there recently, do you have decent locks, security?" I suddenly felt quite vulnerable.

"Well, I've got window locks, mortice locks and a chain on the door, no valuables on show, is there anything else I could do that might help?" He laughs, putting me a little more at ease after the, 'don't have nightmares do sleep well' approach.

"You could always move in a police officer, hey Princess?"

I was speechless, blushing wasn't the word, I didn't even know his favourite colour, his star sign, his middle name, where he lived and he was moving himself in as a security device!

"Wouldn't I be safer with a Doberman or Bull Mastiff?" I asked ludicrously. "Maybe you would, but wouldn't you fancy a real dog Princess…woof, woof!" (Had he been drinking?)

"Look, much as I'd love to continue with this primal banter, I'm just in the middle of getting ready and I've got to be out by seven, sorry." He goes silent again.

"Hey, that's okay Princess, I'm just finishing some paperwork and then I'm off out with the lads later. Take no notice of me. Be good tonight, I'll ring again. Bye Princess."

I stood there feeling all starchy in my, okay yes it was a *tight,* pin-striped skirt, as I caught sight of myself in the hall mirror. I felt quite flushed and I *had* actually opened a couple of buttons, I turned to look at myself sideways…. Maybe I *should* just loosen up a bit, try to see what he appears to see. I pout slightly at my reflection, blow myself a kiss, then turn doing a Marilyn Monroe wiggle back down the hallway into the kitchen. Not that Marilyn would have been wearing grubby, fur-lined moccasins, but hey Durham's not Hollywood!

Why *can't* I see myself as sexy? Why do I embrace the prude in me. My mind goes straight back to that night with Charlie. Yes, I'd had a couple of Martinis but every moment was memorable. His eyes said everything, the way he held me, the way he touched me, the words he used, it all made me feel *so* good. I had loved and enjoyed every wonderful moment…... but I'd assumed it was just a night of fun. Realising he'd meant what he'd said, I was embarrassed. I didn't know how to respond to his apology, genuine interest in me and of course him wanting to see me again. Why can't I believe that someone can find me worth pursuing? Well, I suppose if I knew *that,* would I be having this conversation with myself in my kitchen, with my cat looking at me like I'm mad.

I was relieved tonight wouldn't be a full blown, 'party' party. My party mood had suddenly waned earlier, but I tried my best not to let it show.

Bina had a huge family and with them going to Denzel's family in Ireland this year, everyone was here, the house was choc-a-block. They had a big, thirties semi up Newcastle Road, Whitesmocks, but at this rate they'd be spilling out into the garden. As Denzel opened the door with a huge cheery welcome, I squeezed through the huge crowd of colourful people in full throng. So many different languages were being spoken all at the same time.

Bina had five brothers and three sisters and with mum being white, dad Indian, all the offspring had grabbed at this diversity. No arranged marriages in sight, most of them had met and married through family and business. So, there were Indian, Pakistani, Greeks, Italian, Polish and a French girl, who Bina's youngest brother had fallen for while at university. Most of the women were in colourful saris, which just added to the beautiful ethnic, Celtic, Indian come Irish decoration of Bina's house, she had exquisite taste. (Apart from the Picasso in the downstairs loo!)

Denzel loved it all but insisted on plenty of green, every shade. It reminded him of the rolling Irish hills and the farmland he was brought up on. This was a small concession in Bina's eyes, she loved those Irish hills too and had said if it hadn't been for their family closeness and the children they'd have moved over there like a shot.

"You okay Pen, you look miles away?" I hadn't seen Suse and Simon arrive.

"Fine, I think the late nights are catching up with me. I think I'll just perch here and people watch tonight. What are you and Simon doing for Christmas then?"

Susie smiled broadly. "Yes, well Suse, apart from that!" I grin back.

"Actually, I *was* going to say, he's staying at mine a couple of days before Christmas, we'll be going round to mum and dads for tea on Tuesday."

"I bet they're thrilled you've found such a fantastic man…finally?"

"Oh, they love him, Pen. He and my dad even went off to the golf course Sunday afternoon. Mum keeps hugging me and saying, 'you see, I said, all comes to those who wait.' I can't believe how safe and secure I feel Pen. Christmas Eve, he's taking me and the kitties up to his place. Pen, you'd love it. Huge, detached stone house just on the outskirts of St. John's Chapel."

She looks down coyly. "He told me, he loves me Pen and when I feel the time is right, he'd love me to move in…we've *even* looked at rings. Can you believe it? After all these years of waiting, I just feel so….*so* lucky and this is *so* right."

Her face is positively glowing with pride and happiness and as much as I feel the same for her, there is a deep pang of loss and I'm ashamed to admit it, envy. Her circumstances are changing. She's finally got the future she always wanted and the man of her dreams. Our friendship will now take a back seat, I bite my lip, not wanting her to see the anguish I feel and how much I'll miss her.

"You *so* deserve this Suse. Don't forget if you're going to have a Spring wedding, subtle dresses for the bridesmaids please! No Little Bo-Peep meringue creations, or Peach Melba combos, I just haven't got the height, I'll look like that doll thing that covers the toilet roll at your Grans!"

She laughs and hugs me tightly. "Ever the joker! You're not getting away that easily. I shall make it my mission to get you tied next! You never know, Fraser does seem like my Simon."

I think back to the conversation earlier, in looks and style possibly, but his personality? Can't put my finger on it….. maybe that's the problem? Susie's right I need to loosen up and get some! Bring out the real woman inside and knock his socks off. Like Suse did to Simon. I mean the man wants her in his life, *permanently*, we've both dreamed of this for the past twenty years. I try and put relationships out of my mind and start to do a little festive mingling. I bump into Bina, carrying a sleepy Alfie towards the stairs.

"Can you believe this bubba, he'd sleep through a hurricane, I'll just take him up, I'll be down in a min Pen."

I head towards the large kitchen diner, now appearing quite small with at least twenty people's arms stretching this way and that, for plates, bowls, dips, salads, curries, lasagne, cold meats and fish, all covering a huge pine table.

"Ah, I am seeing the beautiful Penelope, push your way through my girl, you don't get anything in life standing on the side-lines." Bina's ever philosophical, dad.

"Hi, Mr. Khan, this is a fantastic spread, you must have had the day off work to get all this ready." I say tongue firmly in cheek, knowing this man never has a day off.

"Shame on you girl, religion and death are my only reasons

for time off work."

"You big fibber, Ash Kahn! Take no notice Penny love, I had him away for a fortnight in the South of France in July, he told his friends he was checking a possible new line of stock!" Bina's mum appears with a large plate of food in one hand and her grandchild Cosima clutching the other.

Mr Khan puts his finger quickly to his lips, tilting his head towards the munching crowd, then grins. "She's right, we all do it you know. Vijay who owns, 'Star of Bollywood' had three weeks in the Canaries saying he was head hunting a new chef. But to answer your question Penelope, no I didn't produce this wonderful food. Bina and her mum had most of it done by Saturday and we men think we're the ones in control and in charge here. Never!" He hugs Bina's mum, then disappears into the crowd chuckling.

Paula couldn't make it tonight, working late and Morry and Roger are at a big restaurant do with some arty pals in the city. I chat to as many members of the Khan clan I can remember the names of and a couple I can't. It's a warm and convivial night, but I keep looking over towards Suse and Simon. He's gazing at her lovingly, listening intently, her conversation becoming brightly animated. He laughs with her, every now and then leaning in close, or just touching her hand gently as they talk to others, as if reassuring her whoever is in the room, she is the only person that matters.

Oh, to feel *that* special, to feel *that* wanted. To think I may get the chance to feel those things with Fraser....Oh wow! Right, that is me well and truly hyped up and positive for some real Christmas romance.

"You trying to escape from us already?" It was Denzel,

who'd caught me slipping my jacket on and trying to make some headway through the lounge. "Hey Bina, Penny's trying to leave, can I go with her, I'm outnumbered, I'm the only Irish ginger."

"That's fine by me, we've never been racist here, I quite like being married to a minority." Bina looks at Denzel, trying to keep a straight face.

"Think of yourself as my, bit of red instead of bit of rough." He playfully makes a grab for her saying.

"That's all I am to you Bina Khan, you only married me for my looks and child producing loins I know you." She tries to cover his mouth quickly, giggling.

"You two were made for each other and you know it. Have a fantastic Christmas in Ireland, well I know you will." I hug them both and rush to my car as the cold air whips through my flimsy jacket.

"You have a good 'un too Penny. Hope you get *all* you want this Christmas, we'll be back on the twenty-seventh, so don't forget to ring us, we'll want to know absolutely *everything*".

I grin and wave, as I drive off into the night. Here's hoping I have some, 'absolutely everything' to tell them by then.

By Thursday we'd had a fluttering of snow, it was beautiful to wake up to. As I opened the curtains, I noticed the old cherry tree in my little garden had a line of snow on each branch, the bird feeders which I'd topped up at the weekend were a welcome find for a couple of Sparrows and a tubby Robin. I smiled, wrapping my arms round myself. I love Robins, they glow in the white of winter, how wonderful is Mother Nature, putting such cute little things out there to cheer us up on an otherwise cold and dank day.

I hadn't heard from the other cute thing that Mother Nature had put in front of me to brighten my winter. Fraser hadn't rung for two days. It had passed through my mind to ring him at work, but I didn't have a number, work or home.

I was a little worried that would smack of desperation. Or, worse, I would ring in the middle of an important case briefing. I could picture me trying to be casual and non-committal. 'Hi Fraser, Princess just ringing to check what time you'll be at my place Monday?' Silence, then…I'm sorry, this is……DS Grant, I'm afraid this line is only being used for incoming calls for witnesses. We have an ongoing serious crime case at present…' He'd get a ribbing from colleagues and I'd be the shade of pickled beetroot trying to justify my reason for ringing. Cringe.

I nipped out ten minutes early to scrape the frost off the car windows, then decided it would be hell getting a parking space, the shoppers would be out. I'd get my boots on and walk. As I came round the car, I glimpsed something under the wiper blade, a plastic bag on the ice-cold window.

Back inside, I reached in and pulled out a small piece of paper from the bag, unfolding it quickly.

'HI PRINCESS.
IT'S 1AM. I WAS IN THE AREA ON A NIGHT SHIFT. EVERYTHING IS QUIET SO I TOOK A MINUTE TO THINK OF YOU ALL SNUGGLED UP AND WARM IN THAT HOUSE OF YOURS. I'LL RING SOON.
YOUR PRINCE X

I held the note tightly to my chest………Oh wow, how romantic is that! I sighed and leant against the hall wall smiling from ear to ear. Wait till I show Morry this, I may even show Anna,

I'll definitely show Suse when I see her at Parker's for lunch. I didn't even feel the cold. I must have smiled broadly and said hello to everyone on my walk to work. Blimey! Robins, snow, a new man and romantic notes…....could this week *get* any better?

I rushed at Morry as he came towards me from the stairs along the corridor.

"Look at this Morry, isn't it just so romantic, a love note.... from Fraser." He flipped over the piece of paper quickly.

"Oooh! Let me look babe...oooooerr, I don't know sweets, bit creepy?" I stare at him in disbelief.

"*Creepy?* How can this be creepy, he's taken time to think of me and leave me a lovely hand-written note on my windscreen." Morry seeing that some reassurance is needed, quickly adds.

"Well, yes, it could be romantic but... the man has driven round at 1am in the morning, to your front door, known which car is yours. I'm thinking a couple of checks been made there? I don't know Pen, call me a cynical old fart, but surely, he must get the odd tea-break at sociable hours, with a minute to just ring you and *tell* you he's thinking about you. Have I put me Russell & Bromleys in it again, I have, haven't I?"

I felt a little deflated, but not for long, I waltzed away from Morry. He looked suitably guilty that he'd upset me. I saw Anna in the office on her own.

"Anna, what do you think of this, I got a romantic note left on my car windscreen, by Fraser, he was passing on a late shift." She quickly scans the note.

"Oh, that is romantic, he must have made a special trip, you're in a cul-de-sac, aren't you?" I look puzzled.

"Yes, but if they're doing their rounds they have to check all, burglars don't ignore a street because it's a cul-de-sac." I say indignantly, getting annoyed at everyone's negative response.

"Sorry Penny, I wasn't trying to imply anything, other than he must think a lot of you, making that *extra* effort." My turn to look guilty at snapping her head off.

"Sorry Anna, it's just, well, some people are a bit cynical about it all." Morry had long gone, skulked off back upstairs.

"Take no notice Penny, they're only jealous you've got yourself a gorgeous hunk." That thought had crossed my mind. I wouldn't be deterred and was like an excited child by the time Suse appeared in Parker's.

"Check this out Suse, what do you think. Fraser left it on my car windscreen in the early hours of this morning." She read it slowly then smiled.

"That's sweet babe. Simon leaves me little love notes, all over the place, wait till you find one under your pillow…or in your top drawer. Wonder why he just didn't post it through your letterbox though, you might have missed it, you don't take your car to work much do you?" Hadn't thought of that, but I thought quickly to give Suse an adequate response.

"He probably didn't want to risk the letter box making a noise and disturbing me, he'd assume I'd be scared, you know, me being on my own?" She agreed instantly.

"Of course, just being considerate, what a lovely bloke he's turning out to be babe, did you say he hadn't rung for a couple of days."

"I think he's just so busy, it's that time of year isn't it. Christmas, good for some but a nightmare for others."

I quickly changed the subject and chatted about her and Simon. She was staying with his family over New Year.

"We'll have to catch up in the week in between Pen, I need my quota of gossip and your sense of humour." I raise my eyebrows.

"You mean I'm not a redundant best-friend if you move in with the gorgeous Mr Forbes?" She leans back aghast.

"You've got to be kidding! Woman cannot live by man alone! Gorgeous though he is, we want to keep our own hobbies and interests. He's got his golf and buddies in the club and I've got………you."

"Well, first time I've been referred to as a hobby. You mean your interests are gossip and I'm the main source." She laughs.

"Yes, but you're my bestest friend first and that means more." I felt better after my silly maudlin thoughts the other evening. We chatted over a cuppa and a toastie, hugged and parted, she turned and said loudly. "Enjoy your Carol Concert tonight, give my love to the family and sing one for me." I made sure she'd walked a little way so I reply even louder.

"Would that be, 'God Rest Ye Merry Gentleman' or, 'Ding Dong Merrily On High'?" She retorted. "Well, it's not likely to be 'Silent Night' now, is it?"

Chapter 17

It was a really cold night. The snow was starting to freeze. I wrapped up warm, a thick scarf around my neck and my new woolly hat pulled well down over my ears.

I rushed up Crossgate Peth, to St. Margaret's church. It was mum and dads local and she always says they have a better carol service than the Cathedral. Not *quite* true, as obviously the Cathedral has, visiting dignitaries, four choirs, several hundred candles, festive floral arrangements, (none of which Paula had been asked to do which surprised her!) the Bishop of Durham and possibly ten times as many people!

St. Margaret's only dignitary is Colonel Peebles, owner of the V.C. a wooden leg and his over-weight Labrador called Monty.

The choir is four small boys and six members of the Neville's Cross Players. The festive floral arrangements are courtesy of, Mrs Brook and Mrs Peebles, members of the WI and both knocking on ninety. But of course, that is *exactly* why it probably *is* better. Every single person had been involved and arrives tonight engulfed in, not only the need to sing some traditional Christmas songs, but also a need to be together, to remember the community and the real spirit of Christmas, past, present and future.

I see my family gathered at the side of the little snow-covered church. As I gaze at the light streaming, magically through the stained-glass windows, I'm frozen to the spot and just for a split second I see my family differently.

No, nothing spiritual…..but all standing there in………full wedding attire.

Dad with my brothers, standing proudly in top hat and tails, maroon satin cravats and gold waistcoats. Molly with my sisters-in-law Jill and Kay in simple, classic maroon dresses. Mum in a cream suit, huge, feathered hat and maroon accessories. Nephews, Robert, Frankie and Jerome as pageboys and of course, Lily, Felicity and Kezia in layers of cream and gold with baskets of maroon roses…and there I am…the bride, in a beautiful jacket style dress in maroon velvet, down to my ankles, with just enough gap at the front to show the hand embroidered gold bodice with cream lace and satin layered skirt and by my side my groom……

"Penny, will you hurry up, we're freezing out here and mum wants a front row pew, she's got a thing for the new vicar!" Mum shoots Mike a look. "Michael! I said he has a lovely speaking voice which holds your attention that's all, shame on you, what will people think?" I'm pulled back well and truly from my dream and rush over to proffer hugs.

"Maybe you have the same effect on your class Mike, I bet there are a few girlies with your name on their pencil cases and a secret crush?" He grins broadly, but quickly pulls himself up on seeing Jill giving him, 'the look' from over the top of her glasses.

"He teaches science Penny, if I can remember rightly, we thought science teachers were far too clinical, nerdy and boffin-like. We decided Geography teachers were best, they'd always know where they were going and the very best route to get there." Her face smiling wickedly.

"Sadly, I was never that well informed to know that. I had a crush on my Maths teacher. I thought if I smiled and brought him enough apples, he might just forgive the fact that I was so useless at the subject and may just give me something resembling a pass, the grade sort, not the other!" We rushed out of the cold and into the church, our laughter echoing in the night air.

The vicar *was* rather nice actually, distinguished, but possibly a touch too old for me. Never really gone for the older man, maybe I should, worldly wise, experienced. Well, I wouldn't turn down Tom Jones if he offered, or Lewis Collins, or Paul McCartney and worryingly Alan Titchmarsh has a rogue-ish twinkle!

I suddenly realise I'm imagining getting up close and personal with some hunky older men and I'm in God's house. I quickly get my thoughts back on track and ask for forgiveness, after a few Hail Mary's under my breath I realise I'm not Catholic and mum is nudging me. She tuts and tells me in a very loud whisper to stop mumbling and listen, I suddenly feel fifteen, yet again.

I *am* listening though and as I gaze at the candles we begin to sing after the four small boys have reduced us to tears with, 'Away In A Manger'. Everyone belts out 'We Three Kings' and 'While Shepherds Watch'. I smile and think of Suse and Simon as we sing 'Silent Night', but then I start to think a little deeper.

The Vicar gives thanks, gives prayer and makes us consider our worth, poverty in the world and the plight of those less fortunate. I suddenly get a heightened feeling of how much my simple, easy life means to me, how lucky I am to live where I do, to have my family around me, to feel safe and loved. How precious is that.

We all look at each other and smile, I can only think that we all feel the same as we almost put paid to the Vicar's roof fund by blowing a few tiles off with our singing. The whole church suddenly crescendos in the final chorus of 'Ding Dong Merrily on High' and everyone appears to be engulfed with emotion, wishing each other a very 'Merry Christmas' with robust handshakes, hugs and cheery waves.

This of course gives mum the excuse to gush enthusiastically at the Vicar, as he stands at the doors wishing everyone well. Dad looks on in amusement as my mother's voice takes on a cross between the Queen and Hyacinth Bucket.

"Oh Vicar, that was so moving, if there is anything our ladies can do to help the plight of the homeless? We do have a few jars of Rhubarb and Ginger left over from the Autumn market?"
The Vicar smiles politely, obviously used to such offers, however strange. "You are very kind, thank you, but maybe a few small, knitted vests for the African babies, that would be a great help at present. Everyone knows me as Reverend Beadnell but do call me Giles." For a moment my mother blushes, we are trying our best not to ruin her moment, but she doesn't seem to need our help.

"Oh, Vicar, Rev...Bead....erm.... Giles, yes vests, yes..... I myself am a great knit. I mean the ladies......we're all.... very big.... big knitters!"

I hope the poor Vicar hadn't misheard my mum, as she grabbed dad's arm and hid herself behind him rushing down the path. I heard her saying under her breath to my dad, who by now was obviously dying to laugh, but wouldn't dare for fear of having Christmas cancelled.

"Geoffrey, I will never be able to look the Reverend Beadnall in the face again." Dad tried, not very well, to placate her.

"Don't worry love he's a man of the cloth, he'll have come into contact with many a, 'big knit knitter' in his time. More four-ply Vicar?" She glares at him. "Oh, Geoffrey!"

We grabbed the children's hands and walked behind them trying not to giggle and set a bad example to the youngsters, but it was so difficult when we were all together. It's as if twenty odd years vanish and we all revert back to childhood.

Needless to say, after two hours at mum and dad's, three cups of tea, two mince-pies, endless jokes, jibes, stories and quips, I walked home with an aching jaw.

It was ten-thirty when I stepped back into my cosy little house. I put the radio on to keep the festive theme going, clicked on the kettle, gave Ferdy his supper and sang along with Bing, warbling the classic, 'White Christmas'. I was just trying to hit the high notes and do some, 'Walking in the Air' with the ever-cute Aled when the phone rang. It'll be mum, checking I'm home safely.

"Hey! Princess, how's your week going, are you missing me like crazy?" My heart lurched, is he fishing for compliments, conceited, or just worried? Stay calm, play it cool, be like Suse.

"Well, you haven't rung for over two days, of course I'm missing you." (Oh, very cool! No smacking of desperation there then.)

"Princess, there is nothing I would have loved better than to have spent the last couple of days whispering sweet nothings to you. But I had three TWOCs, two domestics, several drunken assaults and a suicide to deal with, difficult to find time for romance in that agenda, babe?"

He was so matter of fact about it all. Assaults, suicide, romance, all in the same sentence, it really was another world, maybe Morry *was* right.

"Oh my God, I can't comprehend what you have to deal with on a daily basis, most people see no more than one dead body in a life-time, it must be so difficult getting the images out of your head."

"You get used to it Princess, think of the Doctors and nurses, who struggle to keep them from being a dead body. Think of the morticians that have to put the 'jumpers' back together for ID, think of the relatives left behind. Now you see why, in our job we want to enjoy our leisure time, we need to live the contrast."

I suddenly felt the urge to *be* that contrast.

"Look, no pressure, but our office party is tomorrow, after work, only round the corner from you. Why don't you pop in?"

I hadn't even had a proper date with him and here I was inviting him to the office Christmas party, certainly would be a contrast!

"I know where the office is Princess, I'm a friend of Tiffs remember. I'm working days this week, but if I don't get tied up with paperwork, or overtime I'll try and get there, can't promise anything. Are you willing to share me with all those beautiful women, or is it a case of, look but don't touch?"

I thought about Anna, June, Eunice on reception, Prue and Beryl in the typing pool, not blowing my own Penny whistle, but there wasn't a lot of competition.

"I think you may find quality rather than quantity would be the order of the day in our offices." He laughed, fortunately it appeared with me, not at me.

"I like a confident woman, Princess. You make sure you keep all those blokes at bay. You are one woman I'd really like to take.....out and about." For one awful moment I thought he may use the classic comedy Police line, 'take down my particulars'. I'd die of shame.

"Look Princess, like I said I'll see what I can do, if I don't turn up, I'll try and ring before Monday okay, stay sexy babe. Bye." He'd gone and I was on cloud nine, left with my Mona Lisa smile, going over every word and sentence, again and again. Tired but content I slid into bed, drifting off to sleep I picture him walking through the office door, looking gorgeous, every head turning, but he only has eyes for me......'all the better to see you with, Princess'.

Er, haven't I heard that somewhere before?

Morry had done his best to get round me Friday morning, after knocking my confidence over Fraser yesterday. After his apology and a little box containing four caramel truffles appeared, I told him about last night.

"He's coming here, to the office party, oh babe, that is fantastic. I hope you've brought the mother of all party dresses for tonight then, you've got to positively shine girl, think what you were wearing when he first saw you, how are you going to top that?" In one sentence Morry had almost demoralised me enough to send me running for home. How *could* I top that creation, he had to see I wasn't a one trick Penny. He had to see I looked *that* gorgeous all the time.......but how?

"Oh Morry, I just brought my little black dress, you know the one that's pretty, comfortable and I wear it every year. I'm never usually here to impress, I was so busy picturing him, I didn't bother to picture myself." I slumped over my desk in defeat.

Everyone just wore their little black dresses, even June. There was only Dot who teamed hers with a home knit festive cardi, with bauble bell buttons and Christmas tree earrings. We all wore the same, every year.

"Don't worry, leave it to me babe, I'll nip out at lunchtime, I'll get a little something to zizz it up, you leave it to your Uncle Morry."

"Oh God, Morry are you sure?" He grins like the proverbial Cheshire.

"Absolutely lovey, I'll give my Rojere a quick ring, he'll keep me right, what shoes have you brought?" I rummage through my bag, noticing Mr Jenkins making his way towards the office, I show Morry quickly. "Black suede, ankle strap."

He rushes towards the door clutching a couple of pieces of prop paper to his chest, as he passes Mr Jenkins.

"Right you are, Miss Wiseman, I'll process that information and have the finished results to you by *three*, is that okay?" I nod, trying to look convincingly efficient.

"Thank you, Mr Wild, look forward to merging our results." Mr Jenkins watches Morry leave the room, then clears his throat.

"As you lovely ladies will be aware the office Christmas party is this evening. I have obtained several boxes of red, white, Asti, some soft drinks and two crates of ale of some description. The caterers are coming in with some comestibles at four-thirty and I feel we should close shop at four to allow, changing of clothing and the beautifying of faces. Is that agreeable to all?"

We smile politely and chorus. "Yes Mr Jenkins, thank you."

His eyes then twinkle as he gazes round at us.....'ladies'.

"Of course, you are all beautiful already and I look forward to some Christmas spirit, I have my mistletoe at the ready and hope to pop a few corks....eh Juney?" As he winks suggestively in her direction, poor June almost dives under her desk with a look of sheer panic.

I think she'll be spending this afternoon phoning poor Barry, persuading him to leave *his* office early. We give her some helpful hints and tips on what she could promise Barry if she wanted him here on time. The expression on her face told me that it was a tough decision between Mr Jenkins and his wayward corks and the promise of wanton lust with Barry. I must say, I wouldn't want that choice.

Now corks and mistletoe with Charlie, or wanton lust with Fraser...another tough one...try both, *then* choose? Mmmm...

My concentration was a little easily led to say the least today. The bosses knew there'd be an obvious lack of focus on party day, they were pretty good about it all. There was only Mr Preece who believed it was a waste of wages. He felt that it should be a quick drink, preferably somewhere else on the last day before breaking up for Christmas. This year, with the twenty-fifth falling on Wednesday means we are here on Christmas Eve, cheers Ebenezer.

I stared at my watch it was ten past three, no sign of Morry. Just as I'd resigned myself to looking like an office bookend, I heard gasps and panting, feet clattering up the stairs, he made a meal of almost collapsing in the doorway.

"I tell you what, you *owe* me girl. I have run myself ragged.

I have been round the lot. I could accessorise all the Spice Girls and still have enough left for Lisa Stansfield and Celine Dion!" He piles several bags onto my desk and grabs a cup of tea from the tray. "How much have you spent Morry? Just a nice necklace would have done."

"Sorry, nothing personal babe but it'll take more than just a necklace to make you look like Audrey Hepburn in that dress." Then he stops himself, realising the cutting remarks should be saved for after the event, not before it.

"No, honestly babe, just hang fire, see what lovely bits and pieces there are first. You can keep the stuff you use, I'll take the rest home for pressies, with seven nieces to buy for they're bound to come in handy, it's not a problem." I give him a hug then we start to go through the bags.

By five fifteen we're all ready. I can't quite believe how clever Morry has been. He's almost as resourceful with clothes, hair and accessories as Susie, now I'll have someone else I can call on when she becomes, Mrs Forbes of St John's Chapel.

"Well, I'm well chuffed babe, you look a proper little Christmas cracker Pen, not too much sparkle, but just enough oomph to turn heads." He looks truly proud of his efforts as he steers me towards the mirror in the rest room.

"Oh, wow, Morry…thank you…… You've got it so right, sets off the dress perfectly." I stare at the classy looking woman in front of me. The dress had been plain, long sleeved with a scoop neck and a slight swish to the above knee skirt. Morry had removed my bra straps, pulled down the neck across my shoulders then placed round the same, a narrow caramel shade, faux-fur tippet, fastened with a gorgeous ruby and emerald clip at the front, so that it looked like an off the shoulder fur collared dress. Then added beautiful, ruby glass, choker necklace and earrings. He'd found some fantastic tights with thin threads of gold in the pattern. For my shoes he'd got tiny sparkling gem hair clips, pinning one either side of my ankle straps. He then put the leftover clips in my hair. Just those little sparkles catching the light and catching attention made so much difference. I felt fantastic.

Maybe, Fraser would have the same feelings, if he walks into the room, hope so. The party was well and truly in full swing by six-thirty. Dot and Beryl were doing a form of Lindy Hop and Jitterbug to every record, no matter what the era, it was fun to watch though and they were having a wail of a time.

George and Toby were the drunks for the evening, having bet each other a tenner who would be the first to down a pint glass of half red and ale, they were now onto the best of three. George had already been sick in Prue's prized Aspidistra so she wasn't best pleased. Eunice ordered George a taxi and Toby several black coffees.

We pushed back the last couple of desks in the boardroom, the bosses had said we could use it this year, although I think Mr Harkass was regretting the decision after seeing George's state. We assured him no one else was anywhere near that inebriated and that George was like that every Friday night, not just Christmas! We breathed a sigh of relief when he actually smiled and clicked on the huge boardroom sound system saying.

"Right, everyone, get on with your party, that's what you're here for. I'm off home now for a decent meal, not curled up sandwiches and a bowl of cheesy what-sits, see you Monday, *everyone* nine o'clock sharp."

I kept looking at my watch, even with overtime I really was hoping Fraser would make it tonight. I tried to keep my mind occupied. I resisted the temptation to dance. I didn't want to look all lank-haired and rosy faced, I wanted to keep myself looking just right, in case he walked through that door.

"Not like you Penny, you're usually ring-leader on the dance floor." It was Danny our post-boy-cum-general-assistant. He was young, fun and loved dancing.

"Just waiting for the right tune Dan, I'll be up there soon don't you worry. Think I'll just have another sarnie, you keep that dance floor warm for me."

Morry had done his best to convince Tiffany that her, 'fruity' photos were safe with him and that no one else knew, so she'd decided to make an appearance. They were both dancing and giggling away, but I couldn't help but notice that for the first party ever, she was wearing trousers. A safety measure perhaps? They of course were beautifully cut over her long willowy legs, with an expensive jewelled belt fastened loosely over her tiny hips. She must live on cigarettes and coffee....meow!

I felt instant guilt for considering food and put down the sandwich I was about to consume hungrily, my eye caught a tall, dark suited male, through the frosted glass in the corridor. My heart lurched. The door opened slowly and there stood....... Barry? He had a big grin on his face, which got even wider as he caught sight of June. She must have promised him the works to get him here so early to save his damsel.

"June! Barry's here, are you ready to continue your party at home?" June rushed across the room, amazingly still pursued by Mr Jenkins clutching his mistletoe, who surprisingly didn't seem to let the sight of Barry put him off the chase.

He bustled up beside Barry keeping June out of his reach.

"May I just say Mr Oliver, you are a *very* lucky man. This woman is an *asset* to this company, her efficiency knows no bounds. She is *firm*....but fair. Is she *firm* with you Mr Oliver, at home, you know.......*very* firm?" He says with a rogue-ish look in his eye. He has obviously been on the Asti well before four, risking the unknown wrath of Barry Oliver and a possible punch on the nose. Barry stays calm.

"My wife maybe a demon in the office Mr Jenkins, but she is an angel at home. She is my world. She is the one woman I respect and love with all my heart....so if you *don't* mind, I'd like to take her home now."

He smiles gallantly at June, who is by now gazing at Barry, seeing him in a totally different light.

"Oh, Barry..... I never knew, I mean....I feel so....please, just take me home... now...just.... *take* me!" With a sense of urgency, she shouts a quick goodbye grabs Barry's hand, her bag, coat, a bottle of wine from a nearby table and they're off.

"Oooh, err! Looks like June's finally found true passion at last...our Barry's going to be in for a shock. That grin is going to be stamped all over his face till New Year now!" Said Morry giggling. I tried to laugh along and felt well pleased for June. But I couldn't help feeling a little disappointed that it hadn't been Fraser walking in, to slight the demons and claim *his* damsel.

I really tried my best to mingle, but it just wasn't happening. I was annoyed at myself, putting the evening on hold in case *he* arrived. Anna, Morry and several others tried to inveigle me in to party mode.

"Come and have a dance, Penny. If Fraser does turn up, I'm sure he'd rather see you enjoying yourself not standing there like a wallflower." Anna shouts gleefully, as she bounces round the dance floor, squeezed between Toby and Dan. Toby, it appears, enjoying every minute of being pressed against her ample bosom.

"Come on party-pooper it's the Christmas mega-mix, get those sparkly shoes on this dance floor and shake it sister. I won't take no for an answer!" Morry grabs my hand and twirls me round.

It's nearly nine, the party will soon be over I may aswell make the most of the time left, what the heck, it's Christmas, I'll see Fraser Monday. He made no promises for tonight. The temptation of the music and fun is too much, I dance solidly for the last fifteen minutes. We are all shattered, but everyone is full of festive spirit and has made the most of the evening and of course the free plonk.

Dan makes a grab for me just before the lights go on.

"Mind if I steal a little Christmas kiss Penny?" I'm passed caring and fling my arms round his neck. He's actually a really good kisser, but I don't remember it being quite this passionate last year. I'm enjoying the moment. So is he, possibly a little too much, well until the charming Toby shouts over.

"Oi, put her down Danny, she's old enough to be your mother!" I quickly push Dan away feeling totally mortified at such a suggestion, but Dan surprisingly springs to my defence.

"You're only jealous Toby. Anyway, *that* kiss beats some dodgy snog with a seventeen-year-old any day....I believe that's the age of *your* current isn't it, fret face?"

I walk away feeling quite proud of my kissing ability, leaving Dan and Toby squaring up for a, boys squabble, two minutes later they're best mates again, as we all start tidying up and

sharing out the leftover food and drink. I was just hunting through by
bag for my little phone book to call a taxi, when Morry runs back up the stairs squealing like a pig in potato peelings.

"Pen, babe, I think you've got a lift home, come over here, quick, quick……. Look!" Morry clicks off the office light at the front of the building and rushes me towards the window. I look down, there standing next to his BMW is……. Fraser. I have butterflies on butterflies.

"Morry, he's here, why didn't he come in, I can't believe he's *here*." Morry is already dabbing my over shiny brow with a tissue and tidying my hair.

"Never mind analysing the finer details girl, just saunter out slowly and wow the bugger!" I could see Tiffany rushing over and hugging him, she looked back towards the office, I hope she knew I was still here. I'd better hurry he might think I've gone home already. I grab my bag, Morry drapes my coat over my shoulders, very fifties movie star, and I carefully descend the stairs then out of the front door. He sees me, as he looks over Tiffany's shoulder, I'm gazing around pretending I'm expecting a taxi.

"Princess! Sorry Tiffany, bye. Have a good Christmas if I don't see you before…Princess, Princess!" He's now rushing over trying to attract my attention. Morry winks at me and whispers loudly as he disappears up the road.

"Give a convincing performance, you've got him hooked!"

Like Susie gets her men perhaps, hook, line and sinker?

"Fraser, sorry, I didn't see you there, I ordered a taxi, I think someone's taken it. You didn't make the party, it was fantastic, are you just passing, or still on duty?"

He shuffles his feet and for the first time I see him look a little awkward and unsure of himself.

"Sorry I couldn't make it Princess, I've just finished. I just drove round on the off chance the party was still going on and that you'd still be here. Look, can I give you a lift home?"

This was a dilemma, if he drives me home, he'll expect to come in…for coffee? If I say no, will he be insulted, will he cancel my…*our*, evening at 'The Straw House'? If I say yes, I haven't tidied away my trashy books and magazines, there's a pile of ironing and….I didn't put on matching underwear! What's that got to do with it? I'm not going there….*he's* not going there, I scold myself!

"Er, I don't know, I should wait for my taxi, I'll have wasted his time…." He tilts my chin up towards his face.

"I wouldn't do you for wasting a taxi drivers time, it's not an offence Princess. Giving you a lift home is the least I can do, for letting you down by not turning up at your party. Come on, you'll be home in five minutes, you'll be standing in the cold that long if you wait for your taxi…lighten up…...I'm a police officer, not Neville Heath." Wish he hadn't said that. I knew exactly who Neville Heath was. My dad had a real interest in classic murder cases and when I'd casually flicked through one of his books, the pages dropped open at Heath who was a particularly sadistic killer. Not the best image to have in your mind as you get into an unfamiliar car. Having said that who is to say the taxi driver would be any safer?

As I sink into the luxurious, soft leather of the passenger seat, he checks my seat belt leaning a little closer than he has to, then looks at me, smiles and kisses me.

"I've been dying to do that ever since I saw you appear at

the door, you look so sexy in that black dress and fur drives me wild, you really know how to push a guy's buttons." He winks and playfully pretends to mistake my knee for the gearstick.

"Bet you didn't see that one coming hey Princess, corny or what?" I couldn't help but laugh and relaxed as he clicked on a tape. It was soul classics, real luurrve songs, Barry White, Roberta Flack, Alexander O'Neal, Marvin Gaye....

Songs for a very sophisticated seduction, I felt flattered, he made so much effort to make me feel like a real woman. But, I am a real woman, this is how I *should* be treated.

He took the 'scenic' route, telling me about the new CCTV systems, pointing out a doorway where a section 18 had taken place. Then gave he me a cheeky look saying.

"I won't press charges if you want to commit a bit of distraction crime on me?" I looked down, trying to be coy and flirty.

"Yes, well as long as it doesn't involve taking down my particulars......" Damn and blast!.......I can't believe I said that....why did say that?!

He looks at me obviously desperate to laugh very loudly.

"Princess! I can't believe you just said that! You little minx!" I blush, what possessed me?

He pulls up outside my door. I do feel I want to run from the car as quickly as possible and hide, but I think that's the last thing I'll be able to do. I see the curtain twitch two doors down, well at least they can see number twelve is finally managing to pull, so they can put the rumours to bed that, I'm a cat loving spinster with only gardening, DIY and car-booting for hobbies. If I can keep Fraser chatting long enough, we may be able to steam the windows a little, give the cul-de-sac it's first 'sex in a BMW' scandal. Me, sex and scandal, not words that readily come to mind…....but Fraser seems to think I'm hot stuff so who knows! I unclick my seat belt and turn my body slightly towards him, my coat falling from my shoulder.

"Sorry for my embarrassing remark earlier, sounded like some naff police sit-com. I'm not very good at the, 'flirtatious' stuff, as you can see." He has already undone his seat belt and moves closer, bringing his knee up against the gear stick, reaches for the fur tippet, stroking it gently, holding my gaze.

"You are being very modest Princess, that's what I find so attractive about you. I love a woman that is unaware of her, sexual power. What fur does to a man's senses, the beautiful jewellery draws my eyes to your slender neck and downwards."

Hell fire, that is *another* big hug I owe Morry! I could feel my breathing almost stop, as he leaned closer, his potent after-shave once again almost overpowering me. His lips gently sweep across mine, then slowly across my cheek and down towards my neck. I could feel his breath, then his mouth on my skin, kissing me gently. I shuddered, sighed and closed my eyes as his hand cupped the back of my head and his mouth seized mine. I felt as if I would melt slowly and fall through the soft leather seats. As his kiss got more passionate, I vaguely considered what the neighbours may be thinking, but then it was a case of..... Sod it, this is truly worth every ounce of gossip!

His breathing became heavier as his hands moved slowly from my waist, up to my breast, he gently circled the area as if instinctively knowing exactly where to touch, to make me weaken. (I don't think that manoeuvre is in the police manual.) Oh heavens! It really had been so long. Nothing had felt this good since Charlie had taken me in his arms nearly three years ago. I'd let him show me what passion should be, I gave myself up to him, totally and it was sheer ecstasy. But, I slowly pulled myself out of the realms of the past and came to my senses. I felt Fraser's hand above my knee and moving up my thigh…...His grip was firm and his breathing loud. I couldn't… I just couldn't……. not here….I drew my mouth away from his, almost dizzy with the feelings rushing through me.

"Look, erm, I should go…I'd offer you a coffee…but…"

He winks then slaps my thigh gently.

"I know, you'll want to have your wicked way with me on the hall carpet, you'll be putting that chain on the door before I can even get my coat off…. You little sex kitten you!"

My nose visibly wrinkles. "Well, no…actually no, I should..." He grins and runs his fingers down the side of my face.

"Don't worry, just a little tease Princess. I'd like to get to know you a little better before divulging *my* bedroom secrets, but from what I've seen and *felt* so far, I think we'd be pretty compatible on that score." I feel myself blushing again and need to explain as his eyebrows raise.

"Hope you didn't get the wrong idea. I'm pretty old fashioned really. I do want all the love and romance bit too, I mean…"

He reaches for the glove box and begins to rummage through his tapes.

"Don't you worry yourself Princess, patience is a virtue, play this and think of me and Monday. I couldn't come in for coffee even if I wanted to, I have to get home."

I turn, looking puzzled. "It's only quarter to ten, I thought you said you were on days?" He shuffles back into his seat, kissing me quickly on the cheek and pulling his seat belt quickly across his chest.

"Er...I promised I'd give my old mum a ring, she's not been too well recently, you know how it is. Just a call from her son, says it's the only medicine she needs."

I feel guilty at having a slight pang of suspicion there.

"Oh, sorry, I hope she gets better soon, especially with Christmas round the corner."

"Yeah, thanks Princess, knew you'd understand, you've got that sweet, caring nature. Bet you'd make a great mum, have you ever thought of having kids?" Woah! Another out of the blue, low baller. Where the hell did that come from?

"Well, yes....er, of course, I've thought about it, would be wonderful...but....." He cuts in quickly.

"There's a lot of, 'buts' in your life Princess, maybe it's time you kicked some! I know when a woman gets to your age, you're either scared of commitment, or just love putting in the practice." He smiles wryly. "I hope it's a good measure of both, then I'll be a very lucky man. Must love you and leave you Princess... look after that sexy little bod for me till Monday."

With that, he turns the engine on, leans across and opens the door for me, he skims his mouth quickly over mine, he's already checking the rear-view mirror. As I feel obliged to get out from the car he adds.

"You're a good kisser though babe, very sensual mouth......" And with that, he winks again and drives away. Leaving me with feelings so confusing, I sit in the darkened lounge in total silence for over twenty minutes, going over and over the last hour, in minute detail.

Eventually with poor Ferdy demanding to be fed and my

need for a strong cuppa, I curl myself up in my favourite chair and click on the tape he gave me. Soul classics again, sexy, driven, passionate songs of undying love, unrequited love and deep and uncontrollable love. Does this make him romantic? He didn't push me any further, then again, he implied that's obviously what I wanted him to do. Does that make him think he is irresistible…....or does that make him think I'm sexy enough for him to want to?

I still can't put my finger on it……. although *he* had a damn good try! What is it about this man? He's gorgeous, good job, house, car, loaded, sexy, funny and he's taking me to out to dinner at, 'The Straw House', isn't that enough?

He turned up tonight, after a long shift at work, just to drive me home, to see me for half an hour…....if that's not romantic, what is? I need to ring Suse quick, get her to give me a good shake and make me see the wood, not the endless forest of trees. Susie's voice trills sweetly out of her answer machine. I hate that thing but needs must. "Suse… sorry, I know you're probably out with Simon. If you're not too busy tomorrow, can you pop in for a quick chat. I'm in a bit of a dilemma. It's nothing serious…. don't worry…see you tomorrow… hopefully. Sorry I'm prattling now. Bye Suse…Oh, hope you had a good…whatever… bugger. .sorry...bye!"

It's a *just* tape recorder, why does it reduce me to a waffling wreck? Now I've probably ended up worrying her. What is wrong with me? Thirty-seven years old, being pursued by a man most women would climb barb-wired for. He not only thinks I'm sexy, I'm his Princess, he also thinks I'm a great kisser. I catch sight of myself in the mirror and run my hand across my fur tippet. Wonder if they make underwear in this? I sigh complete my night time routine on auto-pilot and head for my bed.

All the better to…and as I drift off into dreamland, a huge, fairground carousel appears, my big Magic Roundabout! Which one of you adorable men are going to jump up and squeeze up behind me on this carousel horse. Fraser?…Charlie?...Jason?… Alan Titchmarsh!!…*Aled* Jones!!….Tom Jones!!…Davy Jones?! 'Here they come, walking down the street, get the funniest looks from everyone we meet…hey hey we're the Hunkies!?!'

I *really* do need to speak to a dream analyst!

Chapter 18

I could hear the frantic ringing of the doorbell. I'd barely slept a wink so was wide-awake enough to run and open the door, before Susie took it off its hinges.

"Pen, are you alright babe? What's the bastard done! I'll string him up by his truncheon if he's hurt you!" Susie pushes her way in, grabbing me in a bear-hug, pulling me protectively into her soft Angora sweater.

"Sorry Suse, I knew this would happen. He isn't a bastard and he hasn't hurt me, honest. Well not yet anyway." I prise myself from her vice-like hold.

"I didn't mean to worry you, damn answer machine. I'll put the kettle on, I think we could both do with a strong cuppa."

Suse sighed with obvious relief.

"Thank God babe…I just couldn't get the jist of your call, you seemed worried, wasn't sure if something had happened to you. Thought you'd maybe succumbed to his charms and had given in to wanton lust on your rose covered rug and now regretting it!…. Oh, sorry, you don't do that sort of thing do you?" I catch her wry smile. I raise my eyebrow in submission and look towards the ceiling, before I can think of a witty reply she adds.

"Ooo! Except that waiter fella you told me about, thingy, whats his name? In York, at the hen-do, but that was yonks ago and he doesn't count though, in a hotel room and you were drunk?"

"Yes, thanks Suse, he was an assistant chef, called Charlie actually and I wasn't *that* drunk. Some of us just aren't confident sexually. We may well have it…but haven't a clue how to use it. You don't know how lucky you are, the way you attract men, the way you look, the things you do to keep them enthralled." She listens carefully, watching me feeding Ferdy, making the tea and putting a couple of rounds of toast on.

"Is that what this is all about Pen? Do you truly believe I'm any different to you? Why on earth do you think I drag men home, if I think they tick all the right boxes. I've no more confidence than you have. It's just I don't have your insight, or your patience. I've always been so scared I'd miss my…. Mr Right. I end up trying, Mr Possible, Mr Maybe and sadly, Mr Highly-Unlikely, for fear if I didn't go through them all, my perfect guy would slip through the net and I'd end up with a Mr Make-Do, or worse…a…..*Ms* Parks, spinster of the parish!"

We sit down in silence, then Suse smiles.

"Come on then pass that toast and tell me all about your dilemma, though why you think you need my advice. On fashion maybe…….but men?!" I lean back into my chair, take a couple of bites of toast, a sip of tea, sigh loudly, then tell her…….. *everything*. I can't look her in the eye when telling her about the, 'almost' intimate details, so by the time I do look up she has a strange, bemused expression on her face.

"And your dilemma *is*…?" She asks looking exasperated.

"Well, does he think I'm that sort of ….I mean was he testing me….or would he actually have …..you know…..if I'd let him."

She sickeningly picks up a fourth slice of toast, while I guiltily toy with my second.

"Think you've answered that question yourself Pen, it's quite obvious. Fraser definitely thinks you're sexy, he definitely would if he could. He's probably used to charming the pants off most of his conquests. But you Pen, you've shown him you're worth just that bit more. He's covered himself, by convincing you, that *you* would have, if he'd continued his touchy-feely charm offensive. But you left him wanting, no doubt about that. Why do you think he rushed off so quickly, he'll of been well…frustrated…had to get home to…..you know." I look shocked.

"He said he had to ring his old mother, she's not well." Susie visibly chuckles.

"Come on babe, I've heard every excuse…it's an original I'll grant him that…. Usually, it's…I must get to a cashpoint, I must get home and finish some work, I've got a deadline to meet…... Fraser was clearly wanting to finish what you had so obviously started." I wince at the sudden realisation.

"You mean…….Oh! You don't mean…ewwww!"

"Think of it as a compliment babe, you so obviously turn the man on. He didn't put any pressure on you, he backed off, he's giving you time to make up your own mind. Come on Pen, what do you want from the bloke? He's only human and a damn nice human at that." She disappeared into the kitchen, to pour another couple of cups out, leaving me to ponder my…. 'Sexiness'?

"So, what do I do on Monday, at 'The Straw House'. Do I just play it cool, or should I be encouraging and flirty?" I look to Susie for some clues.

"Pen, only you know what you want from a bloke, how you feel when with him. Just enjoy the evening. It is such a special place, it is really romantic, classy and stylish. The evening will just wash over you. The handsome date, the wonderful food, the beautiful ambience and the conversation."

She sighs loudly, leaning back. "My first evening there with Simon was just so fantastic. Little table for two. Simon's brother is just the best chef ever, even when the conversation isn't flirty the food seduces you. You can't fail to just have a really memorable evening, stop worrying so much, just go with the flow babe." She sinks into her chair, obviously lost in her own experience.

"You're so good for me, you just put things into perspective. I don't know why I'm worrying so much. Fraser just seems that bit more special than other blokes. I don't know why I'm so nervous about impressing him so much…silly isn't it? But what about after the meal, you know later, when he drives me home?" Susie looks at me sideways with that little twinkle in her eye.

"Depends how frustrated *you* are by then babe. It might be you throwing caution to the wind along with your frillies, if he ticks all *your* boxes. If he's anything like Simon, you wouldn't want to leave him sitting there checking his own rear-view mirror that's for sure!" I burst out laughing, Suse follows.

"I can't believe you said that." Suse points at me, hardly able to get the words out.

"Taking down your particulars… *no one* can believe you said *that*!" I wince as I re-live the moment.

"That is so what I needed Suse, a real good laugh. I feel so much more relaxed now. Sorry I dragged you over here, I don't know why I panic so much."

"Pen, like I said, we're more alike than we let on, nobody wants to lose the possibility of true love, it is out there……

somewhere, for all of us. We all just have different ways of finding our nugget of gold. I'm more your bite every stone, grit and pebble in the pan until it feels right, I eventually stop to check if it has any glints of value. You're the one that patiently sifts out all the crap, picks out the shiny piece, but is never convinced of it's worth till you've bitten it, analysed it and got an expert opinion. We'll both get there in the end." She smiles reassuringly.

"Just hope it's in time to do a bit of melting down to produce some little gems of our own. Don't you just long for a family Suse?" We both gaze at the Christmas tree as if lost in our own worlds. Then Susie sighs loudly.

"Oh Penny, wouldn't it just be the icing on the cake, wedding cake hopefully. Simon would love children, as soon as…well if we can that is…oh yes, definitely." We both sigh in unison.

"Look I'll have to get away Pen, Simon is over at mine, we're going out for lunch, doing a bit of…. Christmas Shopping." She smiles knowingly. I give her a knowing look.

"In and out of a few jewellers perhaps?" Her smile grows.

"Maybe, who knows."

I spent the rest of Saturday in a pre-Christmas clean and tidy round. Stopping every now and then to consider a word, or a look from last night. Why do I insist on analysing it so closely? Susie was right, it was about time I threw caution to the wind and just enjoyed the moment.

I kept myself fully occupied, on Sunday too. Had a long phone call with Molly, who after twenty questions thought Fraser sounded like, 'perfect husband material.' As a Police officer he would be law abiding, honest with high standards, values and morals, preaching the doctrine of law and order, not unlike her Donald she felt. Somehow, I couldn't quite see Donald in an Armani suit, wafting of Polo aftershave, driving a BMW and rushing home from church after gazing at Molly in the front pew. Then claiming to have to get back to put in an emergency order of communion wafers. (Knowing those two, behind the pulpit would be their next port of call!)

Molly gushed about how wonderful it would be if I got married and pregnant all in the same year, maybe 1998 is going to be *my* year, she tells me enthusiastically. Maybe she should be putting that one to Fraser, not me.

Or, maybe I'll be doing the same as the last year, counting down to New Year with Ferdy and a cup of Horlicks, feeling as if another year has passed me by and I don't know what the hell the next one will hold....and of course, the resolutions. Go on a diet, find a better job and make more effort to get out more, same old, same old...?

I spent the evening rooting through drawers and wardrobe. I had to find another 'perfect' outfit for tomorrow night. Being positive now, third time lucky...I was going to knock that man's socks off, make his eyes come out on stalks.

After trying on almost a dozen combinations of possible... sexy and seductive, I gazed at myself in a far too tight and too short purple number that made me look as if I should be auditioning for a low budget, porn movie. I sat down in total exhaustion and just wept.

Why was I crying? For what I saw in the mirror, for what I *wanted* to see in the mirror, for time lost, for the complications to come, or the fact that when I looked down all I saw were pale unshaven legs and thick woollen socks. Bet Fraser wouldn't find *that* sexy. I wiped my eyes and began to slowly put the array of clothes back on hangers. Where had, 'being positive' gone?' Get a grip girl,' that's what Morry would say. I smiled. Why was I putting myself through all this grief? If Fraser *really* liked me, he would find me attractive no matter what I wore. Ben had thought I looked great without make-up, jodhpurs and a woolly jumper. Looking like Tiffany every day of my life just isn't me, why make so much effort to be someone you're not. Be true to yourself as they say.

My hand ran over a favourite dress, very Grace Kelly. I really do love that look. I suit that look. The bodice is fitted making the most of my modest, but pert assets. Sleeveless, but not stringy straps that you worry will fall from your shoulders, the full layered skirt, calf-length.

It makes me feel feminine and confident. I calmly hang it up on the back of the door, sort out a couple of bits of jewellery, bag, shoes and jacket, then still calm, nonchalantly run my bath, not giving the dress a second glance.

Without Susies, or Morrys help I have been positive and decisive and if Detective Sargent Fraser Grant is not impressed with the real me, then the River Wear beckons and he can take a running jump. Stay positive. If he truly thinks I'm sexy and gorgeous, he'll probably adore what he sees. Yes, he'll be hooked, lined and well and truly reeled in…wonder where I'll have to remove the hook from?.......Would that be a section 18, or common assault?

Monday morning, I was still calm and happy and so looking forward to this special night. An evening in the most stylish restaurant in Durham City. All these years of passing it and

wondering what sort of people dined there, now I knew…….
Very lucky people, like me!

"Are you going to sit there all day with that strange faraway look in your eyes. You haven't even been on the date yet and you're away with the fairies." Morry saunters in clutching two cups of tea, he pulls a chair up close.

"What you wearing tonight then? This is it girl! Were you out scouring the shops Saturday, or have you borrowed something from an upmarket friend?" I tut loudly.

"Thanks Morry. I know I'm not exactly the best dressed woman in Durham, but I'm no bag lady. I'm wearing one of my favourite dresses and that's it. I want him to see the *real* me and still find me irresistible." I say matter of factly. Morry looks just a tad uncomfortable.

"It's not that purple creation is it, I think considering the real you in that one might cause a difference of opinion." Morry looks genuinely worried.

"Actually, I never really liked that one." I lean forward whispering loudly.

"Anna chose it last year when she was trying to help me with a date. She likes everything a bit clingy, she thinks it holds her in, makes her look slimmer." Morry grimaces, his face is a picture.

"Urgh, nothing worse than trying to squeeze yourself into a size too small, you end up looking like a deformed caterpillar." Anna suddenly looks up.

"Deformed caterpillars, where?" She looks startled.

"They will be if they pop out in the middle of December that's for sure." Anna chirps up, before Morry merrily quips.

"No, sorry Anna we were on about something else popping

out in the middle of December, Penny's got her big date tonight."

She giggles naughtily. "He's a cheeky one Penny love, you just enjoy it all, whatever the evening holds, it's meant to be. Remember what I said, fate, that's what it is…fate."
I spent the rest of the day wondering just what 'fate' had in store.

I couldn't get home quick enough. Ferdy was fed and fussed and my bath was running. I *was* feeling positive now. Only three days to Christmas and I have a truly romantic date with a gorgeous fella at 'The Straw House'…how fantastic is that? With a huge towel wrapped round me, my hands clutching, a large mug of tea, I gaze at my dress. Yes, it *still* felt right. It *had* to be right, he would be calling for me in an hour.

I swiftly dressed, applied make-up, put my hair up, with Susie's tips. I even put in a set of daily contact lenses. I didn't want to miss a thing. It all seemed so easy, coming together, beautifully. I wasn't my usual stressed, panicky self. Maybe tonight fate *was* now helping me to captivate and capture the man of my dreams……I really hoped so.

The house was tidy and festive. Ferdy was being the perfect cat, curled up, on a large cushion. The stage was set. I was just putting a last dash of lipstick and some cash in my bag, (just in case fate decides to desert me. I'm being positive but the tiny cynic in me is also being safe.) when the doorbell rings, waking Ferdy who gazes towards the door. My heart starts to thump again. I swallow hard, give myself a final check in the mirror and open the door smiling confidently.

"Hi, Princess, ready or not here I come." With that he kisses my cheek and walks past me and into the front room.

"Hey, this is comfy-cosy isn't it, like stepping back in time, very old fashioned, bit like you Princess." He looks me up and down as I smile sweetly.

"There's nothing wrong with a bit of nostalgia, I just like the style and colours, rich, classy and sophisticated, *bit* like me?" I say hoping for his approval, as I swish across the room to put out the Christmas lights and leave a lamp on.

"A touch old hat for me Princess, I like all me mod cons. Be a squeeze to get a big surround sound TV in here, wouldn't it? Have you just got the one moggy, or are you one of those women that has to have dozens creeping all over the house?"

I quickly stroke Ferdy's head covering his ears, for fear he'll feel insulted.

"Ferdy was a rescue cat, he's lovely company, he's a real character, he's no problem." Why do I feel I need to justify my cat's existence.

"Hey whatever. I've got an ex-police dog, called Todd."

I can't help but laugh.

"He'll be a big hairy waste of space then?" He visibly bristles.

"Todd is a *real* pet, protective and loyal." I quickly explain.

"Sorry, I knew a Todd that's all, the last thing *he* was protective and loyal." He heads towards the door.

"Right, come on then, let's get to this meal, don't want to hear about your past conquests Princess, not good for a man's ego." Before I could put him right on who Todd belonged to, he had ushered me out of the house and into the car. He talked about his work for the short journey into town. I felt like a real celebrity as we pulled up outside, people taking a second look at the car in case someone important, or famous, was about to climb out, I felt fantastic, really special.

As the doors to 'The Straw House' are opened by a smart doorman, I just stand-still for a moment, taking it all in.

The entrance landing has a huge Christmas tree, must be at least twelve feet high. Gold climbers with huge gold leaves entwine the balcony. Huge gold framed panels of green and pink marble line the walls. Fraser speaks to the Maître d, who then swiftly clicks his fingers for cover, as he takes us down the grand staircase into the restaurant area.

It is just wonderful. Very bright, in white and gold with very stylish festive centre pieces on every table, covered in fresh holly, mistletoe and huge candles, which were lit quickly as soon as we were seated.

Menus are proffered and Fraser orders wine before I'd even found the list. (Obviously au-fait with the house red.)

"This is so fantastic, better than I could have ever imagined." He sighs, looking at me as if I'm Eliza Doolittle.

"A shame you had to wait this long to be brought to a place which is *so* you." He reaches over and strokes the back of my hand. I can't quite tell if this gesture is slightly condescending.

"I don't know, I think this is a mature and stylish place, I don't think I would have appreciated it all years ago." He smiles warmly.

The waiter appears with a bottle of Cabernet Sauvignon. He pours a drop in Fraser's glass to taste. Fraser presses his nose into the glass, sniffs the bouquet, swirls the glass looking at the liquid then slurps…. I try not to snigger. Simon had shown me and Suse how to do it properly and it wasn't like this, but I bit my lip and let him have his moment.

"It's a touch warm but a good flavour, you can pour."

The waiter duly obeys, catching my eye as he does so. I'm sure he was biting his lip too!

"Now I don't want you worrying about your weight, or anything silly like that, we're here to enjoy ourselves you treat yourself to something nice Princess."

Was it just my imagination, or was that said to *make* me think about my weight? Treat myself, I had eaten in proper restaurants before, not *just* Harry Ramsdens and the Porthole.

"I think I'll have the salmon, sounds lovely with the baby shallots and dill and lemon sauce." I smile broadly, gazing round, still taking in the opulent surroundings.

"Are you sure you wouldn't prefer the lobster?" He flicks his finger towards a huge glass tank, covered in jewels and shaded by a huge tree growing from a gold pot.

"You can choose which one you want." I gaze at the poor captive lobsters awaiting *their* fate.

"Heavens no, all God's creatures and all that. Poor things are stabbed through the head, or boiled alive, I couldn't condone them being killed like that, they have a right to a natural life." He looks at me suspiciously.

"You're not one of those God botherers are you? Or worse, one of those friends of the earth, tree hugging, women's lib types?" I felt that remark told me a lot more about him than me.

"Why? Don't you like, strong, opinionated women, or..... religion?" He suddenly grins broadly.

Well, I don't know who'd come off worse in an arm wrestle with Mother Superior, but I wouldn't mind having a tussle with you up a church path!" I shake my head, but can't help but laugh.

"You are *so* predictable. Why up a church path anyway?" He winks. "How else would I get a gorgeous woman like you to come into a church with me." I can feel my heart thumping...is he considering.... could it be... possibly...a...

"Can I take your order sir?" The waiter appears. I hope his timing isn't going to be this bad all evening. I so want Fraser to cut to the chase. Just imagine if he proposed, here, tonight.

"You fancied the salmon, didn't you Princess, well amongst other things eh babe?" He winks, not at me but towards the waiter, I feel a little uncomfortable.

"I'll just have, 'The Straw House' steak special, rare thanks." He says passing the waiter the menus. The waiter leaves quickly.

"Right Princess lets drink to us." He raises his glass, I do the same, waiting for his toast. "Here's hoping we both have a night to remember and a special Christmas for the two of us...cheers babe." His eyes are twinkling in the candlelight.

"To *us*...cheers." I say almost overwhelmed with happiness. The waiter comes and goes, catering for our every need. I try to drink slowly but Fraser insists on filling my glass at every opportunity. The wine is getting the better of my bladder rather than my brain, I excuse myself after the wonderful main course, but before the dessert, which will be profiteroles, (mini eclairs how good are they?)

The waiter seems to instinctively know where I'm heading before I get time to ask, his gloved hand is waving towards a narrow corridor and the, 'Powder room'. As I head through the huge, panelled door, a plume of expensive perfume hits me.

The cubicles are huge, gold flower holders adorn the walls. Everything is so extravagant. Eight sinks set in a marble surround, a decorative guilt mirror above each. The sound system with its piped music, playing the same as in the restaurant.

Not the usual Christmas numbers, just classy romantic stuff, perfect for this place. I listen carefully to the words of Mick Hucknall singing, 'New Flame.' I look at myself in the mirror… maybe this *really* is it. I can barely keep my heart from pushing its way up and out and screaming for joy. My smile is almost from ear to ear, I feel incredibly lucky. I do a last twirl and positively saunter with smugness back towards the table taking in the handsome dark suited man, who is *my* fella.

"What have you been doing in there? Whatever it is it's put a big smile on your face?" I crinkle my nose and give him a flirtatious little smile. "I'm just happy, with all this….and of course with you." He leans closer.

"You're a little tease, don't worry you can show me your appreciation later Princess." Before I could even begin to worry about that one, he asks.

"So, what you doing over Christmas, are you one of these saddos that feels eternally obliged to spend it with the old fogie parents? Or are you going to see who appears on your door on Christmas Eve and I'm not talking Santa and his reindeer. I did say I'd find you something special for your stocking." Just as I was about to extinguish his, 'New Flame' of passion, the waiter appeared at our table again.

"Profiteroles madam?" I smiled, couldn't have put it better myself.

"Large fruit boat sir?" If only he were, I thought. I might be in with a chance of coping with his over-active mind.

"I actually enjoy Christmas with my family, I only spend the day there. Anyway, what about your poor mum, you wouldn't leave her alone would you, surely?"

He looked a tad awkward as if thinking of an acceptable answer.

"I don't have to, she likes to go into the Meadows over Christmas, they have parties, sing-songs, Tombola, you know the sort of thing oldies love. So, it's me that'll be all alone for Christmas. Of course, that's unless a certain gorgeous little creature sitting across this table from me fancies being the centre of my attention for a couple of days? I can safely say you wouldn't regret it babe." He winks again, but this time with a slightly self-satisfied smile. I think I already was…regretting it. If this had been Suse, she'd be playing footsie under the table and licking her licks with rampant desire. But I was panicking again, eyes wide, like a rabbit caught in headlights. I regained my composure and as sexily teasing as I could I manage said.

"Well, we'll have to see what Santa brings won't we…." He was obviously getting quite excited at the thought, he loosened his collar slightly and leaned forward almost singeing his hair on the candle.

"Which does my Santa baby like…good boys…or *bad* boys?" The look in his eyes told me, if I said, 'good' he might let me open his present first before carrying me upstairs for several hours of carnal lust…But if I dared to say, 'bad' there is no doubt I'd be stripped naked and straddled over the hostess trolley before I had time to switch the light off… or tell the poor waiter to look away!

My heart was not only thumping with panic, but also the thought of such raw passion, could I do it, really? Throw caution to the wind Suse said, was it how to keep this man. But when I was in Charlie's passionate hold, he had such a different look in his eyes, something really connected between us. As I looked across the table at Fraser, it wasn't the same expression. It was just desperate and lustful, what if that's all he wanted?

Suddenly, my thoughts were interrupted by a very loud, shrill voice, that appeared to be getting closer.

"Oh, might have known, you'd be in here again!" I looked up from my dessert to see a tall, curvy blonde, striding towards our table. Oh my God, I knew it, he has a girlfriend. My heart now began to thump out of fear.

"Hey Princess, I never promised you a rose garden, nothing was carved in stone babe." Fraser calmly turned slightly as she came in close.

"A *rose* garden! More like a bed of weeds and a weeping willow." She then turned to me. I leaned back in the hope her heavily, jewel encrusted, handbag was not going to be used as a weapon.

"Have you ever wondered pet, why he calls his.....'girls'.... Princess?" I tried to speak but nothing came out, she carried on.

"So, he doesn't have to remember their names. Suppose his poor old mother will be conveniently going into the Meadows for a couple of days, is she?" Confused, all I manage is.

"Er, she enjoys it there, Fraser doesn't make her go, do you?" I look towards Fraser, who is now looking at me as if I've signed his death warrant. The blonde swishes her long mane back and laughs.

"His mother died seven years ago, it's his *wife* who's at home. He picks an argument with the poor cow, then tells her to go to her mothers till he can forgive her. This man is by day, a pillar of society, honest, hardworking, law-abiding DS Fraser Grant. By night he is a serial, adulterous bastard! A classic Jekyll and Hyde eh pet?"

I stare at Fraser in disbelief. "You're...you're married?"

He straightens up defensively.

"Technically, we're as good as separated."

The tears are now bristling the corners of my eyes, but I bite my lip hard, I won't give him the satisfaction of seeing me cry.

"Is your *wife* actually aware….'you're as good as separated'? How can you treat people with such little respect and regard?"

He still doesn't see it, calmly sliding his fingers through his hair.

"Hey, don't get all heavy on me Princess, we're all adults, it's just a bit of fun."

I duck slightly as the blonde brings her handbag up in front of her, but instead of imbedding it in his skull, which would have been reasonable revenge in my present frame of mind, she reaches inside and pulls out a tape cassette. Dropping it by my plate of now sad and soggy profiteroles.

"Soul Classics, just a lucky guess, but I reckon you might have a copy of that one pet? He drove you home, before he left…… 'think of me Princess while you listen to this tape'….and wa *all* did didn't wa? Wa all fell for yer charms eh." She turns to Fraser and leaning in close almost spits the words.

"You are so full of bullshit you could *manure* a rose garden, never mind *promise* one. Do that poor wife of yours a favour and divorce her quickly and invest in some Bromide for your tea…. Shame no one told you, but aroused gorilla in a thong is not a look us girls find sexy……don't you agree pet?"

She was looking at me for back up.

"Er, I didn't…. we haven't…I mean." I was still trying to get that vision from my mind, my nose wrinkling. (Might have known he'd be a thong kinda guy)

"Oh, he hadn't got to that bit wi' you pet. You must be the *romantic* type. You're one of those he has to spend out on, to reap his return…You've had a lucky escape love. If nothing else, at least I've saved you from becoming his Christmas bonus!" And with that she casts him the, evil eye and strides away towards a group of friends at a table, fortunately, at the far end of the room.

The waiters who had stood at a safe distance, in case of trouble but really so they could earwig the conversation, had all moved off too. I was left completely numb.

As I came to my senses, the feelings of hurt, anger, disbelief overwhelmed me. How could the gorgeous man in front of me be such a conman…He was a Detective Sergeant for God's sake. But as Suse had said, he's still a man. I suppose he hadn't broken the law, just his wedding vows…. His poor wife. He just saw me as….a conquest, a bit on the side…Me! Miss Cautious, a bit on the side! Keeping my jaw firm, I finally looked up at him.

"Haven't you got anything to say to me…the truth perhaps?"

"Hey Princess….er Patsy, isn't it? I never meant for this to happen. If she hadn't come along, you'd be none the wiser, pretend she never came in. You know where we'd both be now if she hadn't walked in………loosen up babe…it's only sex."

I leaned forward and hissed at him. "*Only* sex! *Only* sex! You said it was fate that brought us together that night, you talked about babies and churches, how gorgeous I was, how different...how"… He put his hands up.

"Woah! Princess, it's just chat, it's what you girlies want to hear isn't it?" With that my rose-tinted specs were well and truly gone, I saw the man in front of me for the selfish, self-obsessed, male-chauvinist pig he really was, I had to leave this table…right now.

"Hey babe, where are you going, you haven't finished your dessert. It's bloody expensive in this gaff, especially when I'm not being offered a fourth course at your place. If I'd known you were such a prude, I wouldn't have wasted the money."

I gritted my teeth. *Nothing* would have given me greater pleasure at that moment, than to pour the contents of the cream jug over his over inflated head, but, 'The Straw House' was for calm, elegant, sophisticated people with a sense of restraint and respect. But something told me with the doorman and two waiters moving in on Fraser, *he* would no longer be welcome at this high-end establishment.

I walked as sedately and as calmly as I could to the, 'Powder Room.' Once I had made sure the place was empty, I entered a cubicle, locked the door, put the lid down, pulling both knees up under my chin like a Pixie on a toadstool, I wrapped my arms round my legs and let the tears come. I rocked back and forth and bit my lip, so as not to sob out loud. I grabbed some paper to cover my dress as the, mascara-stained tears dripped on…and on.

I went over all the little things that I'd heard him say, but subconsciously put to the back of my mind. The quick, barely noticeable digs about age…weight, his dislike of cats….it was quite obvious he didn't really think I was gorgeous. He just saw me as an easy target for a quick tumble…. The blonde girl was right…he just saw me as a Christmas Bonus …Wonder what she had been, a Spring quota…a Summer special?

God! How could I have been so naive. *She* didn't look naive though and she fell for it, many more by the sounds of it…I felt so cheap. But nothing to how his poor wife would feel if she ever found out, there she is probably blaming herself for every row and trying her best to make him happy every-time he lets her return, how cruel is that? I then cried for her too. My whole body hurt with the pain of realisation of being well and truly duped.

Oh, I'd have to tell Suse, I feel *so* stupid. She'd have seen right through him... How can I tell mum, dad, the family. They finally thought I'd found Mr Right, not a chance, Mr Rat possibly. The tears kept coming as the piped music played such helpful tunes as, Alison Moyet singing 'This Old Devil Called Love' and Whitney singing, 'Saving All My Love For You'..... The mistress's ballad! Thanks.

I finally let my legs fall, exhausted, I had no more tears to cry. I wiped my sore red eyes, completely forgetting I had contact lenses in. I could feel the lens in the left eye dislodge and ping off onto the wall and down. My sight now mismatched I leaned forwards almost toppling off the toilet seat towards the floor. I could hear voices.

"Hello, are you alright?" I didn't want anyone to see me in such a state. I swallowed hard before speaking, trying to sound calm.

"I'm fine, just lost a contact lens, I don't want to tread on it, so I'll just stay here till I find it." There appeared to be two voices, they whispered between themselves, they sounded older. Both used the facilities then went to leave. "Are you sure you don't need an extra pair of eyes to find it dear?" Just an extra pair of eyes that worked would be an asset.

"No! Honestly, I'm fine, really, I'm......fine."

As I heard the door close behind me, I knew I felt anything but fine. All I had to look forward to was sympathetic looks from family and friends, no Christmas romance and a New Year with Ferdy and mug of Horlicks. Bugger! I also had to get out of here without Fraser, or anyone else preferably, seeing me looking like

Alice Cooper in drag. I squinted with my one good eye to try and find my contact lens. I finally found it covered in mascara and fluff. I don't think a bout of conjunctivitis would be a plus to an already downward spiralling festive season, so I took out the other lens and tried my best to cool my eyes, that by now, resembled two currants in a lump of pasty dough.

I tidied myself up, took a couple of deep breaths as I headed towards the door. There was bound to be a back way out of the place. I could then wait for ten minutes, check Fraser's car had gone, the thought of him still there waiting, still thinking I might be stupid enough to convince that he was right. I couldn't bear it. I turned into a narrow corridor, instead of back towards the restaurant.

I squinted round the first corner, there was a sign, fortunately in huge writing, for a fire exit. That would be my escape plan. The corridor finally opened out to a small, quiet hall area. An old ornate staircase led to what the sign said were, Chef's Quarters. I had to climb several steps to get close enough to read it.

Carefully opened the fire exit. I could vaguely make out several dark cars, so went to close the door till my eye caught sight of an old classic motorcycle. I peered at the old BSA emblem and smiled. At least someone had taste. Fraser was just so *not*..... 'The Straw House'. I closed the door, deciding to wait awhile.

I peered up the staircase, suppose this must be where Simon's brother lives in. This building would have been a grand family home at one time, how wonderful to live somewhere like this, even if you were only part of the staff.

The cool air from a ceiling fan made my eyes feel so much better. I felt weary and sat down on the stairs, I felt a wave of despair hit me. I wrapped my arms around my knees again, pulling in tight, rocking slightly to stay calm, urging myself not to cry again. He wasn't worth it...He just *wasn't* worth it....

I was just repeating this useful mantra when I heard a door open behind me and footsteps coming down the staircase.

"Are you alright, can I get you anything, can I call someone for you?"

The voice, Simon's brother, of course, that would be why he sounds familiar, how embarrassing. I couldn't let him see me in this state, he might think I've had a reaction to his cooking, or something.

"No, really, I'm fine, just had a bit of a fall out with my.... my.... the person I was having dinner with." Without looking up, but with quick sideways glance I caught the black and white check of Chefs trousers, as he stopped by the wall on the step behind me.

"Yes, your table waiter actually told me, as I was finishing your dishes, he was a little concerned for you, as was I."

His voice, so kind, so familiar. I continued the conversation as naturally as I could. "You must be Simon's brother?" I felt him sit down, staying on the step behind me.

"I am, you must be Susie's friend...Penny. Simon told me you were coming in tonight. How was your food?" I tilted my face the other way, as I felt him lean forward slightly.

The thought of him telling Simon his version of events and that I ended up resembling something that had gone ten rounds with Mike Tyson was too much to bear, mortifying, after such a 'difficult' evening.

"Your food was excellent. It was definitely just the company that let the evening down a little…no…a lot and I never got to finish my…profiteroles, I do love profiteroles"

That sounded so pathetic, how old am I?

"My favourite too, actually." He says casually.

"You must have been with the enigmatic… DS Fraser Grant then?"

I couldn't believe it! Those waiters must have been having a field day, back and forth telling the staff everything, how embarrassing, I was the laughing stock of 'The Straw House'…. not quite as sophisticated as I'd hoped.

"We've always kept an eye on his……'dates'? Always wondered what it was about him that all these beautiful women go for. Well, apart from his looks, status, money and charm, obviously. Suppose I've answered my own question there really."

I sigh heavily and try my hardest not to let anymore tears come, but I feel one solitary tear well up and I put my hankie to my eye quickly.

"Oh God, that was really insensitive of me, I didn't mean to upset you, you must have really liked him a lot. *Did* you?"

I couldn't bring myself to tell him. It wasn't just because of the lack of love and humiliation from Fraser Grant, but that I could hear the East 17 and Gabrielle hit, 'If You Ever' wafting through the speakers. It got me every time. I could feel him rest a hand on my shoulder,

I began to feel a calmness wash over me and strangely compelled to tell this person…. *'almost'*… everything.

He listened, every now and then squeezing my shoulder gently, especially when I got to the embarrassing and difficult part of the story so far…...

"I can't believe I'm telling you all this. It must be because you are so like Simon. Suse says he's so dependable, patient, caring, a great listener and nothing is too much for him. You seem to have that same kind, familiar way with you. Thanks for listening. I feel awful, I must be keeping you away from your work, your kitchen. Am I?"

I felt a pang of disappointment as he stood up.

"No. I'm lucky being in charge of the kitchen, I can knock off early, after the last plate leaves, which was half an hour ago. I was just going to make a cup of tea, can bring you one and a couple of profiteroles, if you like? I often take some leftovers from the sweet trolley, perks of the job."

He turned striding back up the stairs. I tried to take a quick sneaky look at him. Damn! Without lenses, or specs, he's just a checked blur. Maybe, he *looks* like Simon too.

Why do I care what he looks like anyway? But I hear myself saying.

"I should order a taxi really. Well, maybe just half a cup? Thanks."

While he was gone, I quickly rummaged through my bag, squinting into my tiny mirror. I could see my eyes had gone down and the redness had faded, but not quite enough to let him see my face close to….not yet. I could hear him returning, I kept my head lowered as he passed me, exactly half a cup of tea and a little bowl with several profiteroles, cream and a small spoon.

"I've called you a taxi, it'll be here in about twenty minutes, is that okay? I'd offer you a lift home, but I don't have a spare helmet for the BSA."

Aha! That old motorbike out there was his. I so wanted to turn round and thank him properly he seems so kind, so easy going, so like…...

"At least I've had time to calm down, I haven't done anything rash, or silly in the heat of the moment." I find myself thinking out loud. "Well, you know……it's a good job I found out now, imagine what might have happened. No, best not to think about that, definitely best not to think about that" …

He waited till I had sipped my tea, then spoke.

"I don't suppose you'll be wanting to date blokes for a while after this episode, it'll have put you off the male of the species for a while…has it?" He sits down on the step behind me again. I sigh heavily.

"Oh! I know deep down inside, in my heart of hearts, that not all men are like that. You can't let the few men who treat women badly tarnish you're outlook, or change you into something you're not." That sounds a bit maudlin, so I try and lighten the mood slightly.

"Did *you* make these?" I say putting the last delicious round of choux pastry into my mouth.

"Of course! As Head Chef I like to do *all* the desserts, they are my speciality. It's taken me a lot of years and hard work to get to somewhere as fabulous as, 'The Straw House'. I've put a lot of things on hold in my life. In fact, I almost gave up the search, until…."

I didn't know why I was starting to feel the way I did, or why I had to resist the now urgent need to turn round and look at this man sitting behind me. But as my body started to tingle, the realisation that destiny, yes….. 'fate', whatever magical powers that be, had taken over my senses.

He began to move, not away from me, but slowly squeezed himself down a step, to sit beside me, all the time talking in that lovely, soft voice.

"It wasn't just the searching it was all the comparisons, I mean listen to this song playing now, this could be, *'our song'* …… Joe Cocker singing, 'Feels Like Forever.' It *has* felt like forever and just in case you've left your glasses at home, again, Penny… I am Simon's brother. My name is, Charles Forbes, but special people…… *very* special people, can call me……..Charlie."

And with that his hand turned my face to his, he was close enough for me to see *every* inch of that gorgeous face, that smile, those twinkling eyes and that deep sense of connection.

Three years disappeared, we were back in York and along with my jaw…... the Penny dropped.

THE END

Catherine B. Sedgwick – author and artist.

Born in Nottingham, now living in North Yorkshire.

Has written and painted for many years between working full-time and family time.

Had careers in many interesting fields including, Anatomical Pathology Technician and as a Scenes Of Crime Officer.

Likes to write two books concurrently, one crime, one feel-good.

First published novel was a gritty crime story, 'Taking Out The Trash' in 2020.

'The Penny Drops' being the feel-good.

A sequel to TOTT is on its way!

Printed in Great Britain
by Amazon